CLARET AND CYANIDE

A WINE DETECTIVE MYSTERY

ROBERT STONE

Chapter 1

THE DINNER AT THE Savoy was drawing to an end. The Master of Ceremonies knocked a spoon against a glass to signal for silence.

'My lords, ladies and gentlemen! The time has come to announce the results of this evening's Grand Wine Tasting Challenge. Before I do so I should of course like to thank and congratulate...'

Harry looked across at his fellow contestants, seated, like him, at the top table in between the officials of the Wine Society. Peter Hill, wine correspondent of *The Times*, caught his glance and smiled at him.

He's good, thought Harry, as he smiled back, I bet he'll score in the eighties. The other two, Sarah Morgan of *Wine* magazine and Geoffrey Angmering of Angmering Bros, one of London's top wine merchants, were studying their tasting notes, possibly trying to forecast their scores.

'... So, may I remind you, the maximum score possible is 100, that is one point for each grape variety or varieties, one point for the country, one point for the area, one point for the property and one point for the year, of each of the twenty wines tasted.'

The assembled crowd of wine buffs, there must have been around 200 in all, quietened as the MC prepared to announce the results.

'In fourth place, with the excellent score of 68 points, Mr

Geoffrey Angmering!'

Angmering stood and bowed to the polite applause from the audience.

'In third place, with 74 points, Miss Sarah Morgan!' She waved in response to loud cheers from two tables full of her magazine colleagues.

'The runner-up, with a magnificent 86 points, last year's winner, Mr Peter Hill!'

Harry tried hard not to let his face show any emotion now that he knew he had won, as Hill stood and bowed to the enthusiastic applause. 86 points was a very good score, enough to win the Challenge most years, and Hill wondered about the man who had beaten him.

He was surprised that Harry had won, because from the amount of wine he had appeared to have swallowed, rather than spat out, he had guessed him to be a real amateur. He knew from their brief chat before the event had begun that Harry had been involved in the hotel trade in the East and had come back to England to retire.

'Obviously done pretty well for himself,' he thought, 'if he can afford to retire at his age.'

He estimated that Harry was about 50, fit-looking, slightly under six foot, brown hair slightly receding but no sign of grey. A slightly shy man, he had concluded, but with an arresting habit of looking at you very directly when talking or listening.

'The winner, my lords, ladies and gentlemen, and Wine Society Champion Winetaster for 2017 is...... Mr Harry Benson, with the quite incredible total of 93 points.'

The announcement of the score stunned the crowd into a momentary silence, which gave way to a mixture of loud applause, cheering and an excited hubbub of conversation.

No-one had ever previously scored more than 90 points in what was regarded as the world's hardest wine-tasting event, with many extremely old and rare wines.

Harry stood and smiled as his fellow competitors came over to shake his hand. 'Beginner's luck,' he said modestly as each of them in turn expressed their congratulations. Then, as the MC motioned him to come to the microphone, he picked up his glass and went across to the podium.

'Mr Benson, when I said your score was incredible, I think everyone here, before this evening, would never have believed that such a score was possible. This is a feat unparalleled in the history of the society!' He put his hand on Harry's shoulder and smiled mock-conspiratorially – 'Come on now, sir, admit that you saw a list of the wines to be tasted beforehand!'

Harry laughed and said 'Curses! How did you guess? No I assure you, and all the committee,' – a stage whisper – 'I'll give you the money afterwards,' – 'that I had no prior knowledge of the wines.'

'Of course, of course! Perhaps I can remind the audience that five different members of the committee of the Society each, quite separately and individually, choose four wines and that all are sworn to absolute secrecy. It is absolutely impossible for anyone to know which wines will be tasted in advance. But, Mr Benson, your score still brings the world incredible to mind. Can you tell us your secret?'

Harry realised that he was a bit too tired to go into any lengthy speechmaking.

'Well,' he said, 'the fact is I seem to have the equivalent of a photographic memory, for tastes. In most cases, where I have tasted the wines before, I know immediately what they are. I suppose tonight I was lucky, there were only three that were new to me and I was able to work them out pretty well.'

Peter Hill came over and said that he would like to carry an interview with him in *The Times*, but Harry had demurred. 'One of the few principles I stick to,' he had said, 'is never to knowingly put a penny in the pocket of that evil man Murdoch.'

Hill had rather been taken aback at Harry's use of the word evil. 'That's a bit strong isn't it, Mr Benson?' he said. 'I don't know our proprietor personally and I don't really care for his politics but I don't think you can exactly put him in the same league as Hitler!'

Harry laughed and apologised. 'No, of course not, I'm sorry, a fair bit of wine tonight, anyway, please call me Harry.'

'Peter,' smiled Hill.

'But, to be honest, I don't really want any publicity. I like a quiet life and, besides,' his hazel eyes twinkled, 'too many skeletons in the closet, Peter!'

The more he heard from Harry, the more intrigued Hill became. He saw Harry looking at his watch and said 'Well, anyway, come out to lunch some time, I'd like to know more about your wine-tasting technique for purely personal reasons.'

'OK,' Harry replied, 'here's my card, give me a call, or my e-mail address is on there. Now I must make a move, I've got a bit of a long drive home.'

'You're driving yourself? Haven't you had a bit too –'

'No, it's OK,' smiled Harry, 'the car knows the way, and anyway, Sandra will keep me awake, won't you darling?'

Hill became aware of a very attractive girl in a décolleté dress who was standing a couple of yards away holding a man's coat.

'Yep, don't worry 'Arry, there's not many falls asleep when they're out with me for the evening.' She gave Harry his coat and wriggled her shoulders, in a way that made her very large bust strain upwards in an attempt to escape, and winked at Hill.

'No indeed, I should think not,' he murmured. 'Well goodnight, Harry, I'll be in touch soon, goodnight, my dear.'

A decent sort of man, thought Harry, as he pulled off the road into a brightly lit late-night garage and eased the gleaming, aged Rover to a halt besides the petrol pump. Eton and Oxbridge type, he supposed from his accent and self-assurance. There was a time when Harry would have envied him, but not now. The English pre-occupation with class now seemed quaint and even faintly endearing.

He supposed that he could become a bit of a celebrity if he chose to. Goodness knows, the papers and television are full of wine and food these days, he thought.

He wasn't short of money and, being by nature a rather indolent man, didn't really relish the thought of giving up the leisure he had retired to enjoy. However, he also had a feeling that maybe he should do something more with his life than just enjoy himself.

He had strong opinions on a lot of subjects that he wouldn't be sorry to expound to a wider audience than just his friends, most of whom agreed with them anyway. A man of independent mind, he liked arguments, but disliked confrontations. He prided himself that he was always willing to listen to someone else's views, no matter how much he disagreed with them, and to try, at least, to understand the point they were making. But he found that virtually all the English people he met, who had views contrary to his, had closed minds and were unwilling, or unable, to try to understand him.

I suppose there are some intelligent conservatives, he thought, I just never seem to meet any of the buggers. Consequently, he tended to avoid the company of a lot of people he met and spent most of his time with like-minded friends.

He realised that perhaps this made him mentally a bit lazy, perhaps it would do him good to meet some new people.

He decided he'd give some thought to meeting Peter Hill again.

As he got back into the car, Sandra said 'Ere, wrap this round your neck,' and passed him his dark cashmere scarf from the back seat, 'nothing more certain to attract the rozzers than a dickie-bow!'

'Good idea,' he said. 'Thank you, darling, I suppose I have had a bit to drink. But don't worry, I spat most of it out and I took a breathalyser test before we left, I keep them in the car, and I'm perfectly legal.'

'What if you weren't though? Wouldn't that worry you?' she asked. 'You could lose your licence.'

'My dear,' he said, 'I've been combining the two activities of drinking and driving quite successfully for over twenty-five years, and can honestly say that I've never caused an accident. If I have had a drink or two I always drive more slowly and carefully, in fact. And besides, you must bear in mind that they have to fix the official limit so as to prevent pimply, bespectacled, adolescent youths, quite unused to

6

driving or alcohol, from venturing out onto the roads in a dangerous state. To people who are used to drinking, the limits are absurdly low. I promise you', he said, 'if I wasn't in a fit condition to drive safely, I wouldn't do it.'

'Cor!' she said, 'that was a mouthful! Keep yer 'air on 'Arry! It's just that most people I know think that drinking and driving is next thing to murdering children!'

He laughed 'Yeah! I know my views are not exactly in accord with the majority of the population, especially youngsters. I suppose it has something to do with having spent most of my life in places where no one thinks about it twice. But,' he said, 'I still do think that the limit, for me, is too low'. A pause. 'Obviously though, they can't set a different limit for everyone, they have to set a limit, as I've said, for the young and inexperienced. That's fair enough,' he looked to see that he was not boring her and, reassured by a little smile, continued, 'but, I really don't see why they have to treat people they catch, who have had perhaps just a couple of pints, and are perfectly sober, like public enemy number one! Sheer hypocrisy!'

'Yeah,' she said, 'I see your point. Anyway, I bet it wouldn't bother you, losing your licence, you must be able to afford to have a chauffeur, living in that great big 'ouse!'

He moved out on to the M3 and set the cruise control to 73, it didn't do to go too slowly, he thought, attracted the police. 'Probably,' he laughed, 'are you trying to tell me that I only think as I do because I can afford to?'

She giggled.

'Perhaps you're right!'

'Anyway,' she said, 'I do like to 'ear you talk, all those long words, you ought to be on the telly! You've got a very sexy voice too.'

'I'm a very sexy man,' he said, with a straight face.

'Are you now?'

'Ooh yes! Wonderful thing sex.'

'You got a theory about that too, 'Arry?' She stroked his thigh.

'No,' he said, 'that's enough theories for one night, it's time for a bit of practical! No!' he said as her hand moved inwards, 'better wait till we get home! But you really do have a splendid bosom, darling, I can't wait to get my hands inside your shirt.'

She giggled again, 'Yeah, all the blokes like my boobs, go mad over them, they do. That's why the agency charges extra for me.'

'Well worth it, my dear. But I hope the evening hasn't been too boring for you?' He changed the subject.

'No, it was OK, first time I've ever eaten in the Savoy. But your tasting went on a long time.'

He realised that she was starting to doze so he put the radio on softly, and stopped talking.

The car left the empty motorway and entered the silent, moonlit north Hampshire lanes. Harry loved this part of the world, so near London yet so beautiful, quiet, tranquil, unspoilt. After years of living among the ceaseless noise and bustle of Bangkok, Singapore, and Jakarta, driving along empty roads, not seeing a living soul, was wonderful. He settled back into the leather seat and guided the heavy car the dozen or so miles to his house, unseen except for the occasional late rabbit.

Left to his thoughts, Harry wondered what might result from

his success. He had always known his gift for winetasting was unusual but he hadn't realised he would be such a sensation. After the dinner he had received many offers to write about wine and it seemed that he would be much in demand.

As the car crunched along the long gravel drive, Sandra woke.

'Mmmm,' she stretched comfortably, 'nice and warm in this old car, 'Arry, I must've dozed off. What time is it?'

'Half past one, my darling. Let me put my coat over your shoulders before you get out. There's quite a frost.'

'Thank you, kind sir.'

They went in, quietly, one arm round each other, breath hanging white in the chill air. The old house, warm and welcoming, the thick carpet silent beneath their feet as they kissed inside the front door.

'Now, my dear, I have a rule on these occasions –'

'Yes,' she said, 'the agency told me, and it's very sweet of you, but it's OK, I do want to stay.'

She put her finger against his lips to stop any further conversation, put her hand in his and slowly rubbed the front of her breasts upwards against him, so that they came out of the flimsy front of her dress as it caught against the cotton of his shirt.

Harry had seen many a fine pair of breasts in his time but he couldn't remember when he had seen better. Sandra was slim and even though her breasts projected well out in front of the rest of her body, there was no sag at all, and her nipples pointed jauntily upwards. Harry was torn between looking, caressing and sucking. He walked round behind her as she enjoyed him looking at her, raising her arms above her

9

head to show her breasts to very best effect, and then brought his hands up and cupped them from below, feeling their weight and firmness, vibrating them a little to feel their flex and bounce, kissing the back of her neck.

Then he moved his hands up and round and very gently squeezed the breasts back towards her chest, flattening them slightly and letting the nipples slip in between the cracks of his middle fingers before releasing the pressure so that the breasts regained their shape, but for the nipples, stretched forward slightly in between his closed fingers. Now he moved his hands from side to side, still with the trapped nipples, lessening the contact gradually between his palms and her skin until the only contact was with her nipples, now dark and swollen, swaying the breasts gently from side to side.

'Mmmm,' she murmured, 'you've done this before, but, take me to bed.' Now he moved round in front and kissed her breasts tenderly, holding them up slightly with his thumbs just where the downward slope of the undersides of the breasts became the upward slope leading to the nipples, cushioning the weight with the edges of his palms, his fingertips in the air, then closing in gently, individually, and opening again in a ripple of fleeting touches.

His movements were so rhythmic and delicate that Sandra had the odd feeling that the skin around her nipples had become magnetised and was attracted to the skin of his hands.

She shivered at the sensation and Harry, realising the time had come to desist for a while, slowly pulled the front of her dress back up so that her breasts disappeared, gradually and reluctantly, from view, leaving the large erect nipples pushing up the silky fabric.

'Ow do you do that 'Arry?', she said dreamily as they climbed the curving stairs

'An old trick I learned in Bangkok –'

'Tell me later,' she said kneeling in front of him and undoing his belt buckle with her teeth.

Later, much later, after her battered old Golf had slipped away into the misty light of the early morning, Harry made himself a pot of strong tea and went and had a long shower, turning on the radio for the early morning news on Radio 4 while he washed.

Looking out of the window at the gradually lightening sky, he decided that the day was of sufficient prospective merit to go out for his morning run. He had installed an electric treadmill in his games room which he used when it was too wet or cold outside, but today looked like it was going to be a good day. He pulled on his tracksuit trousers and an old T-shirt and tiptoed down the stairs so as not to alert his ancient dog, Rosie, to the fact that he was going out without her. She couldn't keep up with him and he'd take her for a walk a bit later anyway.

He ran for around 40 minutes on a circular route that took him through Old Rossett wood and down through the village of Upper Rossett before climbing back up towards his house along the path through the fields and copses of the estate where the estate's owner, Colonel Forshaw, bred his pheasants.

Harry's house had been the dower house for Rossett Hall and it was because of his status as occupier of the house that he was allowed to use the path. Once a year, on Boxing Day, it was closed off though, to prevent anyone seeking to establish a right of way through it. It was exceptionally beautiful countryside, he thought. As he reached the top of the rise he could look back and see a view over the Hampshire countryside which, apart from neat hedges meeting squarely at right-angles here and there, had the appearance of being entirely untouched by man. The village was now hidden from view by the woods to the right and there was nothing, no houses, no roads, no pylons, to spoil the uninterrupted natural beauty of what he could see.

He stopped and looked for a minute, getting his breath back a bit, and then set off into the copse to emerge on the road half a mile or so up from his house.

Halfway along the path to the road he saw an old green Landrover coming the other way, it slowed to a halt. Alan, the Colonel's gamekeeper, lowered the window.

'Mornin', Harry, want to come beating tomorrow? Squire's got a big party coming in from Germany, need all the beaters I can get.'

'Sorry, Alan, can't tomorrow, got a lot on. You going to the match Saturday?'

'Surely am. Want to go together?'

'Yes, great, meet you in the pub for a pint first? About 12.30?'

'OK, see you then. Bye.'

Harry and Alan both had season tickets for Southampton Football Club and often went to the home games together.

He'd been back in England nearly three years now and hadn't regretted his choice. When he made the decision to sell up his restaurants and come back to Europe, he'd thought long and hard about where to go, it was either England or the Languedoc, where he'd spent two years at Montpellier university studying catering and the hotel business.

England had won, just, because of the Saints, and because of pubs.

A good English country pub, with real ale and good, simple pub food was what Harry had really missed about home in all his long years away. You just couldn't find anything like it anywhere else in the world. Harry loved beer almost as much as he loved wine. That was one reason why he had to go for a run every day, a natural glutton who loved to eat and drink, often to excess, it was the only way he could keep his weight in check. Besides he enjoyed running, the pleasurable warm fatigue in his muscles when he had finished was like a drug to him; if he couldn't run, he really missed it.

He let himself back into the house by the key hidden under the flower pot in the porch and gave the front door a good slam, to be sure to wake Rosie. Sure enough he heard her stir from her bed under the stairs and presently she came padding out towards him, golden locks of hair hanging forward over her eyes, long pink tongue hanging down over ancient worn teeth. She looked up at him from beneath her fringe, tail wagging steadily despite the reproachful look in her eye when she saw he had been out without her.

'Come on then, old girl, let's get you some breakfast.' He led her out through the kitchen and into the scullery. She headed to the door out into the garden and turned round and looked at him enquiringly, so he unlocked it and let her out into the garden to have a pee.

When she came back in, the shaggy hairs around her paws and mouth were quite wet from the dew so he dried her a bit with an old towel kept there for the purpose before putting her food and water bowls down for her.

He closed the scullery door and watched her eat for a while before leaving her and going upstairs for a bath. He still had an hour and a half before he needed to leave for the golf course, so he ran a good deep bath and settled in for a soak. He mused upon his love for that old dog. He had only had her since he came to England, he had deliberately chosen an old dog from the RSPCA refuge, he didn't want a puppy that would need lots of looking after, but an old quiet dog that he could spoil in its old age. Rosie was an otter hound, a big gentle dog, shaggy and biscuit-coloured, looking just like Old Boot from The Perishers comic strip that used to be in the *Daily Mirror*. He loved her and she loved him, with a quiet devotion that he enjoyed greatly. He also mused about Sandra, a lovely girl, and wondered if he would see her again. He knew she wasn't allowed by the agency to give him her phone number, so he hadn't asked for it. Neither of them had asked the other any questions really. It was the best way, she knew where he was if she wanted to get in touch again. A sensible girl, but he remembered her saying, 'You ought to be on the telly,' and thought, well, perhaps I should.

Chapter 2

LATER THAT MORNING, AFTER taking Rosie for a lumbering walk through the woods, Harry returned to the welcoming odours of fresh coffee and grilling bacon as he let the old dog into the scullery. Rosie sniffed the air hopefully and went and sat by his chair at the kitchen table. He had a bad habit of giving her scraps from his plate. He knew he shouldn't but, as she never begged, he did anyway.

Pat Cross, his home help, came in five mornings a week. She was already busy in the kitchen. It wasn't really in her job description to cook his breakfast but, as she always said, 'It tastes twice as good if you don't cook it yourself,' and she liked to look after him.

She had been inherited with the house. An attractive, capable woman in her mid-thirties, she worked to help out with her four children's school fees, they went to a private day school. Although not a tremendously efficient cleaner, he had got used to her blind spots and liked her far too much to risk losing her by complaining.

'Good morning, Harry,' she said. 'I got you this bacon specially – from the grocer's in Halldean – you know, he cures it himself.'

'Thanks Pat, it smells wonderful. Let me know how much I owe you for it. And thanks for cooking too, you spoil me, I'll get old and fat and lazy!'

But he was delighted really. If he had a favourite meal, it was breakfast. Although English cooking in general was about the worst in the civilised world (excepting of course America), English breakfasts, he believed, were the best, easily.

Lean smoked back bacon, grilled quickly so the fat was crisp outside, moist within, free-range eggs fried slowly, turned over at the last moment, the white all solidified, the rich golden yolks that sat up in the pan still liquid, malted whole grain bread cut thickly enough so, toasted, the outside was crunchy but the interior was still soft, golden salted butter and bitter tangy orange marmalade, thick with chunks of peel, strong black coffee.

Hard and soft, bitter and sweet, combinations and complexities of taste and texture. A good breakfast has all a great meal needs, Harry thought.

Bacon. Harry the impoverished student was vegetarian for a year. He didn't miss meat at all, except bacon. One night, late after an evening's beer drinking, a friend had offered him a bacon sandwich and vegetarianism was over. One of the worst things about living in the States, he had found, was the dreadful, dreadful bacon. No back bacon, only streaky and wafer thin so that, after being cooked, it exploded on the plate when you tried to put your fork into it! How people with as much good sense as the Americans could endure so much awful food was a mystery to him. And drink. Disgusting, tasteless, fizzy beer!

Harry was a sensitive soul, fairly perceptive too, about other people's feelings. He was a good listener, had worked hard at trying to understand people and had made himself into a reasonable judge of character. But he just could not understand how some people were so indifferent to the quality of what they ate and drank!

How anyone, having access to the truly splendid fresh food that was around now, could possibly buy the dreary mass-produced crap they did was beyond him. The power of advertising, he could only suppose. Harry thought the kind of person who cheerfully said 'Oh, I eat anything,' (as though proud of it), when invited for dinner and asked about anything to avoid on the menu, was either an idiot or totally lacking in discrimination. There were dozens of things that Harry just hated to eat. In fact the success of his restaurants had been largely due, he believed, to his policy of not serving any dishes he could not eat with pleasure himself.

The French now, they were different! They cared about what they ate. The freshest, best ingredients. A feeling, a reverence, for good food. Very insular though, impossible to get cheddar cheese there. There was another thing – cheddar cheese! At its best, mature and sharp, one of the best cheeses in the world, certainly the best for cooking, and yet people bought that disgusting 'mild' cheddar with absolutely no flavour other than soap!

When he'd finished, as he started loading the dirty plates into the dishwasher, Pat came back downstairs carrying his washing.

'How did it go last night?' she asked.

'Fine. In fact... I won!'

'Really?!'

He nodded and grinned.

'Well done! Who were the others?'

'Man from *The Times*, a girl from *Wine* magazine and a wine merchant, can't remember his name, all very professional.'

'Interesting wines?'

Pat and her husband Alistair were wine lovers too, they had been frequent dinner guests of Harry's.

'Yes, very. A tremendous '47 Cheval Blanc, lots of good burgundies. Very enjoyable.'

'So, are you famous now?' she teased him.

'Hardly, hardly. Minor notoriety perhaps. "King of the boozers".'

She laughed. He never said anything really funny, but she liked his dry self-deprecatory wit and the orotundity of his manner of speaking and often found herself laughing at him. An oddly attractive man, she thought, not exactly good-looking, but with charm. Goodness knows why he doesn't have a steady girlfriend, she thought.

'And how was the, er, rest of the evening?'

He knew she would already have worked out, from the state of his bed, that he hadn't spent the night alone.

'Mmmm... mindblowing,' he grinned at her.

He moved out through the side door of the scullery into the four-car garage he had had built at the back of the house and heaved his bag of golf clubs onto his shoulder.

He decided to take the green Rover this morning. He had three. One scarlet red, one dark green and one a light beigy brown. They were the old P6 Rovers, built during a decade or so from the mid-sixties. His three had all been immaculately restored and were as good as, or better than, new. To him, it was just about the greatest car ever designed – noble sloping bonnet flanked by beautifully curved side panels and the sexiest, smoothly inclining rounded boot ever. A car with a real chassis, that floated over the road. The 2-litre versions lacked power but the 3.5-litre V8's he had had possessed all the acceleration he needed. To him it was so outstandingly the finest car of its generation that he had no doubt they would be worth a fortune one day, besides, he just loved them. The leather seats, the wooden trim, the quarterlight window fastenings, pure luxury, from a distant age. Most modern cars looked very much the same to him, although he liked 3-series BMWs too, always hired them on his travels, couldn't see the least attraction in a Mercedes.

He had been lucky when he went to look for his Rover when he came back to England. He went up to the National Exhibition Centre in Birmingham for a Classic Car Show and, while looking at one of the Rovers on show there, he recognised a man he had seen in the village pub, looking at the same car. They got talking and discovered that they both shared the same unlikely passion for the cars. The man, George Andrusewski, turned out to be a retired motor mechanic, whose hobby was restoring old cars. He had a small house in the village, but not enough space for a proper workshop, he explained. He had come up to Birmingham by coach so Harry offered him a lift home. They stopped in a little country pub near Oxford and Harry bought him supper. They got on very well and by the time they had arrived back in the village they had decided to look into setting up in business together, restoring old Rovers.

They found a small warehouse unit in a light industrial estate on the edge of the village, Harry provided the equipment and finance, George provided the expertise and did most of the actual work. Harry loved to go down to the workshop, when he had time to help. George was almost always there, except when some of his vast tribe of grandchildren were visiting. Harry, no mechanical genius, had learnt a lot from George and was already halfway to becoming a competent car mechanic. So far they had restored and sold four cars, as well as the three that Harry now owned, with two more currently under renovation. Once Harry had put in the initial investment, they had been able to finance all their expenses from the cars they had sold. George kept accurate accounts of the costs involved in each vehicle and once they sold a car, they split the profit – 60% to George and 40% to Harry.

George was delighted, he was kept busy in his retirement doing something he loved, and earned a bit of money as well. His wife Vera was glad to get him out of the house. Harry didn't exactly get a commercial return on his investment but he did get the most beautiful cars in absolutely mint condition, at a very cheap price. He knew the whole thing would pay for itself in the end, plus the enjoyment of working on the cars and from old George's company.

This had been his first local business venture, and it seemed to have set the pattern for a couple more. By now he had a share in three local enterprises. He had been very pleasantly surprised to find what an impact his money had had on the village, the place seemed to be thriving.

When he had arrived, people were gloomily predicting the closure of the village school, but this year the number joining had exceeded the number leaving, for the first time in a decade.

The village cricket team, with Harry behind the stumps, had just had its best season in years and the pub darts team had started the season with five wins out of six. There's no doubt, thought Harry, that a good pub is at the heart of village life. It had been a big blow when, a few months after moving to Upper Rossett, he heard that the brewery was going to close it.

One of his specifications to the estate agent who had done the preliminary search for the house for him was that it had to be within twenty minutes' walk of a good country pub. The

Hunters Arms certainly fitted the bill, a fine spacious old building with interesting rooms, high ceilings and huge fireplaces, just across the road from the cricket pitch, it was comfortable, friendly and had good beer and reasonable food.

It always seemed to Harry to do a reasonable trade when he went in, which was often, certainly no worse than other pubs in the area he had visited. For various complicated reasons the brewery that owned it was doing a swap of around twenty of its pubs in the area with a national brewery chain; the Hunters was on the list to be exchanged but the new brewery did not see it as a viable concern. Although the old brewery had been happy enough with it (the Area Manager lived nearby and came in frequently) it did not want to complicate its exchange deal and so agreed to the closure.

However Keith Maynard, the Area Manager, did persuade his bosses to get the other brewery to agree to give Tony and Rose Anderson, the tenants of six years' standing, the chance to buy out the freehold.

They had asked a pretty steep price of £400,000, an amount which Tony and Rose had little chance of raising. They were talking to Harry about it one night when he was sitting alone at the bar in the saloon.

'We tried the bank,' Rose said, 'but they reckoned we're not making enough to repay the interest on the loan. Of course we said we could make more if we had a free hand here but they didn't go for that. They said we hadn't been making enough on food. It was a bit depressing really, wasn't it, Tony?'

'Mmm,' said Tony, 'they reckoned we need to do at least three times our current turnover in food to make a go of it.'

He refilled Harry's glass without waiting to be asked, they knew he always had at least three pints, he had only had one so far.

'What do you think, Harry?' Rose asked, 'you used to be in the restaurant business, didn't you? What do you think of our food here? Do you think we could make more on it?'

'Well, my dear,' he said, 'I think you give good value for money. In my personal opinion a small team, such as you have here, should concentrate on a small menu and make sure that everything on it is excellent. That way you can charge more, you get less wastage and it's also easier to manage. Your menu has, how many? About twenty hot dishes?'

Tony nodded.

'I think it's very difficult to maintain a good quality control with that number. I speak honestly, my friends, please don't be offended, but you did ask me!'

'No, we don't mind at all,' Rose replied. 'It's nice to discuss it openly with someone who knows what they're talking about.'

'Well,' said Harry, 'I suppose I've got a fair amount of experience of pubs, but only from this side of the bar! But that was always my policy in my restaurants – keep it simple and don't do more than you are able to do – with excellence.'

'How many restaurants did you have then?' Rose asked.

'Three. I had one in Singapore, one in Bangkok and one in Jakarta. In fact I've only just sold the one in Bangkok, last week.'

'You didn't run them yourself then?'

'No, I always had a local partner. You have to, you know, in Asia. Besides I was working full time, in the hotel business.

Of course I got involved in training the local people and I also had to spend a lot of time checking and ensuring they maintained standards and so forth.'

'Don't you miss it? Being retired I mean.'

'No... not really. Of course it was exciting in a way but all that being nice to people all the time – very wearing – I'm sure you know what I mean!'

'Well, it is hard work, but we like the life here,' said Tony, 'this is a very friendly place and we'll be sorry to leave, that's for sure.'

'Have you got any other possible sources of finance?' Harry asked.

'I dunno,' Tony said, 'our accountant said it was always possible, but we'd have to pay very high interest rates, plus a share of the profits. Probably not worth it, he said.'

'What you need,' Harry said, 'is a partner, someone local, willing to put some money in as a long-term investment.' He thought for a moment. 'Why don't you ask the colonel?'

Colonel Forshaw was a regular customer, had plenty of money and was well liked in the village. He was a local J.P., churchwarden, chairman of the Cricket Club and took a keen interest in village life. The locals knew him as 'the squire'. He and Harry got on famously, especially when the colonel found out that Harry's cellar contained a large assortment of delectable vintage port, of which he was extremely fond.

He was a man of medium height, with a very red, bloodshot face, a large bristling white moustache with ends below the level of his mouth, which, with his arched eyebrows, gave him a permanently cheerful look, as though he were surprised and pleased at the same time. He had retired a few years ago from something of importance in the Ministry of Defence and came to settle in Hampshire to breed and shoot pheasants. Rossett Hall, which he had bought, was an elegant old Georgian mansion with over 500 acres of farm and woodland. The hall had been rather dilapidated but he had had it completely renovated, at a cost of over a million, it was rumoured locally, and it was now really a very fine country residence. Harry had eaten there several times, in great style. From the great bow windows along the front of the house there were fine sweeping views over the estate and surrounding countryside. The colonel claimed that on a clear day he could see the Isle of Wight with his telescope, Harry told him to let him know the day it was clear enough to see some topless sunbathers on Ryde beach.

His pretty French wife, at least twenty years his junior, had moderated his desire to recreate the interior of the smoking room of his London club in their reception rooms and had created a charming blend, Harry thought, of classical Edwardian furnishing with Mediterranean chic. An interesting couple, Frank and Geraldine, very well connected in the County set but not at all the classic huntin', shootin', and fishin' type, both widely read. They never talked about their previous partners or how they had come together although it was clear that they both had been married before. Harry, although not the most sensitive of people in that way, vaguely felt that some dark mystery or tragedy lurked behind them.

She loved to talk to him in French, having little other opportunity when in England, while he was glad to have the chance to stop his French from becoming too rusty. It was a language he loved, so much more expressive than English, and she spoke it beautifully, as only, he thought, an aristocratic Parisienne (or perhaps a Swiss) can. She spent quite a lot of the time away with her family in Fontainebleu and Lyon; during these absences Harry and Frank Forshaw spent quite a few evenings together.

Of course Harry had been asked to shoot, but his refusal, on the grounds of being an opponent of blood sports, had not in the least disturbed the colonel. 'My dear fellow,' he had said, in his normal expansive way, 'didn't think you were one of those animal rights activists!' A great laugh, they were on their second bottle of Warre's 1966 after an excellent Le Montrachet and even finer Chateau Malescot St. Exupéry 1970 with their meal.

He had gone on to explain how his income from raising and shooting pheasants enabled landowners like him to maintain a lot of their land, that would otherwise have had to be turned over to arable farming, in its natural state. Harry, who had never really thought about it, was interested and impressed by what he said about conservation, so much so that he now quite often went out beating for Alan during the colonel's shoots. He had bought a gun and had practiced some clay pigeon shooting, without really getting the hang of it. However he felt he was becoming a bit of a countryman and was grateful for the chance it gave him to fit in to the country scene, having been warned of the congenital insularity of village people.

'Do you think he might be interested?' Tony asked.

'He might,' Harry replied. 'I know he likes coming in here. Look, if you like I'll mention it to him.'

Harry saw the colonel for dinner at The Dower House a

couple of days later and raised the subject with him while they were enjoying a glass of Delamain cognac after dining.

'Mmm, excellent brandy this, Harry, can't beat Delamain, I always say, such a delicate flavour, and so, what's the word I want, what do you wine buffs say... fragrant! You can almost smell the grapes can't you? You can keep all these XOs the Japanese pay a hundred quid a bottle for, if you ask me.'

'Couldn't agree more, Frank. Of course we used to sell a lot of them in the restaurants. I used to keep Delamain, and Hine VSOP too, of course, but they never really went for them. They often used to ask me, you know, what was the best brandy we had, and it was no good recommending them, they couldn't believe that something cheaper could be better! – The most expensive just had to be the best.'

'Yes, I know. Damn good marketing by those cognac chaps of course, must be makin' a fortune. D'you know we went to a wedding in Hong Kong a couple of years ago, must have been a hundred, hundred and fifty tables, and blow me if there wasn't a bottle of Hennessy XO on every table, and more to follow! God only knows what it must have cost them for drink alone!'

'Mind you,' Harry interjected, 'I wouldn't like to be in that business, selling booze I mean, all that constant entertaining and boozing! I went to a golf tournament up in Scotland once, all four days, as a guest of one of the whisky companies. There must have been about forty of us guests, and three or four chaps to look after us. Do you know, those poor sods never got out of the booze tent! Stuck there all four days having to be sociable and drink along with us! You should have seen them at the end – I've never seen people look so ill!'

'Lucky it was whisky,' said the colonel ruminatively, 'whisky's relatively good for you, I always think.'

Harry took the hint and went and got a bottle of Glenmorangie and a whisky tumbler from his drinks pantry.

'Well,' said Harry, after a pause, 'our friends Tony and Rose at the Hunters aren't finding selling booze so easy either I hear, just at the moment.'

'No, so I heard,' the colonel said. 'Damn shame, nice people. Village won't be the same without a pub. I don't understand why the brewery wants to close it. Rose did explain but it didn't make any sense at all to me.'

'You know they've been offered the chance to buy it?'

'Yes.'

'Well, the bank turned them down for a loan. So it looks like they'll have to quit.'

'Somebody else might take it on, I suppose?'

'I don't think so; the new brewery really wants to close it. They've only given Tony and Rose the chance because they've been tenants for a few years. The fact is, Frank, and I won't beat about the bush, if we want to keep our pub we need to do something about it pretty quickly. How do you feel about putting some money into it?'

'Hmm,' the colonel pondered this for a while, pulling at his moustache, ' I don't want to lose the place, any more than you do, but, really, I don't know anything about runnin' pubs and I don't believe in investing blind, you know. How much money do they need?'

'I don't know for sure. But I wasn't asking you to put up all the money yourself, Frank. What I had in mind was that perhaps we could both put up half of what they need. I'd be willing to put some time and effort into helping them to run it better, particularly on the food and wine side, and to keep an eye on things. I think the place has got real potential, could be a good investment. It's got a lot of space inside and plenty of car parking, and there aren't exactly a lot of places doing good pub food round here.'

'So why do you want me on board, Harry? You could do it yourself, surely? – Mind if I have another glass of this excellent whisky?'

'Please, please, sorry, let me fill your glass,' Harry mumbled, he was normally a very considerate host who hated to see a guest's glass empty but the colonel's rate of consumption surprised even him, sometimes.

'Well, to answer your question,' he said after refilling the colonel's glass, 'I suppose I could find the money myself, but I don't think it would work so well if I was "the owner" as I would be, to all intents and purposes, if I put up seventy or eighty percent of the money to buy the place. I've had some experience of partnerships of this sort and I've found where you have one partner as very much the majority partner and the other, or others, as very much minority partners, it just doesn't work very well. Basically all the decisions get left to the majority shareholder and the others feel excluded, doesn't give you the right kind of framework for open discussion, if you understand what I mean. Besides I don't really want to get too involved in running it.'

He poured himself some more Delamain.

'It seems to me that if, for example, you and I both had, say, 40% and Tony and Rose 20%, then they, as long as they could get one of us to agree, could get things done that they wanted to, whereas if it was just me, everything would be up to me. Do you follow what I mean?'

'Mmm yes. Yes, I think so. You're obviously a democrat, Harry – wouldn't work in the Army! Makes good sense to let them run things I suppose, they seem pretty capable.'

'Yes, I think they are. We would only need to get involved in major decisions and, as I said, I would try and keep an eye on things as well.'

'Well, Harry, I'll think about it. Certainly would be a shame for the village if we lost the old place.'

In the end Harry and the colonel had both put in a hundred and fifty thousand pounds, with Tony and Rose contributing one hundred thousand. The pub had been making a trading profit of around thirty thousand pounds a year so they agreed to pay Tony and Rose a salary of twenty thousand and to split all profit above that according to their shareholding.

They had increased the range of real ales and, under Harry's guidance, had improved the food. They had got rid of all the red fake velvet seats and had gone back to the kind of comfortable old wooden furniture the brewery had chucked out when they tarted the place up a few years before. The pool table had also gone and been replaced by a bar-billiards table.

It took a while for business to pick up but once the word got round about the new £17.95 three course lunch, the business trade from Basingstoke and Alton started to come in. There was no choice for this meal, but it changed daily and the ingredients were always fresh and prepared the same day. Harry had found a butcher who could supply really good quality ham on the bone and sausages, the Colonel supplied game and trout. Top quality cheddar and stilton came from a friend of Harry's in Oxford. There was a choice of three puddings every day. The food was simple but very good, quantities were abundant, prices were high enough to make a good profit. Within six months they had more than trebled the previous takings on food, and of course bar takings went up correspondingly. Harry had re-vamped the wine range to include a dozen or so wines from Australia and New Zealand to sell below £16 a bottle, as well as supplying a select range of high-priced classic wines from his own cellar for expense-account lunchers. Tony had had the bright idea of selling wines by the case to people enjoying a bottle with their meal. In all they were now averaging over £3,000 a week on wine sales alone.

In fact the pub was doing so well, with many people driving from miles around, that the locals started to complain that they couldn't find seats. Harry's answer to this was to put the prices up, which they did. Tony and Rose were worried that this would upset the locals so they devised a rebate system whereby the locals got back 10% of everything they had spent at the end of each month. They nearly always spent it on a meal there anyway so it kept everyone happy.

Harry and the Colonel now got a very handsome return on their investment each year, and Harry was happy that Tony and Rose could now run things properly without much help.

Now, in the garage he put the clubs into the boot of the car and went back into the house to pack his golf shoes, wash things and a change of clothes into a grip. He paid Pat for the bacon, and tickled Rosie behind her ear.

'I should be back by about three or four,' he said, 'could you let the old girl out into the garden for a few minutes before you go? Then I'll take her out for a walk when I get back. David's not coming today.' David was Harry's gardener and odd-job man who often kept an eye on Rosie when he wasn't there. Even with the pleasant early spring sunshine it was too cold for the dog to be left outside in the garden.

'OK,' said Pat, 'will do. Have a good round, Harry, see you tomorrow.'

'Yes, see you,' he replied and got into Ramona, the green Rover. The red one was called Rosemary, and the beigy brown one Rhoda. Harry had given his cars nicknames all his life. He pushed the button on the remote control and the garage door opened automatically. He eased the old car out and watched the door silently come down again. He decided it was warm enough to open the sun roof and set off along the lane towards the golf club, a happy man.

Chapter 3

As HE DROVE HOME after his round of golf, Harry became fully aware of how tired he was. His legs ached and driving the car, which normally he enjoyed, seemed like hard work. He even failed to take any pleasure from the beauty of the countryside.

After parking the car and going wearily inside, a lot of wine the previous evening, not much sleep, morning exercise, golf, and two pints of beer in the clubhouse with his partners, had caught up with him. Fortunately Rosie was fast asleep when he got in and did not show any signs of wanting to go for a walk when he tickled her ear, so Harry went and stretched out on the sofa and was soon sound asleep.

He slept until around six o'clock when he was woken by the sound of someone talking into his answering machine, which he had forgotten to turn off when he came in. He got up and walked out into the hall and recognised the voice of Peter Hill.

'Hello, Peter,' he said, picking up the receiver and cutting off Hill's message.

'Oh, hello, Harry,' Peter replied 'I thought you must be out.'

'No, no – just woke from my afternoon siesta, bit of a long night last night.'

'Yes indeed,' Peter murmured, he could well imagine it had been. 'Congratulations again, a remarkable performance.'

'Thanks.'

'D'you know I've never heard of anyone having that kind of instant recall for tastes before, quite amazing. Tell me, does it ever let you down?'

'Not really,' Harry answered, 'not unless I have a cold or something.'

'Well, well, anyway when are you going to be able to come for lunch and tell me all about it?'

Harry hadn't really decided until that moment whether or not to meet Hill again, but something inside him said 'well, what the hell, why not?' and so he said, 'How about next Tuesday? I'm flying down to France in the late afternoon so I could fit in lunch in town before going out to Heathrow.'

They agreed where to meet. Harry took Rosie out for a walk and then came back in and lit a log fire. The central heating was perfectly adequate but reading and dozing in front of a real fire was one of Harry's special pleasures.

Deciding against cooking, he drove down to the pub and had sausages (excellent) and mash with fried onions for his supper with a couple more pints of beer. By the time he got home the fire was really drawing and the room was beautifully warm. Rosie was snoring on the rug in front of the fire, intermittently making the little excited whimpering noises that made Harry sure she was reliving some exciting chase of her youth. He stacked three Bob Dylan CDs into the music centre and settled down with a book for a couple of hours before turning in for an early night.

Harry met Peter Hill again the next week as planned. Hill still wanted to run an interview with him in his paper, but Harry stuck to his guns. When Hill pressed him for a reason for his antipathy to his proprietor, he explained, 'Well, of course there are many tycoons with political views as extreme, or even more so, than Murdoch. The reason I dislike him so

33

much is really because with his media power he has the power to be, even if he isn't yet, a real threat to democracy.'

'In what way?' Hill asked.

'Well, firstly, in that, with his newspapers and TV stations, he can make and break governments, which means that governments tend to do what he wants, what's good for him, rather than what the people want them to do, what's good for the people. Secondly, in that his newspapers continuously espouse right-wing, illiberal, authoritarian positions and views that are, in my humble opinion, very dangerous. You need a balance in society between the haves and have-nots, you need tolerance of other people's opinions, you *don't* need xenophobia, homophobia, automatic support for the interests of big business and vilification of the poor and unfortunate, all of which you get in his papers!'

He paused as the waiter came round to refill their glasses.

'You know,' he continued, 'what really gets me about him, and others like him, is that he has so much power to do good in the world, so much influence, so much money! And yet he does nothing that's good at all, all he wants is to get more power, more money for himself, and screw the rest of the world.'

'Surely,' said Hill, 'the whole capitalist system is based upon just that, only the strong and efficient survive. If Rupert didn't strive mightily to maximise his profits he'd get overtaken (and taken over) by someone hungrier and meaner.'

'Yes, you're right, Peter,' cried Harry, 'that is exactly the nature of the capitalist system. And, because the capitalist system has delivered, we all have to support it and therefore we all have to applaud the most successful capitalists! Well, the trouble with that of course is, what the free-market boys never tell you, is that the logical result of uninhibited capitalism is total economic inefficiency because, when the hungriest and meanest have eventually taken over all the rest, you're left with a monopoly! Or at least an oligopoly, so there's no competition at all. This is why there has to be some regulation of the market, by the government, for the public good.'

Hill was considerably impressed by Harry's vehemence.

'You obviously feel strongly about it Harry,' he said, 'but surely most government interference just does more harm than good.'

'No, I don't agree - look at pensions, look at unemployment benefit, look at the National Health Service - all government schemes imposed upon unwilling capitalists, what kind of country would this be without them? I know it's fashionable to attack social provision today and say we can't afford it, but I think that's baloney. We can afford it if we want to and anyway who wants to go back to the days of the workhouse?

'Don't get me wrong though, I'm not at all opposed to the market system. It's absolutely essential to a successful and efficient economy, I just feel that it has to be controlled so that it works for the benefit of everyone. However, I know that drawing the line between enough, and too much, interference in the market is extremely difficult for any government to get right. I suppose that's in part why I get so annoyed with people like Murdoch. If they would voluntarily try to act in the public interest, rather than in their own selfish one, what a difference they could make! How much easier it would be for governments! After all, you know, at the end of the day, it's obviously in the interests of big business to try to make everyone prosperous, isn't it? The more people there are in work and making a decent wage, the more customers there are for their products. It's only common sense.'

'That reminds me,' Hill said, 'of a wonderful cartoon I saw once. It showed a very prosperous-looking gent, fur-trimmed coat, big cigar, etc. who was standing by, and obviously running, a one-man Punch and Judy stall. Another rich man is passing by and says, "Why! Stanley Fraser! Last time I saw you, you were running a business empire of 100,000 people! Whatever happened?" "Well," says the other chap, "it's funny, I started downsizing and once I got started, you know how it is, I just couldn't stop!".'

'Exactly,' laughed Harry. 'Anyway, I mustn't bore you too much with my economic theories, Peter. I know I do tend to blether on a bit about it all.'

'No, no! I agree with quite a bit of what you say, Harry. Anyway, I really wanted to talk about wine today. You know I'm still not quite sure if I can believe you about your memory for tastes, it really does seem incredible. Although I have the evidence of my own eyes from the Savoy, so I suppose it must be true. You *didn't* have a quick look at the order of battle in advance, I suppose?' he said jokingly.

'Scout's honour,' said Harry.

'But,' said Hill, stroking his chin, 'but, wines *change*! Just because you've tasted a wine ten years ago, how can you recognise it if you taste it today? It's not the same wine, surely?'

'It is the same wine, you know,' Harry responded, 'of course the taste is not identical but it's similar enough for my brain cells anyway. In actual fact it can be very difficult if the first tasting was when the wine was still young and immature and the second is when it's mature, but even then I can normally get it. I could liken it to the way someone's face changes as they get older, perhaps, the skin gets less smooth, it sags here and there and wrinkles appear, but it's still the same face. If you have a clear picture of the young face then it's not hard to recognise the older person and my mind seems to keep a very clear picture of the young face, or the young wine.

'In fact, the biggest problem is when a chateau does two bottlings or something or when there has been some failing in the vinification or labelling or cellaring so that in effect they issue two different wines, but with the same label. It happened a lot in France before World War II, particularly in Burgundy.

'Anyway, if you don't believe me, why not put it to the test? They have a lot of good wines here, I know. You can try me out if you like.'

'Well, Harry, in actual fact I was thinking of suggesting it, but I didn't know if you'd be offended. You must get fed up with people always trying to catch you out.'

'It can be a bit tedious, especially if they want me to identify some anonymous Hungarian cabernet they bought in Asda for £3.99 a bottle!'

Hill laughed. 'Can you?'

'Not unless I've drunk it previously and bothered to look at the label on the bottle. Which is pretty unlikely in the case of Hungarian cabernet. Also the chances are that those really cheap wines are mass-produced by blending together different wines and of course it is likely that the blends will vary over time so that, to me, they are not the same wine. Of course, I'd be able to make a stab at it, the same as any other experienced wine-taster would. I daresay I'm not as good as some, you for example! with new wines, but I'm not bad.'

'OK, right then,' Hill said, 'I'll get it organised. I did in fact alert the sommelier here, old Gerard, that the Wine Society's champion winetaster was coming to lunch here with me today. I rather fancy he may have prepared something a bit special. Waiter!' he called out to the young man who had been serving them, 'could you ask Monsieur Leclerc if he can spare us a minute?'

'Of course, Mr Hill.'

The sommelier, a rotund man of about fifty-five with a large red bulbous nose, rather greasy grey hair and his silver tasting spoon on a chain round his neck, came to their table.

'Harry, may I present Monsieur Gerard Leclerc, Chevalier d'Honneur du Confrerie des Tastevins,' he bowed to Harry, 'Gerard, Mr Harry Benson, Wine Society Challenge Champion Winetaster.'

The two men shook hands. Leclerc sat down at the table.

'An honour,' the sommelier said, pronouncing the 'h', 'I have already 'eard all about your score at the Savoy. *Incroyable*!'

Harry smiled, he was getting a bit bored with the word 'incredible', he thought.

'*Je ne me suis pas débrouillé trop mal, merci, monsieur.*'

'*Ah!, Mais aussi vous parlez bien le francais! Vous habitiez en France, je crois.*'

'*Mais oui, pendant trois ans.*'

Leclerc smiled at him. Harry knew he had a friend.

'So,' Hill said, 'have you prepared something for Mr Benson to taste, Gerard?'

'Yes. It is a wine that 'as never appeared in our *carte des vins*. Because we only 'ave two bottles. Shall I order it to be brought now?'

'Harry?'

'Sure, as long as it's not a sweet wine, I haven't had my cheese yet, Peter.'

'It is a red wine, monsieur 'Arry.'

The waiter brought the wine, carefully wrapped in a white napkin. The sommelier carefully opened the bottle and poured a little into his tastevin and sniffed it. 'Ah, it is good still!' and tasted it. 'Mmmm, a wine worthy of you, monsieur,' he said and nodded for the waiter to pour a glass each for Harry and Hill.

Peter Hill swirled the wine round in his glass and watched Harry do the same and then sniff the wine's bouquet. He noted Harry's look of intense concentration.

Harry, conscious of them both watching him, put his glass down and smiled. 'What do you think, Peter?' he asked.

'Sorry, Harry, no clues!'

Harry laughed.

'You've got it already?' Hill asked.

'Surely *non*!' put in Leclerc.

'I think so,' said Harry, 'but let me taste it to make sure.'

The old sommelier looked incredulous, as Harry took some wine into his mouth, swirled it around and then gently sucked some air in through it, before swallowing.

'A lovely wine, Monsieur Gerard,' he said teasingly, 'but not perhaps as good as the '52!'

Leclerc spluttered into his glass.

'Well?'

'Musigny, Clos des Jacobins,... 1953,' Harry said.

'*Mon dieu, exactement*!' Leclerc got up excitedly and shook Harry's hand. He withdrew the napkin from around the bottle and exposed the faded label, revealing the wine to be just what Harry had said.

'Bravo! Harry,' Hill twinkled, 'I never doubted you for a minute. You've drunk it before?'

'Must have done, can't remember where, though. The memory doesn't always seem to stretch that far.'

After the sommelier had left them, Hill said 'You know, Harry, your talent could make you a fortune. Everyone's interested in wine these days.'

'There's certainly enough about it on TV at the moment,' Harry agreed. 'But I don't really want to make a fortune, Peter. I've got plenty of money and I enjoy my life as it is.'

'Lucky man!' said Hill 'But you really shouldn't hide your light under a bushel you know. OK, you won't give an interview for *The Times*. I also write a monthly column for the *American Wine Review* –'

'Yes, I know,' Harry said, 'I take it.'

'How about letting me write up a profile of you for it? It'd make a great article, they'd love it.'

'OK,' said Harry. 'Now how about that cheese? You could probably persuade old Gerard to let us have some decent port too!'

He hadn't prevaricated about it. He liked Peter Hill and anyway he knew there hadn't been any point in meeting him for lunch if he wasn't going to agree to something of the kind. They had arranged for Hill to come down to Harry's house the following week and the feature in the American magazine came out in its June edition.

Chapter 4

SOME MONTHS HAD PASSED, Harry had been busy without doing very much. The profile of him had appeared in the *American Wine Review* and several friends had been in touch with him about it. However, apart from an increase in the number of emails from Nigerian bankers and Russian ladies, nothing had really come of it.

He wasn't really disappointed, as, he told himself, he had all he needed to be perfectly happy, but there was still a nagging feeling that life might be passing him by.

It was a Tuesday early in August; Harry had just come in from his morning walk when he heard the landline ringing in the kitchen. By the time he'd wiped Rosie's paws and reached the receiver, whoever was calling had rung off. The phone's memory showed a London number he didn't recognise so he didn't attempt to call back. If it's important they'll try again, he thought.

A minute or two later his mobile rang, same London number, he noticed. Flicking across the screen to answer it, he said 'Hello?'

'Mr Benson?'

'Who's calling him?' Harry answered cautiously.

'This is Detective Inspector Pelham, of Scotland Yard.'

'Really! How can I help you, Inspector?' said Harry, intrigued, 'it wasn't me, honestly.'

He heard the inspector chuckle. 'Sorry, you must hear that all the time.'

'Yes, I have heard it before a few times. The fact is, Mr Benson, that I got your numbers from Peter Hill, who writes for the *American Wine Review*, I believe you know him?'

'I've met him a couple of times,' said Harry.

'I read his piece about you in the magazine a couple of weeks ago and it occurs to me that your wine-tasting skills could help us solve a puzzling case. In fact, I'd go so far as to say that you might be the answer to our prayers.'

'Goodness gracious me!' Harry replied, 'has someone else been flogging fake Chateau Petrus?'

'No, it's rather more serious than that, sir. It's a case of murder, I'm afraid.'

Harry, completely taken aback, went quiet for a few seconds.

'I don't know what to say, Inspector, but of course I'll help in any way I can. What on earth has happened?'

'It's rather a long story, and quite complicated to explain on the phone. I believe you live near Alton, Mr Benson?'

'Yes, that's right,' Harry replied, wondering.

'Could I send a car for you now, sir? I could explain properly here and, if you do think you might be able to help us, we could go together to the crime scene.'

'Right,' Harry said, 'I don't see why not. The only thing is that I live on my own with an old dog and... no, that's all right, the gardener's coming this afternoon and I can leave a note for him. I'm your man, Inspector!'

Harry confirmed his address and, seventy-five minutes later, heard the crunch of wheels on the gravel outside. He closed and locked the front door and, turning, found a youthful-looking uniformed police constable waiting for him in front of an unmarked silver BMW 5-series saloon.

'Mr Benson? I'm PC Stephenson, Stewart Stephenson'.

'Good to meet you, Stewart, I'm Harry,' Harry said, shaking

hands.

'Would you rather sit in the back, sir?' the young policeman said.

'No, no, I'd much rather sit in the front and, please, it's Harry, not sir.'

'OK, Harry, hop in!'

After they'd exchanged a few pleasantries about the weather and the traffic, Harry asked whether the policeman knew anything about the case he was being called in about.

'Not really, sir, er... Harry. I know that a man has been found dead, most likely poisoned, in a kind of wine cellar in a posh mews house in Chelsea. Some kind of wine-tasting club involved, I think, but that's all I know, I'm afraid.'

'I see,' said Harry. 'I believe it's Inspector Pelham in charge of the case?'

'Yes, sir. Andy Pelham, one of the youngest DI's in the force. He's known in the office as a bit of a wine buff, that's probably why he's been given this case!'

Their conversation moved on to football and the likely prospects of their two teams the coming weekend and they were soon pulling up beside a side entrance into New Scotland Yard.

'In through the doors, tell the security guard that you've got an appointment with DI Pelham, take the lift to the third floor and the office is through the double doors straight in front of you. You can't miss it.'

'OK, got it. Thanks for the ride, Stewart.'

'My pleasure, Harry.'

Harry got out of the car, had a quick look around and, drawing a deep breath, went in through the door.

* * *

Harry walked into the busy office, noting at least a dozen desks, mostly piled high with files and computers. Everybody was in plain clothes, no uniforms in sight.

'I've come to see Inspector Pelham,' he said smiling at the attractive auburn-haired woman at the desk nearest the door.

She gave him an answering smile as she said 'Oh yeah, come this way please, Mr...?'

'Benson,' Harry replied, 'thank you.'

She knocked on the door of an office in the corner of the large room and said 'A Mr Benson to see you chief?'

'Ah, yes, thanks, Alison. Please come in, Mr Benson. Take a seat.'

'Would you like a cup of coffee, Mr Benson?' Alison said.

'I'd love one,' Harry said, 'black no sugar, please.'

'You, chief?'

'Yes please, Alison, thank you.'

As Alison left the room, Harry studied the man sitting behind the desk. About thirty-five he guessed, no-rim glasses, wiry, black, with short hair and a well-trimmed moustache.

'Not what you expected, Mr Benson?' the inspector said with an amused look on his face.

'Well, to be honest, no!' Harry said. 'I certainly wouldn't have guessed from your accent that you were... well...'

'Black?'

'Yes. Not that it makes the slightest difference of course.'

'Of course.' The inspector grinned.

Harry grinned back. 'I can see that you're not averse to disconcerting people, Inspector. I suppose it must come in useful in your trade.'

'Maybe it does. Some people do have a problem with me so

I find it's useful to raise it and get it out of the way straight off.'

'Fair enough.'

'Good, thanks for coming, Mr Benson –'

'Please call me Harry,' Harry interrupted.

'OK, Harry, as I say, thanks for coming so quickly, I do appreciate it.'

Alison knocked and walked in with two mugs of coffee.

No wedding ring, Harry noted, when she put them down on the desk. Middle to late thirties, he thought, and not hard on the eye.

As the door closed behind her, Harry asked 'You're interested in wine, too, Inspector?' At the policeman's enquiring glance, Harry added 'PC Stephenson told me.'

'Uh-huh. Did he tell you anything else, about the case?'

Harry repeated what he had been told by the PC.

'Yes, that's right, as far as it goes. Word does get around this place. And yes, I am very interested in wine, always have been. In fact, I'd go so far as to opine that a good meal can't be properly appreciated without a good bottle of wine to accompany it.'

'I couldn't agree more.'

'I was amazed at what you achieved at that tasting competition, Mr B – Harry. You really can recognise any wine you've drunk before?'

'Pretty much, yes.'

'Well, your skill could be just what we need. This is the situation...'

The inspector explained to Harry that a man called Simon Oliver had been found dead, presumably poisoned, in the basement of his Chelsea house that morning. They were still waiting for the lab report to confirm the toxicology, but as the man had been found slumped at a table with his head in a puddle of wine from a tipped-over glass, there didn't seem to be much doubt about it.

Simon Oliver was one of a six-man group of wealthy commodity and currency traders who had formed a wine-tasting club. They were all passionate about wine and wealthy enough to indulge their passion by drinking rare, expensive wines.

'Have you heard of the "Twelve Angry Men" wine-tasting group in New York, Harry?'

'Yeah, it rings a bell. Weren't they caught up in that Rudy Kurniawan fraud? The guy who went down for ten years for faking wines?'

'Yes, that's right. It seems that this group modelled themselves on them...'

The explanation continued. It seemed that the group met once a month, in the wine cellar in the basement of Simon Oliver's house, for a competitive wine-tasting. Each man supplied one bottle of wine and they each put up £50,000 to back their tasting skills. The member who correctly identified the most wines collected a cool quarter of a million.

'Whew!' Harry whistled. 'Serious money.'

'Yes,' the inspector replied, 'but these are the kind of guys who get bonuses in the millions and think nothing of running up a drinks bill in the tens of thousands in exclusive wine bars and restaurants, buying top vintage first growth clarets and the like.'

There was to have been a meeting that day. The tastings took place at 11 a.m. on the first Tuesday of each month, and had been running for nearly two years. There was a precise ritual that had to be followed preceding the tasting in order to ensure absolute anonymity for each wine. Each member would come to the house the previous evening at half-hour intervals, from 7 p.m. to 9 p.m. to decant their wines into identical decanters. Simon Oliver would be absent from his house until 9.30 p.m. when he would do the same. Because the decanting process would disturb the wines, the twelve-hour interval before the club met was necessary to let them settle down and be in perfect condition for tasting. After the wine had been decanted, the bottle was deposited, together with the capsule and the cork, into one of six identical small safes for which each member had his own six-figure code.

After the tasting, each member would open his safe and the bottles would be taken out for the marking process. Marks were scored for five wines – not including the wine each member had brought.

'Christ!' said Harry, taking all this in, 'Doesn't look as though they had much trust in each other, does it?'

'Indeed so, the precautions do seem to have been pretty elaborate,' replied the inspector. 'But judging from what's happened, it seems that perhaps their caution was well-founded.'

'Indeed,' Harry mused. 'But hang on a minute', he cried, 'what's to stop me bringing two different bottles in, putting one in the decanter, and a different one in the safe? Or, for that matter putting the contents of a bottle of, I don't know, Chateau Talbot in a Chateau Palmer bottle at home? Either way, all the others would get it wrong and only score on four wines!'

'Hmm,' said the inspector. 'I see what you mean, although I

guess if all the other five correctly identified your Talbot it might be a bit tricky... anyhow, I'll check it out. We've been talking on the phone to Henry Yiu, one of the group, that's where I got the information I've been giving you. I'll ask him about it. But I suspect, bearing in mind the other precautions, they had the possibility covered.'

'Henry is Chinese, is he?' asked Harry.

'From Hong Kong. Seems like a pretty straight kind of chap to me, very shocked about Oliver's death, of course.'

'Was he able to give any reason, or suspicion, about why one of the group should want to kill Oliver?' Harry asked.

'He doesn't know yet how Oliver met his death, Harry. Or, if he does, it's not because we told him.' The inspector gave Harry a sideways glance. 'We keep as much information as close to our chest as we can.'

'Of course, he's still a suspect, isn't he? He might say something, or let something slip, that only the poisoner can know.'

'We'll make a detective of you yet, Harry,' laughed the inspector. 'Anyhow, he did say that Simon Oliver, who hadn't been a regular winner over the course of the tastings, had been the winner in three of the last four months.'

'So, said Harry, thinking out loud, 'one of the others may have been suspicious that he was, let's see, tasting the wines in advance.' He rubbed his eyes. 'It's in his own home, so he would have access during the night, wouldn't he?'

'Exactly,' said Pelham. 'And what better way to test out his suspicions, which were in fact entirely correct, and put a stop to it, than by adding a drop of a lethal toxin to his wine?'

'Oliver was trying all the wines then?'

'Yes he was. Undoubtedly. A little of each had been taken out with a pipette and there were wine reference books open on the table. The browsing history on his iPad showed he'd been to various wine sites as well.'

'So he was right about Oliver. But surely, surely... if he'd been wrong about Oliver, he'd risk wiping out the whole group, including himself, at the tasting? He wouldn't know which decanter was his and he could hardly fling himself at the table and smash them all!'

'Excellent point, Harry, and one that occurred to me too. I checked the decanters and found, just under the lip of the one that it seems Simon Oliver had tasted from just before dying, a tiny blob of hard clear plastic glue. Invisible but you could feel it. My guess is that the killer would, if it came to it, have identified the lethal decanter that way and knocked it over onto the floor, breaking it, accidentally of course, before the tasting started.'

'Makes sense,' Harry said. After a moment's thought he added 'You know you said about keeping your information close to your chest? You're being very open with me, though, aren't you?'

'Well done, Harry. Yes, I am. I wouldn't normally tell you any more than the minimum you need to know. However, I think you, and only you, can help me crack this murder and I'll also most probably need you to testify in court to make the charge stick. So I need you to be completely onside and to trust me. You see?'

'OK, I see,' Harry replied. 'So what is it that you actually want me to do?'

'Well. Let's see. The situation is that we have five unidentified clean decanters of wine. We can be sure that

Simon Oliver supplied one of them but, even when we get the safes opened and know which wines we're dealing with, we won't know which one was the poisoned bottle. And if we don't know that, I don't see how we can identify the killer, do you?'

'No,' said Harry, 'I don't.'

'In a way, it's the perfect crime,' mused the inspector. 'Yes, we know it's one of five people. We could put pressure on each one of them; we can, and will, check if any of them has had access to lethal toxins, but they're all smart, rich guys who can afford good lawyers, and my feeling is that we'd be clutching at straws.

'Whereas if you can identify the five clean wines, the person who opens his safe to reveal the bottle that contained the other one, the poisoned wine, is the murderer.'

'Logical,' said Harry, starting to feel a bit nervous. 'Quite a responsibility.'

'No doubt, it is. There's something else, though. If you can do your stuff, we'll know who the killer is for sure, but the question is, will we be able to prove it in front of a jury? Unless we can link him up with access to the poison, we won't have a shred of proof. It'll be, in essence, your word against his. That's why I said I might need you in court.

'Now, I want you to picture the scene, Harry, at the Old Bailey. You're in the witness box and the defence barrister is cross-examining you. "Come, come, Mr Benson. Do you really expect the jury to accept that you're infallible? We all make mistakes, don't we? I put it to you that it is entirely possible that the Chateau Lafite 1982, supplied by the defendant, which you say contained the poison, was in fact the Chateau Latour 1985. It's notoriously difficult for even the greatest wine expert to differentiate between these wines, isn't it? Why should the jury accept your word," etcetera etcetera. You get the drift, Harry?'

'Mm, yes. I can picture it, Inspector. A good barrister could certainly put a considerable amount of doubt into the minds of the jurors. But,' he paused for a moment, 'you wouldn't be telling me all this if you couldn't see a way round it, would you?'

'Quite right again, Harry. The scenario I've just outlined makes sense if, given the six bottles, your role was just to decide which decanter matched which bottle. The jury might quite reasonably conclude that you might possibly have mixed some of them up. However, and here's the something else, Harry, it seems to me that if you've independently identified the wines,' he paused for emphasis, '*without seeing the bottles,* the mixing them up argument holds no water.' The policeman sat back and regarded Harry.

'If it's conclusively proved,' he went on, 'that you were able to absolutely identify the five clean wines, with no prior knowledge of the bottles, any attack on your competence to make the judgement must surely fail.'

'I see,' said Harry, thinking it through. 'It would look completely different.'

'In fact,' Pelham continued, 'in such circumstances I think it highly likely that the defendant's solicitor would advise him to just plead guilty and hope for a lighter sentence.'

'And I wouldn't have to go to court!'

'Absolutely. So you can see why I said you might be the answer to our prayer, and why I've laid all the cards on the table. It all depends on you, Harry, and your amazing gift. I'm afraid I'm putting a great weight on your shoulders but, if you

51

can do what I think, no, what I *believe*, you can, the dead man at least gets justice. If not, the killer will probably walk free.'
'No pressure then,' joked Harry, trying to cover up his nervousness. 'I don't see why I shouldn't be able to do it. Although, of course, it's possible that there might be a wine, or wines, that I haven't come across before, which could make things difficult. I've tasted an awful lot of wines, but of course by no means absolutely every one of the best wines and there's a lot of cheaper wines I wouldn't know. Do you know what kind of wines they tasted, and in what kind of price range?'
'Yes, just clarets and red burgundies, Yiu said. Minimum price £300 a bottle, no maximum.'
'Good,' said Harry, 'that makes it less likely I won't know them. I appreciate your faith in me, but... there are no guarantees, Inspector. By the way, how are you going to be able to prove to the defence that I had no knowledge of the bottles while tasting the wines?'
'Shall we talk about that in the car on the way to Chelsea?...'

As he waited while Inspector Pelham arranged for a car, Harry wandered over towards the desk by the door, where Alison was busy on her computer.
She looked up and smiled, 'All done?'
'Just waiting for the inspector,' Harry replied.
'Ah,' she said. 'You're Harry Benson, aren't you, the wine man? I just Googled you!'
'Really? I hope what you found wasn't entirely discreditable?'
The policewoman leaned back in her seat, uncrossed her arms and laid them on the arms of the chair.

'No, not entirely!' she teased.

Harry could read body language as well as the next man, and so he really just couldn't help saying, 'Well, if you fancy doing a bit more research sometime!'

She gave him a demure smile.

'Coming, Harry?'

'Ready, Inspector. See you later, Alison.'

'Bye, Mr. Benson,' she said primly.

'Let's go then, the car should be outside in a couple of minutes.'

As they went down in the lift, Pelham said 'Looks like you're having an exciting day, Harry. Nice lady, Alison Carter. She's interested in wine too!'

Yes, looks like being an interesting day, Harry thought.

Again the car was an unmarked BMW, but with a different driver.

'You know where to go, Collins?' Pelham asked.

'Yes, sir.'

As the car pulled out into Victoria Street, the inspector opened his mobile and made a call.

'Mr Yiu? It's Detective Inspector Pelham again. I have another question for you, sir...'

Pelham asked about Harry's query regarding switching the wine put into the decanters and listened carefully.

He listened for quite a long while, before eventually he said 'Thank you very much, Mr Yiu, that's very clear. I'm afraid there's nothing else I can tell you at this stage, but we'll certainly be back in touch. Bye.

'Phew. Quite a complicated procedure. It seems,' he said, turning to Harry, 'that Oliver's butler-cum-valet, a man called

Pearson, would check each member as he arrived to ensure he was carrying nothing but his bottle, no bags allowed, no jackets with pockets. The bottle is wrapped so that Pearson couldn't see the label, but the neck is exposed so that he can check that the capsule is intact. Then he turns his back while the bottle is opened and poured into the decanter. This must have been when the poison and glue were added. I guess they would have been easy to conceal in trouser pockets. As soon as the bottle, cork and capsule have been put in the safe, he turns back and puts the decanter, stoppered, into a temperature-controlled wine cabinet. Partly in order to keep it in good condition, of course, but also to prevent the next member coming in being able to see it, smell it or even taste it. Evidently he locked the cabinet each time. It seems that they all trust him – he's an ex Regimental Sergeant-Major in the Royal Marines, but this procedure, a hangover from when they first started, has become a bit of a tradition.'

'Goodness gracious,' Harry said, 'even so, what a suspicious lot! But that wouldn't stop Oliver himself from changing his bottle later, would it?'

'No – I'll check, but it does explain the mystery of the fingerprints on the decanter.'

'Fingerprints!' Harry exclaimed, 'I didn't think of that! But wouldn't it...' he trailed off.

'Oh dear, might have to start you in the uniformed branch after all, Harry! We got quite excited when we found two sets of prints on the poisoned decanter. One belonged to Mr Oliver of course. But then we found the same two sets on all the other decanters and it didn't seem likely the murderer would touch all the other five. Of course we didn't know then about the locked wine cabinet which would have made it

54

impossible. The second set must belong to Mr Pearson.'

'Shouldn't there be three sets?' Harry asked, 'Oliver, Pearson, and the murderer?'

'You'd think so, wouldn't you? But no such luck. At first we thought he must have put gloves on or wiped it clean with a handkerchief, but in fact there were only three sets on two of the decanters, and those third sets were smudged. It's a puzzle.'

Harry thought for a moment, imagining himself decanting wine from a bottle into a decanter. Light dawned.

'Whereabouts on the decanter did you find the sets, Inspector, on the bulbous part, holding the wine?'

'Yes, why?'

'Because if you're pouring a fine wine into a decanter, you won't keep the decanter upright and let it splash down into the bottom, you'll tilt the decanter so the wine runs gently down the side. To minimize the risk of any spills you'll hold the decanter by the neck to tilt it, won't you, so it won't move?'

'Hmm, yes, you're right, Harry. Well done. Back out of the uniformed branch. You'll grip the neck between your palm and your curled fingers, no fingerprints. That explains it.'

'Are you going to fingerprint them all to eliminate the people with the two sets you found?'

'I don't think so; it's not really going to get us anywhere and, as I say, they're smudged.

'Anyhow I'll just check about Oliver changing his bottle.'

He called Henry Yiu again. 'Sorry to bother you again, sir, but I've got another question regarding the arrangements for the tasting. I can see that none of the other five members of the group would be able to change their wines, but can I ask if

there were any precautions to prevent Mr Oliver doing so?'
Again he listened to Yiu's reply before thanking him and ringing off.

'Pearson locked the cellar after he put Oliver's wine into the cabinet. Mr Yiu thinks he had the only key. But, clearly,' he turned to Harry, 'Oliver had another as well as, I guess, a key to that cabinet.'

The inspector stopped speaking and thought for a moment. Then his face cleared and he smiled broadly. 'Hey, thinking about it, it's lucky for us that they were all so suspicious, otherwise it really would have been a perfect, unsolvable murder!'

'How do you mean?' Harry asked.

'If the decanters had been left out as the others came, the murderer could have, and surely would have, unless he was the first to arrive, put the poison into someone else's wine. We'd have been totally snookered. As it is the murderer can only have put the poison in his own wine.' Another pause. 'I wonder where Pearson was when I was there earlier? We were shown in by the cleaner, who discovered the body.'

The car pulled off The Embankment into Oakley Street.

'Pricey area,' Harry commented.

'Well over a million just for a flat, I think,' said the inspector. 'Goodness knows what this house cost.'

They stopped outside a terraced house and got out of the car. Four floors above ground, Harry noted, and a basement. The house had the typical white stucco portico of the area and black metal Juliette balconies on the first floor. They walked up the steps to the front door, where a uniformed PC saluted Pelham.

'Is the butler, Mr Pearson, in, Gardner?' he asked.

'Yes, sir, came in around mid-day.'

'SOCO people still here?'

'Yes, sir.'

'OK, could you get word to Mr Pearson that I'd like to see him? I'll be down in the cellar.'

They went in through the door into a hall with a polished wooden floor and high ceiling. Then into a luxurious grey-flagstoned kitchen from which a granite-stepped staircase led down into the basement.

'Just wait here a minute, Harry, will you? I'll check that everything is in order.' The inspector disappeared downstairs and Harry, feeling distinctly nervous, was left to wonder if he was up to the task of bringing a killer to justice.

Chapter 5

A COUPLE OF MINUTES passed before the inspector reappeared, accompanied by two SOCOs who carried up their equipment in large metal cases. One turned to the inspector and said 'OK, Andy, I'll try and get the recording equipment set up for this evening.'

'Thanks, John,' Pelham replied, 'see you later.'

He smiled at Harry and gestured for him to follow him back down the stairs, at the bottom of which was a heavy wooden door with a Yale lock. The door stood open and Harry followed the policeman into the room.

Harry's immediate impression of the cellar was of just how bare it was – plain white walls and neutral-coloured carpeting, with functional strips of LED spotlights overhead. In the centre of the room was a large rectangular stripped pine table, on which rested five identical glass decanters. Rather to Harry's relief, there was no lifeless body slumped over it.

Pelham caught Harry's inquiring glance and explained 'No, he's been taken off to the mortuary for a post-mortem. And the poisoned wine is at the lab. It might take some time to identify the poison. All the other evidence has been secured but we've kept the decanters, for you to taste.'

Harry gulped. 'Goodness gracious me.' Looking around he saw another table at the end of the room in front of a wooden glass-framed door giving on to the steps up to the street. The door was secured, he noticed, with a metal grille outside over the glass and heavy horizontal bolts at the top and bottom.

On the table were around a dozen glasses and all the paraphernalia associated with wine tastings – bottles of Evian water and water glasses, large jugs for use as spittoons, pens and notepads. Beside the wall was the temperature-controlled wine storage unit where the decanters had been stored overnight. Harry went up to it and saw that it was indeed lockable, which was unusual. The top three racks were missing, obviously in order that the decanters would fit in. On top of it stood a small rectangular mahogany cupboard, containing the six safes, in two columns of three. Each safe had a bronze-coloured metal door containing a digital keypad. As Harry was taking all this in, a constable came down the stairs and informed the inspector that the butler was waiting in the sitting room.

'Excuse me, Harry,' he said, 'I'll go and talk to him up there. I shouldn't be long – please feel free to look around, here and below, but please don't touch the decanters yet!'

He followed the constable up the stairs and Harry realised that there was a door in the wall at the other end of the room from the window. A white-painted door set in a white wall. He opened it and found himself in a small office, with a stripped pine desk, with two drawers either side, a four-drawer filing cabinet, and a bookcase.

There was a well-worn leather chair behind the desk and on it sat a computer connected to a small printer. The bookcase was exclusively devoted to books about wine, and wine magazines.

In the corner of the room, away from the door, was another staircase, of similar construction to the one leading down from the kitchen. Harry had been wondering where all the wine was kept – not much of a cellar without any wine – and now saw that there was a sub-basement.

He'd read about wealthy Londoners excavating below their houses to create extra space for gyms, swimming pools, and the like and, moving down the stairs, he saw that Simon Oliver, or a previous owner, must have done the same to create this large open space. The walls and ceilings were totally smooth and met in perfect right-angles, in contrast to the more elegant rounded cornices favoured by the house's 19th-century builders on the floors above.

The room was totally devoted to the storage of wine, with whitewashed brick and cement bins all around the walls. Each bin had a lower area for the storage of unopened cases, with a shelf above, at waist level, allowing the stacking of individual bottles. Along the centre of the room were two rows of solidly built wooden racks, following the same principle.

Harry wandered around between the bins, looking with real interest at the contents. There were plenty of clarets, burgundies and champagnes but also classic wines from the USA, Australia, and Italy. There were some wines worth a fortune, some 1961 first-growth Bordeaux amongst them, but Harry couldn't help noticing that most of the bins containing these wines were much emptier than the ones containing more recent, less expensive, wines. Still excellent wines, but perhaps not the ones someone with money to burn might have purchased, he thought.

He wondered whether Oliver's motivation for cheating might have been as much financial as for the kudos of beating his friends. Some friends! he thought, as he heard DI Pelham coming down the stairs to find him.

'OK, Harry?' the inspector asked, 'a bit of an Aladdin's cave for a wine lover, isn't it?'

'It certainly is.' Harry replied. He wondered whether he should share the theory that Oliver had been spending rather less on wine recently with Pelham, but Pelham started telling him about his interview with the butler.

'Basically Mr Pearson confirmed what Henry Yiu told me. He checked the capsules and then turned away to let them decant the wine and put their bottles into the safe, before he put the decanters into the cabinet. Pearson didn't notice any of the group being particularly agitated yesterday, or any smell of glue or anything else unusual. He's greatly shocked of course. It seems he's been working for Simon Oliver for four years, liked him, said he was a very considerate employer and found it hard to believe that he would cheat in the tastings. As far as he knows the group are all pretty friendly and he has no reason to suspect any particular one of them.'

'Did he know that Oliver had a key to the cellar door?' Harry asked. 'He certainly wouldn't have been able to get into the cellar from the outside.'

'No, it seems not. The cellar was normally left unlocked so Oliver wouldn't have needed a key. It was only ever locked the night before a tasting. If Oliver had been going down to the cellar in the night before previous tastings, he must have been very careful to tidy up afterwards because he, Pearson that is, was the first person in the room on the morning of the tastings and would have noticed anything different. But he admits that it wouldn't have been difficult for Oliver to get a second key made.

'His apartment is on the top floor so he wouldn't have heard anything if Oliver, whose bedroom is on the floor below, had gone down into the cellar.' The inspector paused to see if Harry had any further questions and then went on, 'So there we are, basically we're as sure as we can be about what happened. The thing to do now is to prove it!'

'Sure,' said Harry, 'but, to repeat my previous question, how are you going to prove I had no previous knowledge of the wines? If, that is, I actually can identify them.'

'Don't worry, Harry, I'm sure you can. But, to answer your question, my intention is to take an official, witnessed video of you doing the tasting, followed by the opening of the safes to reveal the bottles. I've discussed this with the Commissioner, who is going to run it by the Director of the CPS.'

'But couldn't we have opened the safes before and re-closed them?' Harry asked, 'bearing in mind what you said about the defence counsel at the Old Bailey.'

The inspector grinned broadly. 'Very true. So we're going to get the five group members to come and open them themselves!' He chuckled. 'Talk about coming it the Hercule Poirot! All the suspects gathered in one place and the murderer revealed!' another chuckle. 'I'll be the talk of the Force! But only with your help,' he added quickly.

'Good heavens above!' cried Harry. 'You mean that I've got to perform, in front of the... in front of the murderer? And that he's going to see me more or less condemning him? I'm really not sure I'm ready for that, Inspector.'

'Hmm, I see what you mean. But,' he said, thinking quickly, 'it needn't be like that. You don't need to be there when the safes are opened, do you? And, anyway, I'm not sure we'll be able to get all of them to come in person. We need to get on with it before the wine deteriorates. I'm hoping to do it this evening, but it might have to be tomorrow morning. It depends on how quickly we can get hold of the other four and their availability.

'At this stage, none of them are really aware of the situation and we can't force them to come unless we announce that we're investigating a crime. I don't really want to do that just yet. It may be that we ask anyone who can't come to send a personal representative with the code for their safe.'

Harry thought this over. 'That makes sense, and it's quite a relief for me. I suppose the murderer may very well find an excuse not to come!'

'Yes, quite likely.' He thought for a moment. 'Let's see. They probably all know by now from Henry Yiu that Oliver's dead. That means the one who added the poison knows he'll be under serious suspicion, along with the others. But, he'll reason that there's no way we can prove anything, because he's clearly thought all this through in advance. So it might well be that he *will* come to avoid arousing our suspicions if he doesn't.'

Harry's stomach rumbled and it reminded him that it was gone 3 o'clock and he hadn't had any lunch.

The inspector grinned and said 'Yes, time for some lunch. I need to get back to the office and get on with organising this. I'll grab a sandwich there. Do you want to come back with me? I expect there'll be some food left in the canteen.'

'Not really, to be honest,' Harry replied. 'There's a nice-looking pub just along the road and I could do with a beer after all this excitement. It sounds like you'll want me here either this evening, or tomorrow morning?'

'I'll aim for either around 7.00 this evening or, if that's not possible, say 10.30 tomorrow morning. The one'll give you time to get home this evening, the other time to get in here in the morning. Does that sound OK? Although I imagine we could arrange to put you up in Town tonight, if you'd prefer?'

'Thank you, but no, I'd rather get home,' Harry replied. 'I'll go to the pub and grab a meal – will you call me and let me know?'

'Certainly. I'll call as soon as I can.' Pelham was all business again now, Harry could see, and he wasted no time in taking his leave and heading out along Oakley Street towards the pub he'd noticed on the way there.

It was a Fullers pub, serving food all day, he saw with pleasure, and he looked forward to a pint or two of ESB, one of his favourite ales, with his lunch. Better not have more than a couple, he thought, need to keep a really clear head for tonight. He sipped his first pint slowly as he studied the menu, before ordering a Ploughman's Lunch which promised crusty bread, mature cheddar and stilton, with pickles. Just what the doctor ordered, he thought.

As he waited for his lunch to come, he went back over the events of the day. Scotland Yard had been much as he had expected from watching television, a bit shabby but seemed bustling and purposeful; he thought how much he liked Andy Pelham, clearly a very bright guy; and his thoughts turned to Alison, something about her reminded him of Katharine Hepburn, one of his favourite old-time film stars. Something in the poise of her head, maybe. He tried to keep himself from thinking about the test he was facing either that evening or the next day, and about the consequences if he failed, or indeed if he succeeded.

Rather given, as he was, to introspection, Harry instinctively tried to avoid crossing bridges before he came to them. He tried to live in the present and got impatient with people who spent their time either harking back to better days or longing for something good that was going to happen tomorrow, next month, next year. He had faced many difficult and challenging situations in the past and had come to the conclusion that worrying and overthinking only made things worse.

Nevertheless, his thoughts turned towards the kind of person who could deliberately set out to poison someone who, if not necessarily a friend, was at least someone he had a longstanding acquaintance with. Harry wondered if he'd done it because of the money, jealousy, or anger at being cheated. And he wondered how that person would react when he realised what the police, and Harry, were trying to do. He was glad that Andy Pelham had said he didn't have to be there when the bottles were revealed – it might well be a very nasty scene and he really didn't like confrontations.

He supposed that that would disqualify him from being a policeman, confrontations must be an everyday part of the job. Nice as Inspector Pelham seemed, Harry didn't doubt that his friendly exterior concealed an inner steel.

These thoughts kept him occupied throughout his lunch and second pint. He was just wondering whether to indulge himself in a pudding – syrup sponge and custard was on the menu – when his phone rang. It was the inspector.

'It's no-go for this evening, Harry, I'm afraid. One of the other four, a chap named Peter King, has tickets for *Turandot* at the Royal Opera this evening, a box there, no less, and I can't in all conscience make him miss it as he's happy to come tomorrow morning. It looks like everyone can come then, just waiting for final confirmation, so unless you hear from me otherwise in the next couple of hours, it's set for tomorrow at 10.30, OK?'

'OK. You want me to come to Oakley Street?'

'Yes, please, it'd be good if you can be there 15 minutes early. Would you like me to send a car again?'

Harry thought quickly. 'Er, no thanks, it'll mean getting a taxi back from Alton station again afterwards. I'll find my own way in.'

'I'm glad you said that! It's all hands to the pumps here at the moment. But do let me have your receipts for the journey back tonight and for the return trip tomorrow, take taxis, they'll be reimbursed.'

'OK, thank you, will do. See you tomorrow, Inspector, or should I say - Poirot?'

Harry heard the inspector chuckle down the phone. 'No, better not! See you tomorrow. Bye.'

'Bye.' Harry shut off the call and sighed. It meant another half a day of anxiety, but at least he could have another pint and that syrup sponge.

Chapter 6

HARRY HAD BEEN VERY tired by the time he got back from London and went to bed early. He didn't even feel up to a run in the morning, so he just took Rosie for a quick walk before driving in to Alton station.

He decided the Metropolitan Police could probably afford the extra £10 for a first-class fare and relaxed in comfort reading the sports pages of *The Guardian* for the 70 minute journey into Waterloo.

Emerging from the station into a beautiful summer morning, he waited in the taxi queue for ten minutes before his turn came. He gave the address to the driver and sat back in the seat, intending to enjoy watching the bustling life of London on the way to Chelsea. However, thoughts of what he was heading towards intruded and he barely noticed where he was until the cab pulled to a halt outside Simon Oliver's house.

There was still a policeman on the door and Harry could see the cab driver, intrigued, was about to ask about it. He wasn't really in the mood for chatting so he said 'Sorry, mate, got to dash.' He handed over a note and, not waiting for change, or a receipt, climbed out of the car.

Checking his watch, 9.55, he found he was 20 minutes early so he took a turn down to The Embankment and looked at the river for ten minutes before taking a deep breath and heading back down to Oakley Street. Here goes! He thought.

The constable on the door recognised him from the previous day and took him straight in to the study, where Andy Pelham was talking to the SOCO Harry had seen coming up the stairs yesterday. The inspector turned to him. 'Harry! Good morning. Very punctual. John, this is Harry Benson, the wine expert – our star turn today. Harry, this is John Morris, our senior Scene of Crimes Officer.'

'Morning, Mr Benson,' Morris said, 'DI Pelham has told me about you. Some gift you have. Personally, I couldn't tell a Chablis from a Chianti.'

Harry grinned weakly and said hello.

'John has set up all the video recording equipment for this morning.' Pelham said. 'See you downstairs in ten, John?'

'OK, my friend,' Morris said, heading down the stairs to the cellar.

'Right, Harry,' Pelham said, 'let's sit over here in the corner for a minute, shall we?' He led Harry over to a red leather two-seater sofa next to a window looking out on to the garden.

'They're all here. Henry Yiu, Peter King, James Courtenay, Mike Ellison and Guillaume Benezet are their names. Guillaume is French. Apart from Henry Yiu, the others are English. They've all been told that we need to identify the wines as part of the investigation into Simon Oliver's death. They don't know about the poison, apart from the murderer, obviously. They've been told that you're going to taste the wines. I'm sorry, Harry, but they've all been asked to attend the tasting. It's not ideal for you but the guidance from the Commissioner is that the video must run continuously from the introductions, to the tasting, to the opening of the safes.'

Harry gulped nervously. 'OK, Inspector, if that's the way it has to be. By the way,' he continued, 'how are you going to open Oliver's safe? Does Mr Pearson know the code?'

'No, I'm afraid not. Although in a way it's a good thing,

because it proves no one could have changed his bottle. No, we've got to do it the old-fashioned way – cold chisel, lump hammer and crowbar plus a strong young constable.'

He looked at Harry carefully. 'Any more questions? Are you feeling OK?'

Harry nodded.

'Look I'm sorry to put all this pressure on you. But you can leave as soon as you've finished, before the safes are opened. Your pub'll be open, go there and I'll join you when it's over. OK?

'Yes,' Harry replied, 'I expect I'll be in need of a pint after this. But don't worry, I'm OK and ready.'

'Sure?'

'Sure.'

'OK, let's go down. I'll be doing all the talking, so just follow my instructions.'

Pelham turned and walked down the stairs, Harry took another deep breath, and followed him. Here goes, he thought, thirty years of tasting for pleasure, but this isn't fun any more.

'Good morning, gentlemen,' the inspector said, when everyone was assembled in the cellar.

'Thank you all for coming. I'll make the introductions in a minute. But first, this is Sergeant Imtiaz Ahmed from Scotland Yard, who will be recording this morning's proceedings.'

'Thank you, Inspector. Good morning, gentlemen. Under the terms of Section 32D of the Criminal Justice Act 1988 I am making a video which may be produced in a court of law. None of you are under any compulsion to participate. Would anyone like to withdraw at this stage?'

He paused and looked around.

'No? Good, thank you. The video will be made on this single video camera here, by my side. The camera will roll continuously, with no breaks. I'd be grateful if, when speaking, everyone could look at the camera, and speak clearly.'

He looked across at DI Pelham. 'That's it, sir.'

'Thank you, Sergeant. If you can start the camera, we'll begin.'

While the policemen had been speaking, Harry looked at the other five men in the room, all seated around the tasting table. The man from Hong Kong, Henry Yiu, was instantly identifiable from his appearance. From what Pelham had said, Harry doubted that he was their man. The others ranged in age from mid-thirties to around fifty, Harry estimated. They were all smartly dressed: Yiu and two others in dark-coloured business suits and ties, the other two more casual in chinos and open-necked shirts. The man Harry guessed to be about fifty, caught his glance and smiled at him. Harry smiled back briefly.

If this was a Miss Marple or Hercule Poirot denouement on TV, Harry thought, I'd be guessing whodunnit. But I really haven't a clue, they all look perfectly normal, even though one of them must be guilty of murder. None of them look even slightly tense, do they?

His thoughts were cut off when Andy Pelham, seated at the head of the table, turned his chair to face the camera and started speaking.

'I am Detective Inspector Andrew John Pelham, of Scotland Yard,' he began, 'and I am investigating the death of Simon Oliver, on Tuesday August the sixth 2017. Today is

Wednesday August the seventh. The time is,' he checked his watch, 'ten thirty three a.m. Pursuant to this investigation I wish to determine the contents of these five decanters of wine,' he gestured to the table, 'and to ascertain who provided the wines in question.

'I am joined by six men who have agreed to assist with this investigation. I will ask each gentleman seated around the table to briefly identify himself.' He turned back to the table and indicated the man seated next to him, on the left-hand side. 'Will you start, please, sir? If you could just give your name, age and where you live.'

The man who had smiled at Harry spoke. 'My name is Peter Norman King. I am 48 and I live in London, in Kensington.'

Next was Henry Yiu. 'I am Henry Yiu. I am 38 and I live in London, in Westminster.'

It went round the table, they all lived in the wealthier parts of London. James Courtenay and Guillaume Benezet, the two in casual shirts were both 36, Mike Ellison, 42.

'My name is Harry Richard Benson,' Harry announced. 'I'm 47 and I live in Alton, Hampshire.' He was aware of looks from all the other five when he gave his name.

'Right, thank you.' The inspector resumed. 'I'm now going to turn to the subject why each of you is here. Mr King, if I may again start with you. You are a member of a group of six wine-lovers who meet regularly in this room for competitive wine tastings. Is that correct?'

'Yes,' King replied.

'Could you please say, Mr King, when you last visited this room and what you did when you were here?'

'Certainly. I came here on Monday evening, August 5th that is, and I brought a bottle of wine. After I decanted it, and put the empty bottle in my safe, Pearson, that is Mr Oliver's butler, locked the decanter into that wine cabinet unit, then I left.'

'Thank you, sir,' Inspector Pelham said. 'Can I just confirm which safe is yours, and how it is operated?'

'The middle one, on the left. Each safe has a six-digit code which opens it.'

'Thank you again. Can I ask if anyone else is in possession of the six-digit code for your safe?'

'You mean does anyone else know it?' King queried.

'Yes, that's right.'

'No, I have never told anyone the code.'

'Is it possible that anyone else could have learnt the code, perhaps by observing you open the safe?'

King thought. 'No, no one, apart from Mr Pearson, the butler, has ever been here when I opened it, I'm sure. We all come at separate times. Mr Pearson turns away while I open the wine and put it in the safe, so it would not be possible for him to watch, even if he wanted to.'

'Thank you, Mr King. In your opinion, is it possible that your safe has been opened since you deposited the bottle on Monday evening?'

'No, of course not. Not unless someone has had the time to try out the million different combinations!'

Pelham didn't smile at this pleasantry. 'Yes, indeed. Also, to your knowledge is it possible that anyone else, particularly anyone else in this room, could know which bottle of wine you brought here on Monday?'

'No, not at all. We go to great lengths to preserve the anonymity of the wines before the tastings. That's the whole point.'

'Yes, of course,' the inspector replied. 'So, am I correct in saying that, to the best of your knowledge, you are the only person in the world that knows the contents of your safe?'

'Definitely!' King replied.

'Thank you, Mr King. Now Mr Yiu, if I may turn to you...'

Harry watched while the inspector asked the same questions and elicited very much the same responses from the other four members of the group. Ellison pointed out that the safes were designed so that three incorrect codes entered would freeze the operation of the safe for 24 hours. It had been him who had commissioned the construction of the cupboard.

Did any of them look nervous or flustered? Not really, he thought. None of them appeared to be sweating overmuch or avoiding the inspector's gaze as he looked steadily at them while they spoke. Whoever did it must be a cool customer, he thought. Or perhaps it all was just a huge misunderstanding with an innocent explanation? No, can't be, he decided, the drop of clear glue on the poisoned decanter can't be explained away.

When the last member of the group, Guillaume Benezet, who spoke excellent English with only a slight French accent, had finished speaking, Pelham turned to Harry.

'Mr Benson. You are the current holder of the title of Champion Winetaster of The Wine Society, is that correct?'

Harry was looking at the inspector as he spoke and so was not aware of any change of expression among the others seated at the table as Pelham was speaking. But was that the sound of a slightly sharp intake of breath from across the table? Perhaps he'd imagined it. 'That's correct,' he answered.

'In the tasting competition you won, I believe you scored 93 points out of a possible 100. No other champion in over 40 years has ever scored above 90. Is that also correct?'

'I believe so.' Harry resisted the temptation to be modest or flippant, much though he disliked blowing his own trumpet.

'In a recent interview in *The American Wine Review* you explained your success by saying that you have the equivalent of a photographic memory for tastes, which enables you to identify any wine you have previously tasted. Is that also correct?'

'Yes, I do seem to have that ability.'

'Does it ever let you down? Have you ever wrongly identified a wine you had already tasted?'

'Not to my knowledge. I do try to avoid any tasting when I have a cold as I feel it may interfere with my sense of taste.'

'I see,' Pelham replied. 'Do you have a cold today, Mr Benson?'

'No, I'm perfectly well.' The tension was getting to Harry a bit and he couldn't resist adding 'But thank you for asking!'

The inspector didn't smile or respond. He's really tense too, Harry realised. Of course it would be a big feather in his cap if he could 'come it the Hercule Poirot' – in his own words.

'Right, gentlemen.' Pelham gazed around the table. 'That completes the introductions. Unless anyone has any questions we will proceed with the wine tasting, followed by the opening of the safes.'

He looked around the group of men seated at the table.

Mike Ellison spoke. 'Well, Inspector. This is all very mysterious, I'm sure. I imagine your intention is to match Mr Benson's, er, opinions, to the bottles in the safes. I'm not quite sure why. But, yes, I do have a question. As Mr Oliver is... well, is not here, how are we going to open his safe? No one here knows his code, I'll wager.'

Harry thought to himself how well and calmly the man spoke, but perhaps that's just a bluff? Might it be him?

'Good question, Mr Ellison. I had hoped that Mr Pearson might know the code but that is not the case. We will open it the old-fashioned way, I'm afraid, by physical force. Are there any other questions?'

Nobody spoke and Pelham continued 'Very well. Mr Benson? If you're ready, we'll make a start.'

Harry indicated that he was.

'OK. To avoid any possible confusion,' Pelham said, 'I'm going to affix a number, 1 to 5, to each decanter with these sticky labels and ask Mr Benson to clearly write, in capital letters, on each of these sheets of paper, also numbered 1 to 5, his decision on the identity of each wine.'

He carefully stuck the numbers on the decanters and, moving to the table at the end of the room, brought back five wine glasses, a water glass and a spittoon.

He pushed across the numbered sheets to Harry and asked if he would like a pen.

Harry declined and took a Cross ballpoint from the inside pocket of his jacket. 'I came prepared.'

'Very well. I will now ask you to pour some wine from decanter number one and taste it. Take your time, there's no hurry.'

Harry did his best to shut out all the thoughts and questions, removed the stopper, and poured himself a third of a glass from the first decanter. He tilted the glass sideways and held it in front of the sheet of paper in front of him, assessing the colour against the white background. Next he swirled the wine around the glass for a few seconds, releasing its aroma, before sniffing the bouquet. He instantly relaxed as the memory cells kicked in and he knew he recognised the wine. Consciously trying not to display any outwards signs of his satisfaction to the watching group, Harry next took a small mouthful of the wine. He swirled it round his mouth before drawing in a little air through it. Yes, he definitely knew it. He swallowed the wine and then wrote carefully on the sheet bearing the number one, *DOMAINE DE ROMANEE CONTE, LA TACHE, 1982.*

'Will you sign it please, Mr Benson, and hold it up to the camera?' the watching inspector asked.

He did so, and poured himself some water. He drank a mouthful, cleaning out his mouth, before going on to the second decanter and a second glass.

Following the same procedure he tasted the second wine. His relief at again recognising the wine was quickly followed by a degree of surprise. It was a Chateau Lafite, 2006, a very good wine from a famous chateau in the Medoc but not an exceptional vintage. He felt sure it could be purchased for considerably less than the £300 lower limit Andy Pelham had specified. He tasted it a second time to be absolutely sure and, quite satisfied that he wasn't mistaken, wrote on the second sheet *CHATEAU LAFITE ROTHSCHILD, PAUILLAC, 2006.* Again he signed it and showed it to the camera.

After another mouthful of water, he poured himself some wine from the third decanter. He could see from the colour of the wine that it was really mature. He noted just a hint of brown on the rim of the wine, as he held the glass against the white sheet of paper. It's really old, he thought, and it's aged really well. This impression was confirmed by the wonderful bouquet and his mind took him back to a tasting held at the house of the wealthiest man in Jakarta, a frequent diner at Harry's restaurant there, many years before. It had been the first time in his life that he had tasted Bordeaux from the fabulous 1934 vintage. Well, this wine hasn't cost less than £300, he thought – not much change from £1,000. He tasted the wine reverentially, instantly identifying it as a Chateau Haut-Brion from that remarkable year. Well, that's made it worth coming today, he thought amusedly, what a wine!

He carefully wrote *CHATEAU HAUT-BRION, GRAVES, 1934* on the third sheet, signed it, and showed it to the camera.

The last two wines weren't quite so exciting but he was relieved to be able to identify them quickly as a Chateau Petrus 2000 and a Chateau Margaux 2005. Both wines would have cost well over the £300 limit, as would the first wine, the DRC La Tache, Harry thought. That second wine was a puzzle.

When Harry had finished with the fifth and final sheet, Andy Pelham thanked him.

'Thank you, Mr Benson. You are now free to leave, if you wish.'

Harry was glad to do so and, nodding goodbye to the other men, he put away his pen and headed for the stairs. As he passed up them he met two constables coming the other way, one of them carrying the safe-breaking equipment.

Two of them, he wondered? Andy Pelham might just be anticipating some trouble. Grateful that he didn't have to be part of it, Harry took a deep breath of fresh air as he left the house and headed down the street to the pub.

Chapter 7

THE PUB, THE WELLINGTON Arms, was unexpectedly busy when Harry arrived at around 11.30. It looked like there was some kind of pre-wedding gathering, the men were in suits and the ladies mostly in smart frocks. There weren't many young people, he noticed, probably an older couple getting hitched, perhaps on second marriages? It wasn't a very big pub so he had to squeeze through a press of people to order his pint.

After standing for a while, he saw a small table in the corner being vacated. Moving swiftly he got to it just before a couple of wedding guests did, and settled down to wait for Andy Pelham. He tried to sip his beer calmly but his mind was whirling. He wondered what was happening back in that whitewashed cellar, what drama was unfolding? Was one of the five men being led away in handcuffs? He didn't really have any doubts about his identifications of the wines. Apart from the 1934 Haut Brion they were all wines he had come across on more than one occasion. He went back over the inspector's chain of reasoning step by step in his mind. He couldn't see any flaws in it and concluded that the guilty man must be revealed when all the bottles were brought out.

On the other hand, they'd all seemed so normal, so unconcerned, hadn't they? There had been that intake of breath, which he thought had come from the other side of the table, so either Peter King, Henry Liu, or James Courtenay. Mike Ellison and the French chap, what was his name?... Guillaume... something, that was it, had been on his side of the table. But perhaps he'd been mistaken about the breath.

He wondered how long he'd have to wait for Pelham and was considering if he'd be able to keep his table by leaving his newspaper on it while he went to the bar for a second pint when he saw the policeman coming in through the door. He stood up and waved as he saw Pelham looking for him through the crowd of people. Pelham saw him and came over to his table.

Harry tried to read his expression as the inspector sat down. He certainly wasn't giving off the air of someone who'd just notched up a major triumph.

He met Harry's enquiring look with a grimace and Harry knew something had gone wrong.

'Well,' Pelham began, 'I'm pretty sure I know who did it.' He paused and looked directly at Harry. 'But there's a problem.'

'The Chateau Lafite 2006?'

'You guessed? Yes,' Pelham said. He looked around at the crowded bar. 'This isn't really the place to talk about it. Can you come back to the office?'

'Yes, of course,' Harry replied.

'There's a car coming for us in five minutes. I'll meet you outside? If you'll excuse me I must talk to the boss.' The policeman got up from the table and headed for the door, taking his mobile phone from his pocket.

Harry finished his pint, went to the Gents, and walked outside. The inspector was still talking on the phone and continued until his car pulled up a minute or two later. He broke off as the two of them got into the back of the car.

'Sorry, Harry,' he said. 'There's a bit of a panic on back at HQ. Please excuse me while I make another call.' He kept talking all the way back to Scotland Yard. 'I'm just arriving now, sir,' he said as the car pulled up at the entrance Harry recognised from the previous day, 'I'll be in your office in a couple of minutes.'

'You know the way to my office, Harry?' Pelham asked. Harry nodded and he continued 'I should only be a few minutes. Alison won't have gone to lunch yet – get her to make you a cup of coffee, and I'll be with you as soon as I can.'

The inspector headed off down the corridor to the left and Harry made his way to the lift and up to the third floor. The pleasant anticipation of seeing Alison again was overcoming his sense of disappointment at the apparent outcome of the morning, and his urgent desire to find out what had happened.

She was busy concentrating on her computer screen as Harry approached her desk but looked up as he began 'Excuse me, er, Alison...'

'Mr Benson,' she interrupted, smiling, 'how can I help?'

When Harry explained that he needed to wait for the inspector, Alison immediately settled him into Pelham's office and got him a welcome cup of coffee. She didn't ask any questions about the morning's events but left him alone, leaving the door into Pelham's office open. As Harry scrolled through the news headlines on his phone he wondered if that was because she wasn't aware of what had been happening, or whether she was just being discreet. Discreet, he decided – if the constable who'd driven him in yesterday was aware of the case, Alison almost certainly was. Smart lady, as well as very attractive, he thought, and wondered how he might set about asking her out.

After he'd been waiting about ten minutes, the phone rang on Alison's desk. She listened for a minute and then came in to speak to Harry. 'Mr Benson, I'm sorry the inspector's going to be delayed. He's asked me to apologise and ask if you would mind waiting for him? He may be some little time longer and suggested that perhaps I could take you along to the canteen with me to get a bit of lunch?'

Harry smile broadly and said 'Why, yes, that would be very kind of you, if you're sure I'm not putting you out?'

'Not at all,' the policewoman replied, 'I was just about to go. If we go now we should beat the one o'clock rush.'

As they ate their lunch in the staff canteen on the fifth floor, they chatted easily about wine, restaurants they liked, the latest shows in London's theatres, all kinds of things. He found his original good impression of his companion was amply confirmed, intelligent and charming as well as very attractive and discreet. She still didn't ask about the morning. Alison seemed to enjoy talking to him too, he decided that he really would have to ask her out. But how, that was the question. He was really quite shy and it was a long time since he'd had any practice in this kind of thing.

He'd spent so long out of England and had become used to living among fairly hard-drinking, fast-living, expatriate sets of people. He'd had girlfriends and the occasional relationship, of course, but, he thought, that was 'Love in a Hot Climate'. Hot weather, pool parties and barbecues, people not wearing very much, people focused on making money, getting on, moving on. A few drinks, a warm evening, a look returned, that was how his affairs had started.

She was still calling him Mr Benson, hadn't asked him at all about his life and, he had to admit, could very well be being nice to him purely out of professional courtesy. On the other hand there was her body language when they'd first met. He was just summoning up the courage to ask if she was free that evening when her mobile rang.

She answered briefly and then said 'The chief. He's on his way back to the office now. Shall we go?'

They collected up their plates and cups and deposited them on a trolley by the door. As they walked back together towards the lift Harry cursed himself for his indecision. However, when they got in to go down to the third floor, they had it to themselves and Harry found himself saying 'Alison, I was wondering if, er, if…'

'Yes, Mr Benson?' She turned and looked directly at him. Was that an amused look in her eye?

'Well, if, er, you'd like to come out for a meal some time?' His face felt very hot, he hoped he wasn't going red.

'Well…' she hesitated, as his heart sank, then gave him a warm smile, 'yes, that would be lovely.' The lift door opened, 'I'll give you my number before you leave.'

Harry remembered to start breathing again and followed her through the double doors and into the office.

'Ah, Harry, there you are,' Andy Pelham called from his room. 'So sorry to have kept you so long. You got some lunch, I hope?'

'I did, thanks. And thanks to Alison.'

'Oh yes. Thanks, Alison,' he called through the door.

'It was a pleasure, chief,' she called back. 'Especially as Mr Benson paid for it!'

'Hmm, did you, Harry?' The inspector looked sidewise at him. 'Anyhow, I expect you'd like to know what happened this morning?'

'Yes, very much.' With a bit of an effort, Harry put the pleasant prospect of an evening with the lovely lady out of

82

his mind and concentrated on what Pelham was saying.

'Let me see, now. The first to open his safe was Peter King. He did it with a bit of a flourish, I must say. It was the DRC La Tache 1982.'

'Ah-hah, good,' Harry exclaimed. 'Had you already looked at my sheets?'

'Yes, I had, so I was feeling pretty good at that stage. However –'

'Sorry,' Harry interrupted. 'Had the others seen them as well?'

'No.'

Harry waited for an explanation, but none came. Still keeping his cards close to his chest, Harry thought.

'So, next Mike Ellison opened his. It was the Haut-Brion 1934.' He paused, 'So far so good. Next came the French guy. Margaux 2005. Next came James Courtenay, he's our man, I think. Mouton Rothschild 2005.'

'Another 2005! But I definitely didn't taste it this morning.'

Harry waited while the inspector gathered his thoughts. 'Even before he opened his safe I thought he was looking a bit flustered. He'd obviously worked out what was going on. Anyhow he opened his safe calmly enough and brought the bottle to the table.

'I was feeling pretty confident at this stage, as you can guess. However, Henry Yiu opened his safe and brought the bottle over. Chateau Lafite – 2005.'

'Not 2006.' Harry closed his eyes, remembering the taste. 'I thought it was strange. The price of the 2006 is way below £300.'

'Yes, I noticed you tasted that one twice,' Pelham said. 'I wondered why.'

'But it definitely was the 2006.'

'You're sure?'

'Yes. I knew it instantly. No doubt in my mind.' He thought. 'Definitely wasn't the 2005, quite different.'

The phone on Pelham's desk rang. 'Yes, sir. No, I agree, we can't proceed. Sorry. Yes, I will.' He rang off and sighed. 'That was the boss. We're not charging Courtenay. He asked me to thank you for your efforts.'

'Very kind of him.'

Pelham smiled. 'Anyhow to cut a long story short, Oliver's safe, when we finally got it open, revealed the Petrus 2000.

'So. I know, and you know, that you identified all those wines correctly. Courtenay's wine was definitely not there. The poison is in the Mouton Rothschild. But, as far as a defending barrister is concerned, as far as a jury is concerned, you failed to correctly identify one of the wines. "The prosecution's case, ladies and gentlemen of the jury, is that none of the decanters contained the defendant's wine, the Mouton Rothschild 2005. However, there is no proof that the second decanter did not contain it. Mr Benson, when all is said and done, failed to identify the contents of the second decanter, did he not?..." You get the picture.'

Harry could picture it. 'I can see why you can't arrest him. So, what happened at the end, once all the bottles were revealed?'

'I had to think quickly. My instinct was to confront Courtenay but the doubt was there about the Lafite and I decided not to. I wrapped things up pretty quickly, thanked them all for their assistance, and officially ended the video. I could see that one or two of them were going to start asking questions so I asked Sergeant Ahmed to let them know we'd be in touch and show them out while I busied myself on the phone.'

'Goodness,' Harry said. 'How did Courtenay react – did he look relieved?'

'Hard to say. But, yes, I think so. Of course he doesn't know about the Lafite, none of them saw your sheets. He may think that we're just biding our time, but I don't know.' The policeman paused and Harry thought how tired he looked all of a sudden. Must have been a big disappointment to him. 'But, as far as I can see, he's got away with it, Harry.'

'So, what happens now? About Oliver's death, I mean.'

'We can't really keep it quiet any longer – that he's been poisoned. We won't say anything about the circumstances, we'll just say we're pursuing various lines of enquiry, something like that. But I daresay the papers will start digging and will talk to members of the group. If they do they'll probably find out about this morning's events and will pretty soon put two and two together and surmise that members of the group are in the frame.'

He looked at Harry appraisingly. 'Most likely they'll be on to you pretty soon, Harry. I take it we can count on you to keep it all under your hat? Don't deny you were involved, though.'

'Yes, yes, of course. I'll just say, let me see, that I was asked to identify some wines, no idea why?'

'Right, thank you,' Pelham replied. 'Sorry to have got you involved. Sorry it didn't work out.'

'No worries, I'm glad to have helped, even though it didn't.' He thought for a moment. 'You know, Inspector, someone, somewhere, for some reason has put Lafite 2006 in a 2005 bottle. You didn't get a look at the cork, I suppose?'

'Yes. Definitely 2005.'

'The foil, the capsule?'

'Looked legit. Heavy duty foil, stamped Lafite.'

'Hmm. Who would do it, and why?' Harry mused. 'Henry Liu? To make the others get his wine wrong? But what if they all identified it? Also, where would he get a virgin Lafite capsule from? Doesn't add up.'

'So?' the inspector interposed.

'So, to go to that trouble it must be a commercial venture. Someone who found a way of doing it, in bulk, could make a lot of money. A real top vintage can sell for ten times the price of a lesser one, as you know. And if the lesser one really is from the same chateau, the fraud would be extremely difficult to detect.'

He stopped and considered again. 'That must be it. Someone must be doing this on a commercial scale. Faking labels, corks and capsules, not that easy.' More thought. 'Did the label look genuine?'

'It's not a wine I can afford to buy often enough to be really familiar with the labels,' the inspector said drily.

'Of course, sorry!' Harry cried. 'I don't suppose I could have a look at it?'

'I don't see why not. I'll ask Alison to get it sent up from the evidence store.'

Pelham went out and spoke to Alison, leaving Harry alone with his thoughts. Did he want to be involved in this any more? It might be best just to forget all about it. After all it really wasn't his problem, was it? But Andy Pelham had been so open and frank with him, he really felt part of the team. He could see Pelham's disappointment and wanted to help him. Also, on top of that, he had to admit, his pride had been piqued. He would like to prove that that wine really *was* a

2006. He was pretty sure the inspector didn't doubt him, but, he thought, it was more than likely that word would get out about it, and plenty of people *would* doubt him.

When the policeman came back into the office, Harry had a question for him.

'Inspector, if it could be proved, beyond reasonable doubt, that the wine in that second decanter *was* Lafite 2006, would the case stand up in court?'

'Why... yes, I think so,' Pelham replied, 'but how could you do it?'

'I don't really know,' Harry said, 'but I'd like to try. The thing would be to trace back where Henry Yiu's wine came from. I think the chateau might help – they won't want their best wines being passed off.'

'Yes, they might. But it's not really a line of enquiry the police could pursue, Harry.'

'Why not? You said that proof would help the case stand up?' Harry asked.

'It's too abstruse.' Pelham rubbed his eyes with the back of his hand. 'I could never get approval to send a detective to France, or anywhere else for that matter, to try to prove that the contents of a bottle of wine are not what they should be. And, if you're right that this...'

He broke off as Alison came into the office.

'Excuse me, chief,' she said. 'Here it is.'

Alison put a sealed heavy-duty clear plastic bag on the table. It contained a dark green bottle, a cork and a small circular piece of thin red metal. The remainder of the capsule was still round the neck.

'Many thanks, Alison,' Pelham said.

She smiled an acknowledgment. What a lovely smile she's got, Harry thought.

'Do you need gloves, sir?'

The inspector glanced at Harry questioningly.

'Oh, I see,' Harry exclaimed, 'to handle it with. No, I think just looking will be enough, thank you.'

Alison left them and Harry pulled his chair closer to the inspector's desk to have a good look. 'Hmm, let's see. It all looks kosher to me. Label, yes; cork, certainly. The capsule. That certainly can't be original, no way to get one of these off without damaging it, I'm sure.'

He scrutinised it for a while through the bag. 'OK, if I feel it through the plastic?'

'Yes, sure,' the policeman replied.

'Well, it certainly feels thick enough. The colour though, it's certainly very close to Lafite's red, but is it identical? I'm not sure.'

Harry pondered for a minute or two, then said 'I think the bottle and cork are genuine. Which presumably means that whoever did the switch *did* have a genuine bottle of Chateau Lafite 2005. What did he do with the real wine? It doesn't really make sense.' A pause. 'A restaurant or wine bar. Must be. They pour the real wine for a customer, charging the 2005 price of course. Keep the bottle and the cork, refill it with the 2006 and sell it again.'

'I follow all that, makes sense,' Pelham said. 'But how does the bottle get to Henry Yiu?'

'No idea.'

'Me neither, but that brings me back to what I was saying when Alison came in. The only way to approach this is to first establish that it is happening, that wine is being switched. No detective could do that, I'm afraid.'

'By tasting it you mean? No, that's true. But, let me see, if we could trace the bottle back to a restaurant, by working back through the supply chain, couldn't you, er, put someone in under cover?'

The inspector shook his head, smiling.

'What about by checking their records? Compare how many bottles of a wine they've sold to how many they purchased?' He paused. 'No, I suppose not. Whoever has the brains and ability to do this on a commercial scale, would certainly be able to cover their tracks fairly easily. Hand-written bills, stock records muddled.' Harry had worked in restaurants long enough to be under no illusions about the opportunities for fiddling and the ingenuity with which some staff would pursue them.

'No.' The policeman rubbed his eyes again. 'If you could, with the chateau's help maybe, identify who's doing it, and where, then possibly I might be able to do something. If it's in the UK, that is.

'Harry, sorry if I sound negative. I know that you want to help me, and I appreciate it very much. You've already been a great help and, at the end of the day, this is not really your problem, is it?'

'No, it's not.' Harry made up his mind. 'Nevertheless, I'd still like to get to the bottom of it. I'm really intrigued, professionally, as it were. Maybe it won't be any use in the case, and I do understand why you can't pursue it officially. But it does seem to me, without being too dramatic, that I'm the only person who can do anything about this. I don't like to think of Courtenay getting off scot-free because I couldn't be arsed to do anything about it.'

'Thanks, Harry. What you say is true, I think. If you really want to go into it, I'll certainly give you any help I can and, who knows, we might make a detective out of you yet! The Wine Detective!'

Chapter 8

HARRY PEERED OUT OF the window as the Ryanair flight began its descent into Bordeaux's Merignac airport. Down below he could clearly see the split where the Gironde estuary was transformed into the two great rivers of south-western France: the Garonne and the Dordogne. He kept looking as the plane banked and flew over the unmistakeable green strips and white splodges of a golf course situated on the northern fringe of the city. He remembered having played there a few years before, as far as he could recall the two courses hadn't been particularly interesting, but he'd enjoyed the practice driving range – you hit from a great tiered gallery into a lake, with targets tethered on the water. The range balls floated, of course.

The thought of the lake brought to mind the name of the club – Bordeaux Lac, that was it. His thoughts drifted on to the many times he'd visited the great wine city of Bordeaux, a city he liked very much, with its cosmopolitan air, its fine old architecture along the riverfront and its many wonderful restaurants. He'd come several times to Vinexpo, the great two-yearly wine exhibition, looking for new wines for his restaurants in the East and the small distribution company he'd run in Singapore.

For many years he'd also come each spring for the *en primeur* tastings of the previous year's wines, when the great chateaux opened their doors to their trade customers and wine journalists to come and taste and assess the new vintage. He'd made a fair bit of money over the years from correctly assessing a young wine's potential, buying it before it was even bottled, and selling it on when the wider market had woken up to its potential.

On these trips he'd always stayed at a delightful small hotel in St Estephe, the most northerly of the four great wine villages of the Medoc, called Chateau Pomys. He'd been delighted to find it was still going strong and had booked in there for this trip. Set in the heart of the vineyards, it was practically within walking distance of Chateau Lafite, situated at the northern limit of the neighbouring commune of Pauillac.

It was at Chateau Lafite that he had an appointment for the following day but first he wanted to wallow a bit in the ambiance of one of his favourite parts of the world. He picked up his hire car without too much delay and headed into the city, trusting himself to remember the way rather than putting on the Satnav that came as standard on his BMW.

Despite a couple of wrong turns he was soon parking in the big underground car park by the river. He emerged up the steps into the summer sunshine and walked along the bank for a bit, taking in the strolling tourists, the numerous joggers, and the huge cruise ship moored alongside the promenade. He crossed into the wooded, shady area where the tram stops were and made his way up past the Institut de Vin to his favourite wine shop in the whole world, L'Intendant, on the corner opposite the Grand Opera. He climbed its well-remembered spiral staircase, surrounded all the way round with great Bordeaux wines which got better and better, and more and more expensive, the higher you climbed.

At the very top, in glass cases, were the crème de la crème

of clarets, *premiers grands crus classes*, from fabulous vintages, in magnums, double magnums and jeroboams. If you wanted to find yourself surrounded, immersed, in great wine, this was the place, Harry thought. He had a good look at the bottles of Chateau Lafite, paying particular attention to the colour of the foil capsules. Was it the same? He wasn't sure, anyhow tomorrow should tell. Then he purchased a couple of bottles of a pretty good vintage of Chateau Palmer, a particular favourite of Frank Forshaw's wife, Geraldine, for a gift and made his way back outside. He wandered down the bustling pedestrian shopping street, the rue Sainte-Catherine, towards the cathedral and the old town.

Stopping to buy himself a small box of the delicious Bordeaux cakes called *canelets*, dark golden and crispy on the outside, soft and almost gooey on the inside, he made his way back down to the river. He found an empty bench and sat and ate a couple, just as good as he remembered them. They were based on a kind of batter, he remembered, but they had to be eaten freshly made, when the outside was crisp, once they got soggy they were horrible – he'd better eat the others! He found a table in a café, ordered a double expresso and, rather guiltily, ate the other four.

Looking at his watch he realised he'd better get going in order to beat the horrible rush-hour traffic along the embankment. He remembered that he could get out of town that way, circling round the eastern edge of the city, past the golf course and up the little-used country road into the Medoc, bypassing the big dormitory suburbs north of the city. He had a bit of difficulty finding his way around the new interchange with the Rocade, the city's circular peripheral dual carriageway, necessitating a two-way trip over the giant

Pont d'Aquitaine bridge, but by four o'clock he was driving up past the golf course, content that he was on the right road.

As he drove, his mind went back over the events of the last few days, since the day of the tasting with Andy Pelham. Before he left the office he had two phone numbers – Alison's, which she surreptitiously passed him with a little note, as he stopped at her desk and thanked her for her company at lunch, and Henry Yiu's, which Pelham had a little reluctantly given him.

'Please be tactful, Harry,' the policeman had said, 'and if you can avoid letting him know I gave you his number, I'd be grateful. And please don't discuss the case any more than is strictly unavoidable.'

Harry had nodded and said 'Yes, of course,' but Pelham continued.

'He may well be in touch with Courtenay and the last thing we want is for him to get wind of what we know – and don't know.'

Harry negotiated his way through the little town of Macau, remembering the short-cut past the fire station, and reflected that Henry Yiu couldn't have been more helpful when he'd called him the next day.

He was a member of The Wine Society and had actually been present at the Savoy when Harry had won the society's wine-tasting title. He said how impressed he'd been and they chatted for a while about Harry's gift and tasting in general. Harry worked the conversation round to the morning at Simon Oliver's house and wasn't surprised when Yiu asked him how his decisions had matched up with the bottles.

He'd decided in advance to plead ignorance about it, saying

the police were still keeping everything under wraps. Which was true, up to a point, he thought. Harry also wasn't able to speculate about what had happened to Oliver and what the point of the tasting had been.

He could tell Henry Yiu had his doubts but he didn't press him and was very happy to talk about the wine he'd taken.

He'd purchased a case of Lafite 2005 from a very respectable, long-established wine merchant in Wiltshire, he said. He'd already drunk two bottles from the case at a dinner party with friends. There was a note of doubt in his voice when Harry asked him what he thought of it.

'Well,' he said, 'we enjoyed it. It's undoubtedly a fine wine but, erm, perhaps it didn't have quite the elegance and staying power that I've found in other 2005s. What did you think of it?'

Harry decided that honesty, in this case anyway, was the best policy. 'Well Mr Yiu, although the police haven't told me what the bottles were, they did tell me that you'd brought Lafite 2005. They told me because, well, because I identified one of the wines as a Lafite 2006.'

He paused and heard Yiu whistle down the phone.

'Yes. I'm certain none of the other wines was a Lafite, so I believe your wine was the one I identified as a 2006.'

'Well, well,' Henry Liu exclaimed, 'that would chime with what we thought of it. The case and the bottles all look perfectly genuine, though.'

'Do they? I'd be really interested to have a look at a bottle, if it wouldn't be too inconvenient?'

'Not at all. It'd be really nice to meet you. When would you like to come?'

Eventually, after Harry had set up his date with Alison, he'd gone to Henry Yiu's luxurious penthouse flat the next afternoon. Having admired his host's spacious and luxurious purpose-built temperature-controlled wine cellar and his impressive collection of fine wines, he had no difficulty in persuading him to let him take away one of the bottles for checking.

He'd refused Harry's offer to pay for it, on the condition that Harry would let him know what he discovered. Harry said he would and left, relieved that Yiu didn't press him for any more information. He'd told Harry in passing that he hadn't been in contact with any of the other members of the group since the morning in Chelsea, so Harry hoped he'd stayed pretty much within the inspector's guidelines.

He left the country road and joined the D2 which winds up through the main wine communes of the Medoc. He passed on his left the Tudoresque monstrosity of Chateau Cantenac Brown, constructed by an eccentric Scot, he remembered, and the little road on the right which leads past the church to where Chateau Margaux, architecturally the finest of all the great chateaux, hides behind its stand of trees.

On past the amazing wine shop La Cave d'Ulysse in Margaux itself, owned, it was said, by the Chanel family and on out into the fields, the roads surrounded in well-tended vines as far as the eye can see.

His dinner date with Alison had been pretty much as successful, he thought, as his meeting with Henry Yiu. She'd looked stunning in a crisp white high-collared blouse and an aquamarine skirt, with shoes in a matching colour, and a small leather clutch bag, Lancel if he wasn't mistaken. Her jewellery was discreet, unfussy but expensive-looking. Harry

96

wasn't the world's most observant man but he couldn't help noticing that she was able to look smart without looking as though she'd *tried* to look smart.

She'd only been a perfectly allowable fifteen minutes late outside Piccadilly underground, for which she hadn't apologised. A lady's privilege, Harry thought amusedly. He'd booked a table in a little Italian restaurant in Soho that he knew well, having discovered during their lunch together that she loved Italian food and wine.

The food and the wine had been admirable, they both had a passion for the wines of Barolo, and they'd got on very well. The conversation at first carried on where it had left off in the police canteen, about wine, food and everyday life. Harry had never cared for the kind of conversation that takes the form of question and answer, finding it rather illiberal and intrusive, so he was glad to find that Alison seemed to feel the same way.

Neither asked the other where they came from or what they had done in life or if they had any family, or any of those kind of questions but, as the evening wore on and they relaxed in each other's company, they both spoke about parts of their life, where they'd been, things they'd enjoyed or disliked.

He'd discovered that she was well-travelled, particularly in France, Spain and Italy, fairly left-wing, not interested in sport, a decided and eloquent feminist, and enjoyed her job. What she'd made of him he wasn't sure. He thought maybe he'd seen an amused twinkle in her eye when he expounded one of his theories at perhaps too great a length, but she seemed to enjoy herself.

At any rate when he'd given her a peck on the cheek at the entrance to her apartment block in Marylebone and said he hoped they could meet again, Alison gave his hand a warm, firm squeeze and said 'Yes, that would be lovely, Harry.'

They had spoken about the case, which she was perfectly au fait with. He told her about his meeting with Henry Yiu and his plan to take the bottle to the chateau, to try to confirm his diagnosis and to try to enlist their help in tracing where the wine had come from. He didn't really feel he could phone the Wiltshire wine merchants and ask them. Alison had been full of encouragement for his plans and seemed to think there was no reason why he shouldn't be successful in his quest. She didn't seem to think it at all strange that he felt the need to get so involved, which pleased and relieved him.

He had to wait a minute or two as the road bent round in front of the picturesque Chateau Palmer, right next to the road with its smart black railings and shutters and beautifully landscaped gardens. The small parking area opposite was a confusion of tourist cars and shiny black Mercedes 12-seater tour buses as people stopped to take photos. Some things never change, he thought, but it *is* a beautiful building.

Soon he was heading into St Julien, grandiose Chateau Beychevelle in front of him, and along past the big square hall-like Chateau Ducru Beaucaillou on the right. Down the dip between the two chateaux Barton and then through the vineyards of Chateau Latour, the chateau itself hidden from view, like Chateau Margaux, in a stand of trees. Now he was entering the commune of Pauillac, greatest of all Medoc wine towns, containing three of the five *premiers grands cru classes*: Latour, Mouton Rothschild and Lafite.

In the town itself he took a detour along by the estuary and stopped to stretch his legs with a walk along the wall of the little harbour, crammed with yachts and motor cruisers. Luxury coaches were busy bringing back American tourists to the big river cruiser moored against the outer harbour wall. The coaches had been away visiting the local chateaux, he guessed, and he noted with interest that very few of the returning passengers were carrying any actual purchases of wine.

He walked back down to the quayside and crossed the road to a café to get himself a drink. It was a very warm evening and he decided to have a beer. Not a fan of French beer, he ordered a Belgian Leffe and sat and watched the world go by for a while, deliberately not thinking about his appointment the next morning and what it might lead to.

While driving through the town of St Julien he had seen a restaurant on the right where he remembered eating very well more than once. He hadn't been able to see its name, but a quick Google search revealed it as Le Saint Julien – of course! – and he booked a table for eight.

Looking at his watch he saw it was gone six o'clock and that he could now check in at his hotel. He drove north along the estuary and then took the right turn that would lead him into St Estephe the back way, along by the river. He passed the giant oil-storage site on the left with its array of vast circular tanks and remembered that it had once been a big oil refinery. Rumour had had it that the well-connected proprietors of the grand chateaux had conspired to have it closed down so that the fumes wouldn't affect their vines and spoil the wines.

The locals, who had lost many hundreds of well-paying jobs as a result, had been decidedly unimpressed and, as a result, there wasn't much love lost between them and the businesses on which they chiefly depended for employment. Every corner of paradise has its problems, he thought.

Harry's thoughts ran along these lines as he drove alongside the great estuary, miles wide here, taking in the *carrelets*, the fishing huts on stilts that ranged along the bank, with their big circular nets suspended over the water. Eventually he turned away from the river, up into the little town of St Estephe and found his way through to his hotel, and a very welcome hot shower.

After showering and changing, finding he had 20 minutes in hand before he needed to set off to St Julien, Harry wandered down the lane away from the hotel into the surrounding vineyards. All had been recently thinned, removing the high-growing branches to allow more sunlight to reach the grapes, and they were as neat as soldiers on parade. Looking closely he could see that all the merlot grapes had reached their mature full purple colour, while the bunches on the later-maturing cabernet sauvignon vines were still in the process of turning from green, to pink, to red and on to purple.

He reflected on how centuries of wine-making experience and wisdom in the area had resulted in these two varieties being chosen to combine to make the best wine possible, given the soil, the climate and the topography, what the French call *terroir*. In one year the merlot might do better, in another the cabernet sauvignon, resulting in subtle changes in the wines from year to year that you didn't really find in wines made from a single grape variety, he thought. It all helped to make Bordeaux wines the most complex and most fascinating in the world.

Retracing his steps, he climbed into the BMW and set off for his supper.

Chapter 9

HARRY WAS UP BRIGHT and early next morning, despite having had a fairly late night, sharing an extra bottle of wine with Claude, the owner and chef, and some of the local winemakers who had been dining there. All had agreed that it was going to be a famous vintage but, then again, Harry thought, he'd never visited in any year when any of the Bordelais thought anything different! Prices were bound to go up, demand from China was so strong these days – several properties now had Chinese owners. Hail was always a threat in such a hot summer, more and more top properties were installing shockwave generators, known as hail cannons, to disrupt the formation of hailstones in the clouds, the merlot was doing very well in sandy soils, less so in clay.

Harry had enjoyed the local gossip, it's really good to be back here, he thought as he had a good long soak in the bath. He put on his best cashmere jacket and a nearly new shirt ready for his meeting with Alain de Bossenet, Wine Director of Chateau Lafite, at 10 a.m.

The appointment had been made via the good offices of Peter Hill of *The Times*, who knew de Bossenet well. News of Simon Oliver's death as a result of poisoning and of Harry's involvement in the case had appeared in the London *Evening Standard* so Hill had been intrigued when Harry called him to ask for his help.

'Hello, Harry, good to hear from you,' he'd said. 'Been to any good wine tastings recently?'

Andy Pelham had managed to keep a lid on details of what his involvement had been so Harry was able to deflect Peter

Hill's curiosity to a large extent by repeating what he'd said to Henry Yiu. He could tell Hill wasn't too convinced and pressed on to talk about the discovery of the apparently fake bottle of Lafite.

'Hmm, I won't press you, Harry – as long as you promise to tell me all about it one day – as an exclusive! But it is intriguing about the wine, I wonder what's going on? It's funny, I had lunch the other day with an old chum who'd just come back from Shanghai, Charlie Christianson, do you know him? Wine merchant in New York?'

'The name rings a bell,' Harry replied, 'can't place him though.'

'Anyway,' Hill continued, 'he said he'd been to one of those wine-tasting events the big restaurants hold for their clients and that he'd been given a glass of a very prestigious wine, I can't recall which he said it was now, and he was pretty sure that it wasn't what it was meant to be. Similar, he said, but not the real thing. He'd seen the bottle opened and it had looked perfectly genuine, evidently. He said nobody else seemed to notice anything strange so he half convinced himself he'd been mistaken.'

'But not convinced enough not to tell you about it, Peter.'

'No, indeed.'

When Harry explained what he wanted to do, Peter Hill had called the chateau there and then. He explained who Harry was and that he had a bottle of their 2005 that he doubted was genuine, could Harry bring it to be checked? Alain de Bossenet had heard about Harry's record score at the Savoy and had agreed immediately to see him. He told Hill to give Harry his direct number and said Harry should call once he'd booked a flight.

It being Friday, Harry had decided he'd better fly on the following Monday and booked his flight. When he called he had not been at all surprised to find that de Bossenet spoke perfect English, as so many of the top winemakers in France did. They very briefly discussed the bottle Harry was going to take, Harry saying he was convinced it was 2006, not 2005.

'Let's check it out together,' the winemaker concluded, 'have a good flight!'

Harry had made arrangements with Pat to look after Rosie while he was away. He hated to put her into a kennel and she was used now to Pat's house, climbing out of the car quite happily when they arrived there on his way to Gatwick. He'd told her that he should be back the following evening, but that it was possible it might be a day later. 'No worries!' she'd said.

Harry took the road through the vineyards he'd walked along the previous evening, guessing it would lead him out to the main road to Pauillac.

His guess turned out to be correct and after a right fork and a right turn he found himself emerging between Chateau Cos d'Estournel, with its elaborate oriental-style stonework and famous carved wooden door, and Chateau Cos Labory, on to the main road. He was a little shaken up, having misjudged the speed at which it was advisable to cross the little level crossing at the bottom of the dip before the road climbed up to the two chateaux. What a bone-cruncher, he thought, glad it's not my suspension!

Now he could see the well-remembered outline of Chateau Lafite in the dip in front of him as he turned left on to the main road. He swung round to the right and descended the slope past the little canal that marked the boundary between St Estephe and Pauillac; passing the long whitewashed wall and row of willow trees that marked the boundary of the estate, he turned right and right again to find himself at a gate with an intercom. Not just anyone could get into Chateau Lafite Rothschild, he knew – visits by appointment only.

He'd been a couple of times for en primeur tastings and knew some of the history of the place, where great wine had been made since the late 17th century. Nowhere near as grand as Chateau Margaux or some of the other chateaux, particularly with its kitchen garden going down the slope towards the road. However, it had style - he remembered reading somewhere that it had been earmarked for Hermann Goering during the war.

'*J'ai un rendez-vous avec Monsieur de Bossenet, je suis Monsieur Benson,*' he announced and the gate swung open. He followed the road round behind a long low building he took to be a chai, where the wine is aged in barrels, and parked next to a gleaming Mercedes 4x4. Taking his briefcase containing his bottle of wine from the passenger seat, he closed and locked the door of the poor abused BMW and went into the reception. 9.55, he checked his watch, good timing.

He waited a couple of minutes after the receptionist phoned through to announce his arrival before Alain de Bossenet came through the glass door at the side of the room, hand outstretched.

'Mr Benson, welcome to Chateau Lafite. Alain de Bossenet. It's good to meet you!'

'It's a pleasure to meet you, Monsieur,' Harry replied. 'Thank you so much...'

De Bossenet waved away Harry's thanks 'No, no thanks needed, please follow me to my office. This way, please.'

Very tall, very debonair, beautifully dressed, Harry thought, as he followed his host along a corridor lined with wooden-framed paintings and signed photos of members of the British royal family, past an ornate drawing room, furnished in Second Empire style.

They entered a much more modern room in the centre of which was a big old-fashioned double-sided partner desk. The desk was surprisingly messy, Harry thought, strewn with photographs, office equipment, files and wine memorabilia – a framed label of the 1840 vintage caught his eye.

'Please be seated, Mr Benson, and please excuse the *désordre*, my secretary is on holiday.'

It was Harry's turn to wave away the apology as unnecessary. 'It's really a great pleasure to be here,' he said.

When they'd had coffee and exchanged some small talk, de Bossenet settled back in his chair and said 'Why don't you give me a brief rundown on how you come to be in possession of this mysterious bottle – you have it in your *valise*?'

Harry brought the bottle out of his briefcase and placed it on the desk. While he gave a potted version of the events that had led to him being there, leaving out the death of Simon Oliver, his host subjected the bottle to a searching examination with his eyes and his hands.

When Harry had finished he put the bottle back down on the table. 'Remarkable. It certainly looks genuine, Mr Benson.'

'Please call me Harry.'

De Bossenet raised his eyebrows but, after a short pause,

said 'Very well... Harry. Alain.'

Harry wondered if he'd put his foot in it, the Frenchman was an aristocrat, no doubt about it. Always hard to know whether to *tu* or *vous* a French man, Harry thought. He relaxed as de Bossenet smiled at him, seeming to read his thoughts – 'Ah, we French, *tres difficile*!'

Harry laughed and decided that he liked this man.

'Very well, I will call Gilles, our *maitre de chai,* to check he has prepared a bottle each of the 2005 and 2006 in the *laboratoire* and we will have a comparison. If you are correct about this bottle, as I expect you are, we will have the bottle, the label, the cork and the capsule examined, but I must say it all looks genuine...' He mused for a few seconds while Harry relaxed, knowing that he was going to get an answer to his question. '... But perhaps the colour of the capsule is not quite perfect.'

De Bossenet picked up the phone on his desk, dialled a short number and asked if all was ready. 'Yes,' he said and, picking up the bottle, 'let's go, Harry!'

Harry followed his host out of the office, out into the courtyard and then into the chai, where dozens of oak casks were laid out in long rows and Harry breathed in the heady odour of fine wine evaporating through new oak. In the far corner of the chai they passed through a glass-panelled door into a brightly lit, sparkingly clean room with a stainless steel bench in the middle. On the bench Harry could see two bottles and three groups of three tasting glasses, together with a spittoon.

A youngish-looking man with a white lab coat over his working clothes was waiting by the bench, smiling at Harry. De Bossenet put Harry's bottle on the table a little apart from the other two and made the introductions – 'Gilles, Monsieur Harry Benson, Harry, Gilles Larrieu, our *maitre de chai.'* The two men shook hands and exchanged '*Enchante, monsieur*'s. Gilles produced a waiter's friend corkscrew from his pocket and looked enquiringly at his boss.

'Where shall we start? If you agree, Harry, we'll commence with the real bottle of 2005. Then open your bottle and see how it compares. Then we'll open our bottle of 2006 and compare it again to your bottle?'

'Perfect,' Harry said.

Gilles carefully opened the bottle of 2005 and poured a little into a single glass in each group of three. All three men carried out the same tasting routine as a thousand times before, checking the colour, swirling the wine round the glass a little, sniffing the bouquet and, finally, tasting it, drawing a little air through it through their pursed lips, before spitting it out.

Harry instantly recognised the exquisite wine. '*C'est magnifique'* he said, and the two Frenchmen eyed him with approval.

'No doubt about that one,' de Bossenet said. Gilles nodded his approval.

Right, now for it, Harry thought. He really didn't want to be shown up as a dud in this company, and, after all, perhaps not all the bottles in the case Henry Yiu had bought had been wrong 'uns.

Gilles looked at Harry's bottle appraisingly before carefully cutting the capsule and slowly withdrawing the cork, inspecting it closely. Harry felt the tension rising as all three men carefully regarded the wine in their second glasses.

'Hmmm...' said de Bossenet.

'*Vraiment?*' said Gilles.

Harry said nothing.

Then they each went through the same routine as for the first wine.

Harry held his breath, he was still sure it was the 2006, but these men would know for sure.

The two Frenchmen looked at each other questioningly, before both shaking their heads.

'It's ours,' de Bossenet said, 'but it's not the same. It's not the 2005. *D'accord, Gilles?*'

'*Oui, certainement ,chef,*' Gilles replied.

They both retasted the two wines, confirming their opinion.

'OK, now for our 2006,' de Bossenet said.

Gilles opened the third bottle, again pouring a little into each man's third glass.

Again the same tasting routine. To Harry the second and third wines were identical, he just hoped the other two would come to the same conclusion.

They both retasted the second wine, Harry's bottle, and then the third wine.

Again they looked at each other, this time they both nodded.

'*C'est la meme,*' Gilles said. 'Ze same,' he translated for Harry.

'Absolutely no doubt about it, Harry, your bottle *is* Chateau Lafite 2006.'

Harry breathed a big sigh of relief, he'd been pretty sure of his diagnosis in advance but here, with these two masters of wine, in the heart of the Medoc, he hadn't been able to suppress his feelings of anxiety.

'But how on earth...?' De Bossenet expostulated. Gilles was minutely examining the capsule, cork, and label of Harry's bottle. 'Anyhow, Harry, your diagnosis is confirmed. Gilles will get the details checked but certainly someone has found a way to make a switch.' He paused to think.

'Come back to the office and we can discuss what to do about it.'

Seated again in the office, de Bossenet called for some more coffee. He rubbed together his upright palms and fingertips as he contemplated. Harry thought it best not to interrupt him.

After a few minutes his host asked 'Harry, are you pressed for time? I think I had better make some phone calls to some of my *confreres ici* to discuss this matter and it may take me some time to get hold of them. Do you have to return to England today? Or could we meet again tomorrow?'

'I do have a flight booked for late this afternoon,' Harry replied, 'but I don't see why it can't be changed. The hotel wasn't very full last night so I expect they'll have a room for tonight.' He considered, 'No, there's nothing I have to do tomorrow that can't wait.'

'Where are you staying?'

''Chateau Pomys.'

'Very good. If it's OK for you to stay until *demain* then I'll give them a call, you'll be our guest, of course.'

After the details of his stay and the meeting for the next day had been fixed, Harry took his leave and drove away from the chateau, ordering his thoughts. Plainly de Bossenet thought his discovery a matter of some importance, which surprised him slightly. His main hope had been that he would be able to find out where the Wiltshire wine merchants had purchased their case from, but perhaps more assistance would be forthcoming to trace the wine back to its source.

He arrived back at the main road and realised he'd better make a decision about lunch. Something light, he thought, after last night. He remembered a pleasant meal he'd once had at an unpretentious restaurant down on the quayside at Lamarque, where the ferry went across the Gironde estuary to Blaye, and turned right down towards Pauillac.

It was still early for lunch, only 11.30, so he took his time driving the dozen or so miles south. He parked in front of the restaurant, which he was glad to see was open, and got out to have a walk down to the waterside and to think some more about the morning's events and what might happen the next day.

Naturally, he concluded, it must be vitally important for the owners of very expensive, upmarket brands to protect their reputation. While the odd fake bottle, or case, would hardly be likely to do much harm to the prices they could command for their exclusive wines, they would perhaps need to be vigilant against the possibility of large-scale counterfeiting. He thought back to his conversation with Peter Hill about his friend's doubts about the wine in Shanghai.

Perhaps it's not just the odd bottle or case, he thought. And, of course, it might be disastrous for the first-growth owners if there were a major scandal about it – who's going to fork out thousands of pounds in a restaurant for a bottle of wine that might be fake?

With these thoughts in his mind he went into the restaurant and took an outside table on the covered terrace with a view of the little jetty and the river. Cars were beginning to queue on the approach road to the side of the jetty so he guessed a ferry would soon be in.

He studied the menu – *Moules Marinieres a volontiers*! All you can eat mussels! Just the job, thought Harry. He passed up the help-yourself buffet which, he suspected, from long experience of the catering trade, would consist of whatever didn't sell yesterday, and ordered the mussels together with *frites* and a half-litre carafe of the local rose.

He'd managed a second, but not the proffered third, bowl of the delicious shellfish by the time he'd finished the nice fresh-tasting wine and ordered a coffee. By now the ferry, the *Sebastian Vauban*, had come in and had disgorged a surprising number of vehicles, including a gigantic tractor. Embarkation was just finishing when a car came screeching up the road, raced up the jetty, swung left and boarded just before the gates closed. The driver jumped out, exchanging noisy witticisms with the crew busy raising up the side and casting off.

Wonderful! I do like France! he thought.

Chapter 10

THE REST OF HARRY'S day passed uneventfully. He managed to extend the car hire and altered his flight to the following day. He called Pat, who was very happy to have Rosie an extra day. In the evening he found himself wishing he had some female company and remembered that there was, or had been, a nightclub in Pauillac on the back road up towards Chateau Lynch-Bages.

It won't get going until late, he thought, better have an early night. He decided to call Alison instead, partly to update her but mostly for the pleasure of hearing her voice.

'Hello, Harry,' she said, 'how's it all going?' She sounded really pleased to hear from him so he thought he'd be a bit flirtatious.

'Dreadful! I'm stuck here for another night, all alone, no one to share a nice bottle of wine with, and thinking about you.'

She laughed. 'You should have invited me to come with you! But seriously... what was the verdict on the bottle of wine? I imagine if you're staying longer something must be up?'

'The guys from Lafite definitely confirmed that it was 2006 in a genuine 2005 bottle. I'm going back tomorrow morning after they've talked to some of the other big chateaux.'

'Are you?' Alison said, 'It sounds as though they're taking it pretty seriously, then?'

'Yes, I was a bit surprised, I have to say.'

'Very intriguing, Harry, you really must tell me all about it when you get back.'

'I'd love to. Err, I don't suppose you're free tomorrow evening? My flight gets into Gatwick about five...'

'Well, I don't know, Harry. You don't invite me to Bordeaux, one of my favourite places, and then you want to fob me off with a date here!'

'Ah... I'll definitely ask you next time. But could you get time off work that easily?'

'Don't worry, Harry, I was only teasing. But, yes, I expect so, I've got three weeks leave due and Andy is a sweetie really, beneath that tough manner. So, where shall we meet tomorrow?'

Harry arrived promptly for his rendezvous the next day and was ushered through to Alain de Bossenet's office where he found Alain and another man waiting for him. 'Ah, Harry, *je vous presente* Christian Villeneuve of Chateau Margaux. Christian, Monsieur Harry Benson'.

As the two men exchanged '*enchante monsieur*'s Harry noted with amusement that de Bossenet's desk had been tidied up since the previous day, everything neatly arranged. He wondered if the secretary had come back.

The coffee was brought in by an attractive young woman whom he hadn't seen the day before, so he guessed she had. '*Merci*, Christine,' his host said as she left the room and closed the door. 'You made all your arrangements OK, Harry?'

'*Oui, merci, Alain. On parle en Anglais*?'

'Yes, yes. Christian went to Eton!'

Another aristo, Harry thought, as Christian Villeneuve chuckled and said 'My mother is English and we lived in

114

London when I was young.'

Knightsbridge, I bet, Harry thought to himself and said 'Right, English it is.' He thought about making a joke that he'd been to Eton too – on a day trip from his grammar school for a chess match, arranged by his teacher who was an Old Etonian, but thought better of it. De Bossenet was looking very businesslike, as though there had been enough small talk.

'Right,' he said. 'Firstly, I've traced the case your English wine merchant had. It came from a Sotheby's wine auction in Hong Kong. We will try to find out who the seller was, but that may take a little while.'

'Secondly, I've spoken to, as well as Christian, *ici*, colleagues from Chateau Latour, Chateau Mouton Rothschild and Chateau Petrus. In short, we are of the opinion that this is probably not an isolated occurrence and that there may well be an organised, *comment dire escroquerie...?*'

'Racket,' said Villeneuve.

'*Exactement*, an organised racket, taking place. I won't go into details of why we think this, the question is, what to do about it?'

'Indeed,' Villeneuve broke in, 'there's aways going to be somebody trying to make money by forging high-priced things. My cousins in Chanel spend a fortune combatting it. Of course, in a way, it's a compliment – no one tries to knock off second-rate brands. But...'

'But,' Alain continued, 'it has to be kept within limits. I don't need to tell you why.'

No, Harry thought. Reputation, exclusivity, is hard won, easily lost.

After a pause, de Bossenet continued, 'Probably someone in

Hong Kong is somehow making the switch. Hong Kong is a very big market for our wines, of course, and the distributor also supplies to Guangzhou and Shenzhen, which are also important for us.'

He paused and Christian Villeneuve broke in again.

'We could possibly ask our distributor, Kowloon Fine Wines, to investigate this matter but it is possible that they, or someone they employ, are part of the problem. They do, we know, sometimes use auctions to reduce overstocks.'

'That's not the way to go,' de Bossenet said. 'But, let's talk things through. *Il me semble* that as the 2006 has been put into a genuine 2005 bottle – Gilles has confirmed that, Harry – something must have been done with the original contents. Now, what could that have been? Switched into a bottle of even higher priced 1995 or 1982, perhaps? It seems unlikely. Where would it all end? 1961, 1945, 1934?'

'Highly unlikely, the differences in the wines would be much greater and more noticeable,' Harry said, 'I reckon it must be happening in a restaurant setting. The 2005 is poured out and genuinely sold at the correct price, the bottle and cork are retained and, later, reused.'

'*Oui*,' Villeneuve said, 'that's what we think.' He paused, 'We would like to put a stop to this of course, but we would like it to be handled discreetly. No question of involving the police.'

De Bossenet took over. 'The first thing to do is to identify which restaurants are involved, it must be more than one. It needs someone who is able to, *comment dire constater...?*'

'Verify,' Harry translated for him, 'someone who is able to verify where a switch has been made.'

'Yes.'

The two Frenchmen looked at Harry expectantly.

'Someone would need to visit the big restaurants and order very expensive bottles of wine,' Harry said.

Again, 'Yes'.

'It would cost a lot.'

The two Frenchmen exchanged a glance.

'Let's be frank,' De Bossenet said, 'we think you're the man to undertake this, Harry, you have the expertise – who could be better qualified? – you have the motivation, and, if you will be willing to do this, we will give you a commission and cover all your expenses.'

Seated comfortably on the plane back to England, Harry reflected on the meeting. He hadn't really been surprised at the offer, as Alain had said, he was ideally qualified, but was still gratified by the confidence that had been shown in him by such grandees, as well as by the generous commission terms. First-class flights, five hundred pounds a day and all expenses! He was really looking forward to telling Alison all about it that evening, some excellent champagne might well be justified, he thought. However, he could see a potential difficulty arising – they wanted it all sorted out quietly while he, and the police, wanted proof that might be needed to stand up in a court of law. Well, they'd have to cross that bridge when they came to it, he decided. Perhaps Courtenay would plead guilty if the case against him was overwhelming, as Andy Pelham had suggested.

'So, you're off to Hong Kong then, Harry!' Alison said that evening, 'How exciting!'

She leaned back in her chair, readjusting the recently

replaced crisp white napkin on her lap as she looked at him. She was attracted to him, no doubt about it, but was he really what he seemed? All the really nice men were married with kids at his age, she thought. Why wasn't he? He'd obviously moved around a lot in his life, which might explain a lot. She actually liked the fact that he 'I't been inquisitive about her life, hadn't asked personal questions, as so many men she met did, far too soon, but did it mean that he wasn't really interested in her? Just looking for a casual affair? Her intuition told her that wasn't the case. Andy Pelham liked him a lot and he was a good judge of people, she was sure. Had she been too friendly, too forward? Maybe. She needed to be careful, yes, but… she wasn't sure she really wanted to! 'Looks like it,' he replied, thinking again how nice she looked in her pink and green floral silk dress.

They'd had a bottle of Krug 1976 with their delicious fresh crabs in Wilton's seafood restaurant in St James's. He remembered being at the vineyard when Remy and Henri Krug had unveiled their 1976 vintage champagne. A three-star Michelin chef had been imported from Reims to create a special meal to accompany the new champagne at the trade launch, it had been one of the most delicious meals he'd ever eaten.

The wine, coming from that tremendously hot dry summer, was perhaps his favourite champagne ever, simultaneously dry and fruity, with a hint of digestive biscuits. The price of a bottle now was horrendous but he reflected that a couple of days commission would cover it.

Alison had certainly appreciated it, which pleased him. He was also grateful that she shared his liking for crab – a lot of people didn't like getting their fingers messy with it but she had had no hesitation in using fingers, tongue, and lips together with the little prong to get the last slivers of body meat out from the central shell.

'We used to have holidays in Cromer as kids,' she'd explained, noticing his admiring glance at her technique, 'my parents were big fans. Much nicer than lobster, I always think.'

'Definitely,' he'd said, 'of course lobster is much easier to eat. It's very nice but really fresh crab is absolutely delicious. It's such a shame that, given our coastline, people here really don't appreciate it. Ninety-five percent of the catch is exported to countries that do appreciate it!'

'Good food and drink is really important to you, Harry, isn't it?' she smiled.

'Yes, sorry, I do go on about it a lot, forgive me.'

'Don't apologise, I like it, but what else is important to you, I wonder?'

He'd wondered for a moment if it was a serious question to be answered seriously. Their conversations thus far hadn't really dipped below the surface of friendliness. She seemed to like him, he definitely liked her, but he decided that discretion should be the better part of valour.

'Oh, golf, Southampton Football Club, old Rovers, 1960s singer-songwriters.'

She'd seemed satisfied with his throw-away reply and their conversation moved on to other things. He'd told her all about his visit to Bordeaux – Alison wanted to hear all the details of the meetings and where he'd been and eaten, so it all took quite a while.

* * *

119

Now, eating their desserts, fresh fruit salad for Alison, crepes suzette for Harry, they got on to the subject of Hong Kong.

'So, you're off to Hong Kong then, Harry! How exciting!'

'Looks like it.'

'Do you know it well? Alison asked.

'Yes, a little.'

'I've never been to the Far East, I've always wanted to.'

She looked at him, into his eyes. This time Harry felt valour overcoming discretion.

'Come with me.' He held his breath.

'Wow! Harry!' She didn't look too shocked, though, he thought.

Be careful! 'I'll... I'll need to think about it.'

She moved her hand slowly across the table and put it on top of his, they both felt a tingle of electricity. He was aware of her immaculate scarlet nails, not too long, not too short. No ring. As he felt the light warm pressure of her skin on his, time seemed to stand still.

'It would only be because you'll need an assistant,' she murmured. Careful be damned.

'Of course.' He didn't move his hand away, she gave it a light squeeze and returned hers to her side of the table.

'Excuse me, Harry, I must go to the ladies.' She smiled at him, rose, and moved away from the table.

Harry sat back, a little stunned. Things were moving quickly, much more quickly than he'd expected.

All the doubts, all the reservations, he'd had throughout his life about getting involved, getting tied down, seemed to be melting away.

How did he feel? He decided he felt wonderful.

Chapter 11

HARRY DIDN'T REALLY LIKE to ask Alison about Scotland Yard's progress in the case. She hadn't raised the subject and he could see that she had a duty of confidentiality, the police couldn't just go around discussing confidential investigations, could they? He was also most unwilling for her to think that he was meeting her for any other reason apart from the pleasure of her company.

So he decided not to talk any more about it and to just enjoy a pleasant evening with a lovely woman, and she was lovely, he thought. She certainly seemed to like him, the fact that she wanted to come with him to Hong Kong suggested that she was willing for their relationship to be more than just friendship. But how to proceed? Stop worrying and over-thinking he told himself, just relax!

While she was in the Ladies, Alison was having similar thoughts. Had she been too forward? Travelling overseas together couldn't help but involve some degree of intimacy. Would they have separate hotel rooms? That would be expensive. Did she really want to sleep with him? Was she really ready for a new relationship? She really wasn't sure.

She thought back to her previous lover, Martin. He was a policeman, though not in the Met. Married, he'd promised to leave his wife for her. She'd never really believed it, in a way hadn't wanted him to, she'd thought about his two young children, didn't want the guilt of being a homebreaker. It must be three years since we ended it, she thought. Apart from a slightly inebriated one-night stand on holiday in Corfu, she had been celibate ever since.

She giggled inwardly at the thought of that night, my goodness he'd been good in bed! Good job they'd both been heading off the next morning or heaven knows what might have happened, he must have been ten years younger. YES, she did want a new man, she decided. Harry? Well why not? With these thoughts in their minds they had a very pleasant evening, just enjoying each other's company, leaving tomorrow, and the future generally, to look after itself. They went on to a tiny jazz club in Soho, in a basement where the steam ran down the walls as the three-piece band gave it their all and the closely packed throng of customers drank Spanish beer and danced with increasing abandon until they were ejected at one in the morning. They both danced freely, if not expertly, losing themselves in the music and the moment, frequently holding hands and being pressed close together in the crowd.

In the taxi on the way back to her apartment Harry said that he'd give Andy Pelham a call next day to see how things stood. She said she'd check out how she stood for taking some time off, they'd talk tomorrow evening. Satisfied that they'd only let the future briefly intrude on their enjoyment of the moment, they relapsed into a companionable silence, although they both shared the feeling that something might be about to happen.

Suddenly, the taxi swung to the right to avoid a Mini trying to force its way onto the road and Harry, seatbelt-less, was sent sliding sideways across the bench seat on to Alison. She'd been sitting half facing towards him so, as he raised his hand to stop himself it brushed against her breast before ending up resting on her arm where it met her shoulder. The sudden intimacy, the touch of his hand on the silk of her dress, the slight pressure on her skin, sent another charge between them and it just seemed inevitable that they kissed. It wasn't a sudden or a long kiss, they held each other's eyes for a second before their lips met, closed at first then briefly opening before the tips of their tongues met for a delicious moment. Both a little shocked by what had happened, they drew apart, smiling at each other.

There was a further five minutes journey to her home and, holding hands, they were silent with their thoughts. Would she ask him in? On balance, Harry hoped not. Things had moved very fast, perhaps too fast, and he was, he realised, really tired. Should she ask him in? No, she decided, let's not rush things.

As the taxi drew to a halt she said 'Thank you, Harry, for a *most* memorable evening. Safe journey home and speak tomorrow', a squeeze of his hand and she was gone.

By the time Harry had collected his car from the car park beneath Hyde Park and driven home, it was nearly 3.30 a.m. and he really was tired, exhausted. He fell into bed, went to sleep instantly and didn't wake until he heard Pat vacuuming on the stairs.

'Heavens,' he exclaimed and glanced at the clock on his bedside table – 'ten o'clock, nearly!' He hurriedly pulled on his dressing gown, ran a brush through his tousled hair and went out on to the landing. 'Morning, Pat, sorry, got back very late and overslept – I meant to come and get Rosie first thing. Have you...?

'Yes, she's downstairs, Al took her for a walk, she's fine, don't worry.'

'You're an angel, thanks so much. I never sleep in, normally,

I was just knackered.'

She smiled at him. 'And please forgive my appearance, too.'

He hastily retied the belt of the dressing gown round his waist as he realised it was coming apart a bit and that he was in danger of losing his modesty. Pat grinned at him. 'Good trip?' she asked. 'You changed your flight OK?'

'All went well, thanks. I'll just jump in the shower and I'll come down and tell you about it.'

'Would you like me to start a cooked breakfast, for you, Harry? I've got enough time if you want me to.'

'That would be great, if you're sure you don't mind. Croissants are all very well but...'

'I'll just finish doing these stairs and I'll get going, take your time in the shower.'

'Great, thanks so much, Pat, I could do with a bit of a soak, perhaps I'll have a bath then, be down in twenty minutes?'

'Fine, as I say don't rush. Eggs scrambled or fried?'

'Ooh, fried, I think.'

'Two?'

'Yes please, you know me too well, Pat. Don't know what I'd do without you.'

'You need a woman, Harry!'

He thought of Alison, remembering their brief kiss. 'Maybe. But what would Alistair say?'

Pat made a pretend slap at him. 'Go and get in the bath!'

Feeling much refreshed after a bath and a shave, Harry joined Pat in the kitchen, savouring the delicious smell of toast and bacon. He told her about his trip as he ate his breakfast, describing the hotel and the suave Frenchmen he'd met without going into the reasons for going.

She didn't seem to have heard anything about his involvement with the police, or if she had, she didn't ask him about it, which made him think that Scotland Yard had been successful in keeping a bit of a lid on the publicity.

After Pat had left he put in a call to Andy Pelham. He'd been busy in a meeting but had called back half an hour later. Not much had happened, Courtenay had hired an expensive lawyer who had enquired as to the state of the inquiry and to whether his client was likely to be questioned any more, with the pretext that he might have to go overseas on a business trip.

The poison had been identified as cyanide, which had seemed the most likely as Oliver had evidently died almost instantly. 'I was a bit surprised, though,' the inspector said, 'because normally cyanide, or prussic acid in its liquid form, gives off a distinct bitter almond smell and I certainly didn't get that from the decanter. But the toxicologist told me that the smell isn't always present and that, even if it is, some people can't smell it.'

'I see,' Harry said, 'still, Courtenay was taking quite a risk, wasn't he? Oliver might easily have detected it, unless he could be sure it didn't smell?'

'Yes, don't know how he could be sure. But, thinking about it, it's possible it was intended as a warning as much as a serious attempt to kill him. After all, Courtenay didn't know for sure that Oliver was cheating. Also, Oliver wouldn't have known who'd done it and couldn't have confronted the group to find out without admitting he'd been cheating.'

'That makes sense' Harry replied. 'But, if Courtenay had accidentally on purpose knocked over his decanter next morning Oliver would have known, surely?'

125

'True.' A pause before the policeman continued. 'But even then, what could he do about it without admitting he'd been cheating? Looks like our Mr Courtenay is a bit of a risk taker, though.'

The press seemed to have lost interest as newer murders, sadly, were committed. Pelham suggested that Harry update him by email on his French trip and his future plans.

Harry had said he would and took it as a hint that the policeman didn't want to get too involved at this stage. Fair enough, he thought, there's really nothing he can do to help at the moment. He wondered if Alison would tell him why she wanted to take time off. Probably not, he thought, but it's up to her. Then he wondered if, in the cold light of day, she might decide that she didn't really want to fly to the other side of the world with someone she'd only met three or four times. He was professionally and financially involved, but what was in it for her? A nice holiday? No, if she did come it must mean that she was serious about him.

She liked him, for sure. He liked her, very much, but did he really want to get into a proper relationship? He'd been hurt before. She was younger than him. Did she have children? He'd never asked and she hadn't mentioned it. How much did they really know about each other? Not an awful lot.

He sighed. But memories of the previous evening came into his mind and then he smiled. She was lovely, he didn't need to make any decisions yet. Also, there didn't seem much point in making anything in the way of plans until he knew if Alison was going to come, and, if so, when she could get time off.

He remembered his promise to Henry Liu and called him to confirm that the bottle he'd kindly supplied had also been a

2006. Alain de Bossenet had told him to let Yiu know that the chateau would reimburse him for the case he'd bought and, in return, would be grateful if he wouldn't mention it to anyone else, as it might compromise their enquiries. He'd been very grateful, in turn, and agreed to send de Bossenet a copy of his invoice and his bank details. He confirmed to Harry that he had not, in fact, discussed it with anyone other than Harry, so all was well on that front. Harry felt that he owed Henry Yiu something for his willing cooperation so, when he'd asked if Harry knew what the chateau were going to do, he told him that it looked like they'd be making enquiries among their distributors in China, not mentioning Hong Kong specifically. He promised to keep in touch if he learnt any more, which seemed to satisfy Liu.

He wrote his email to Andy Pelham, summarising what he'd found out in France and said he planned to go to Hong Kong soon, but couldn't yet say when. He sent it off and decided that it would be good to forget all about it for a while, at least until he called Alison that evening.

However, as always he found it easier to decide to stop thinking about something than to actually do it. What would he do when he got to Hong Kong? He didn't speak Chinese at all. Supposing he successfully identified restaurants where wines were being switched, what would he be able to do about it? It didn't look as though his connections in France or Scotland Yard would be of any use to him.

Maybe he was setting off on a wild goose chase. Perhaps he should just forget the whole thing. But no, he was committed to the French chateaux, and besides, there was Alison to consider. Let's go, and see what happens, he decided.

There was another thing, after the article in the American

wine magazine, his name wouldn't be unknown in Hong Kong, would he have to use a false name so as not to be recognised? If he was, there was a good chance they wouldn't switch wines on him. Fortunately, he hadn't agreed to Peter Hill's request for a photograph to accompany the article. He decided to stop shaving and let his beard and moustache grow. He had a credit card in the name of his wine trading company, so he could use that rather than a personal one, he'd have to give the bank a ring and get them to increase the credit limit – a lot!

His mind ran on in this way, to his annoyance, so he decided he'd better get out in the fresh air and do something. Half past one, I'll call in at the pub for a pint and a sandwich and head on to the golf club, he decided. Thursday afternoon, there might be someone around for a game.

Chapter 12

UNLIKE HARRY, ALISON WASN'T having any second thought or doubts the next day. She wasn't much given to introspection, once she'd made up her mind about something or somebody she tended to stick with it. Not that she hadn't often been wrong, but she'd been right far more frequently and, although she would have struggled to put it into words, far less try to explain it to someone else, she had a strong feeling that female intuition was something special and dynamic, making women more than equal to men. She intuitively felt that Harry was the right kind of man for her. She sensed a base of steadiness and balance underneath his rather louche and playful demeanour. She really liked the fact that he hadn't pressed her with enquiries about her life. The past was the past, live in the present.

She was early getting in to work and stopped on the way to buy a packet of Jamaican Blue Mountain ground coffee, Andy's favourite. When he got into work at 8.30 he stopped and sniffed the aroma coming from the coffee machine appreciatively.

'Mmm, smells divine, Alison,' he said, 'what have I done to deserve this?'

'Nothing, nothing, it's a Thursday, the weekend's coming up, I thought we deserved a good start to what is going to be a good couple of days and a marvellous weekend!'

'Hmm, I see, you're in a good mood,' he replied a little suspiciously, 'any particular reason?'

She poured out a mug of the steaming, freshly brewed coffee and set it on his desk. She hadn't made any secret of the fact that Harry had asked her out the previous week. She'd told him the next morning that she'd had a nice evening and they'd both left it at that. However, they knew each other pretty well and she guessed that he suspected that there could be more developments.

'No, not really,' she grinned at him, 'but, well, chief, there is something I wanted to ask you, in fact.'

'Uh-huh?' He sipped appreciatively at the coffee.

'I wonder if I can take some of my leave? I think I have around sixteen days left.'

'Ah-hah! Nice coffee, by the way.' His sly dig at her attempt to get him in a good mood made her blush, just a little. 'When are you thinking of?'

'I'm not absolutely sure, but fairly soon, if it's possible. Of course I don't want to leave you in the lurch, but I'm fairly up to date with everything at the moment. Steven is pretty much au fait with...' she broke off as she became unable to ignore his silent appraising gaze any longer.

The inspector looked at her for a long moment. 'This wouldn't happen to have anything to do with a certain Mr Harry Benson would it? Not that it's strictly any of my business, of course.'

Alison breathed a sigh of relief. She hadn't been sure whether or not to tell him what she was planning to do but, now he'd asked, she was sure it was for the best. 'Yes, it might,' she smiled.

'OK, tell me all about it.'

They talked through the plan to go to Hong Kong and, when he was satisfied that there would be no overlap between her official position and what they were going to do, he agreed to her leave request, as long as she didn't go until the middle

130

of the following week, after handing over her outstanding work to Steven Dell, who worked on case analysis for him, who was due back from a course on Monday.

'I'm sure I don't really need to repeat myself, Alison,' he said, 'but, just to be quite clear, although we would very much like him to succeed in getting proof of the switch, Harry's investigation is *not* an official police investigation. If the two of you get into trouble we won't be able to support or help you.' He broke off. 'That's as your boss. As your friend, if I might put it that way...' he glanced at her inquiringly. She nodded and smiled, 'Of course.'

'As a friend, have you thought it might be a bit dangerous? It sounds like there's definitely some criminal activity, there may be a fair bit of money at stake for someone.'

He paused. 'And whoever it is might not take kindly to you and Harry interfering.'

She swallowed. 'Mmm... I see what you mean. I hadn't really thought of it in that way, I think it's just a question of identifying the restaurants... but I'll talk to Harry about it before making any decisions.'

Harry had found his friend Graham McKechnie on the practice range at the golf club trying out his new Callaway Big Bertha driver and they'd played nine holes together. Graham had been willing to play the back nine as well but Harry demurred. 'Sorry, Graham, I'm a bit knackered, it's been a busy few days.' Graham had suggested a pint but, after they'd changed their shoes and loaded their clubs back into their cars, they found the clubhouse bar was shut, a little to Harry's relief. They arranged to play together in the club's monthly Stableford competition on Saturday and Harry set off for home, in Ramona the green Rover.

After taking Rosie for a walk, he decided that it was warm enough to lie out on the patio on a sun lounger. David had been busy and there was a pleasant smell of freshly mown grass as he settled down with a mug of tea next to him. He was feeling drowsy so he set an alarm on his phone for eight o'clock, when he intended to call Alison.

As usual when he set an alarm, something in his brain woke him up a couple of minutes before it was due to go off. The evening was drawing in so he moved the lounger back into the garage and went inside, closing the patio doors. He was just making himself a cup of coffee when his mobile rang, Alison's name came up on the screen and he took the kettle off the hob.

'Good evening, Alison.'

'Hello handsome!' That made him smile.

'Hmm, don't think so, really. But, how's your day been?'

'Fine. I've got two and a half weeks off starting next Wednesday. I told you Andy was a sweetie. But, Harry, what are we actually going to do there?' She told him about the inspector's misgivings. 'I'd kind of envisaged just visiting restaurants and identifying which ones are doing it, but that's not really going to be enough is it?'

'Firstly, it's great that you can come! Even if nothing comes of it, wine-wise, having your company will be... well you know, great,' he said a bit lamely. He hurried on, 'But yes, I've been giving a lot of thought to that question as well. I don't speak either Cantonese or Mandarin so I'm not sure I'd be any use at all at investigating how it's happening and who's doing it. So I don't think you need worry, all we will be able to do is identify the restaurants. My partner in my restaurant in Jakarta, Jack Chau, is from Hong Kong so I'm planning to give him a call and ask his advice. It's the middle of the night there now so I'll give him a call in the morning.' He paused.

'I see' Alison said, 'makes sense. If he can't help, would you still want to go?'

'Yes, for sure. I'm committed to the chateaux in France, and they'll be happy to have the restaurants identified – they'll have the ability then to put a stop to it, I think.'

'OK, good! I'm looking forward to it. Hong Kong! I've always wanted to go there.'

'It's a great place. I know it a little, as I said, but from a fair long while ago, I'm sure it's changed now the Chinese are asserting their control.' He paused again. 'So no second thoughts, Alison? I'd entirely understand if –'

'No!' she interrupted, 'I'm not backing out now, as I said, I'm really looking forward to it. But I'm glad we're not going to be dodging down dark alleyways and climbing through windows in search of evidence!'

'Me too,' he laughed, 'I don't think I'm really cut out to be Sam Spade or Philip Marlowe.'

'No, but what did Andy call you? The Wine Detective? That fits.'

'Maybe. Sometimes I wonder... what's happened to my nice quiet life, playing golf, restoring old cars, selling a bit of wine?' He spoke jokingly but she detected a note of seriousness in what he said.

'Well, Harry, let's get together this weekend and talk it all right through. I'm meeting my sister on Saturday, but I'm free on Sunday.'

'Good idea. What do you fancy doing?'

'The weather forecast is good, how about... how about a run out into the country and a picnic somewhere? I love London but everywhere's just so full of people and tourists. I'm sure you've had enough of coming up here for a bit, too.'

'You're quite right,' he said, 'anywhere you'd like to go?'

'How about if I come out your way? I could get a train from Waterloo and meet you at a station near you. I'm sure you know somewhere nice for a picnic.'

'Sounds ideal to me. I'll pack up a picnic and –'

'How about doing that together?' she broke in, 'If I make an early start we could do a bit of shopping together on the way, make a real expedition of it!'

He laughed. 'OK. I'll just organise plates, cutlery and glasses.'

'Ice blocks too, Harry. And napkins, please!'

They arranged to meet at Winchester station with the plan to drive out into the New Forest for their picnic. Harry offered to let her know the result of his conversation with Jack Chau but she demurred.

'Let's do that on Sunday, Harry. Have a bit of that quiet life first, what was it? Playing golf and restoring cars?' she chuckled.

'Actually, yes, I am playing golf on Saturday.'

'Good! Have a good round and I'll see you on Sunday. Night, handsome.'

'Good night, gorgeous!' He heard her laughing as she rang off. My word, he said to himself, she really is gorgeous, can't believe how well it's going. Perhaps too well? He looked around for some wood to touch before restarting the kettle and making himself a snack.

Chapter 13

THE PHONE RANG PROMPTLY at nine the next morning. It was Alain de Bossenet from Chateau Lafite. 'Bonjour, Harry, it's Alain.'

Harry, freshly showered and dressed after his morning run, replied 'Bonjour Alain *ca va*?'

'*Oui ca va bien merci, et toi*?'

Goodness, we're tutoying each other now, thought Harry.

'Fine thank you. Busy planning my trip.'

'Ah, very good. Listen Harry, we've traced the seller of the case of wine. It came from The Mandarin Oriental Hotel, in Hong Kong. It's a long-standing and very important customer and, really, there's zero chance that they'd be involved in any way in switching wines. I know the Food and Beverage Director personally, no way.'

'I see,' Harry responded, 'not very helpful.'

'No. They get all their wines direct from our distributor, Kowloon Fine Wines, and, *comment dire*, belief is stretched also that they could be involved. And furthermore, Harry, they sold two cases at that auction. The other case, it so happens, went to a restaurant in Paris we know well, they've already sold it and are sure it was genuine. Their customers would have known for sure, they say.'

'No doubting that The Mandarin isn't involved,' Harry paused for thought, 'perhaps it got mixed up at Sotheby's.'

'I don't think so. These were the only two cases of 2005 in the sale.'

'Right. So we're no further on.'

'No, I'm afraid not, Harry. Sorry not to have been more

helpful. We don't think it would be politic to ask the hotel about it. We would much rather wait for your report before we decide what steps to take.'

'OK, I understand,' said Harry, 'I haven't actually booked my flight yet but I'll let you know when I'm going.'

They exchanged civilities and Harry rang off. He was nearly convinced de Bossenet was right and that The Mandarin wouldn't have been involved. But, perhaps, someone who worked there, in cahoots with...? With who? Or whom? I should say, he thought.

For once he wasn't in the mood for a big breakfast and just had some toast with Marmite with his cup of tea, before settling down at his PC to check out flights to Hong Kong. It looked like there was plenty of availability in the middle of the following week. Two business class seats were considerably less than one first class one. He'd thought about running taking Alison with him past de Bossenet and had decided against it as an unnecessary complication.

Before calling Jakarta, he thought through how much he could tell his friend Jack. He was a good friend, and Harry knew he really needed his help, so he decided to tell him everything. He texted to find out what would be a good time to call and they decided on 11 UK time.

After they exchanged news of each other's lives, Harry recounted the entire story, not leaving anything out. Jack Chau listened carefully, without interrupting.

'What do you think, Jack?' he asked, 'Would it just be a wild goose chase?'

'A wild what chase, Harry?'

'Sorry, a silly English expression! A complete waste of time?'

'Well,' Jack said, considering, 'firstly it's by no means

impossible that this is happening in Hong Kong. So many family interconnections in the restaurant trade. It seems to me that there must be quite a few people involved, in different restaurants, to make it worthwhile. So quite a few people probably have an idea what's going on.

'Secondly, Harry, I don't think you'd have a chance in hell of finding out anything. If an outsider like you was to ask questions, they'd all clam up and, frankly, it could be dangerous for you. There might be some violent criminals involved. But no, it needn't be a waste of time. As I said, there could well be quite a few people in the know. If you can identify some restaurants which are involved... let me see. Harry, I'll have a think about it. Maybe there is someone there who can help. But... even so, you'll need to be careful, Harry my old friend.

'I could try to talk you out of it but, knowing you, you've made your mind up!'

'I think so, Jack. But I really value your advice. If you said it would be better to let sleeping dogs lie—'

'Dogs? What dogs?' Jack interrupted.

'Sorry, another untranslatable English expression! It means to avoid stirring things up. If you said that it's not going to be possible, or just too dangerous, I'd have to seriously consider not going. Although I am rather committed to the French.'

'I see. Give me an hour, Harry. I'll have a think and make a couple of calls – don't worry, I won't tell anyone anything!'

In fact it was more than two hours later when Jack Chau called back. He didn't try to talk Harry out of going and in fact said that, with the number of people who must be in some way involved, it ought to be relatively easy to get to the bottom of it. A couple of calls had established that his ex-wife's cousin's son was a private investigator based in Hong Kong and, by all accounts, a good one.

'I guess he'll be able to find out what's going on,' Jack said. 'But, Harry, you said that you needed proof that will stand up in court. I'm not sure how you'll get that, unless you involve the police, which you don't want to do, I think?'

'There is that,' Harry replied, 'but thanks so much, Jack, you've been an enormous help. I definitely think it's worth going. I'll talk to the police here about the evidence. At least I'll know I've done my damndest.'

Jack Chau chuckled. 'I thought so and... you'll have established a connection in France that could be very useful! I can see you being very valuable to the fine wine trade – flying around the world, sniffing out, if I can use that phrase, trouble. Nice work, Harry!'

Jack promised to give the good word about Harry to his relative and then to send Harry his contact details. They spent a while discussing the restaurant trade in Jack's part of the world before finishing off their call.

Jack's parting words were to tell Harry not to hesitate to call him if in need, 'And, Harry, if necessary, just jump on a plane to Jakarta!'

Harry promised he would and they rang off.

Sunday morning dawned bright and sunny with the promise of a hot day to come. Harry had enjoyed his Saturday, playing reasonable golf and coming sixth in the club Stableford before listening on local radio to the Saints getting a creditable 1-1 draw away on the opening day of the football season.

He'd done a bit of research on the internet and had decided on Emery Down, in the New Forest, as a good place for a walk through the forest and a picnic. After an alcohol-free evening and an early night he was up bright and early, in good time for a short run and to take Rosie for a walk before getting organised for their picnic.

He got out his wicker picnic hamper and checked that all its crockery, cutlery, and glasses were clean and presentable before adding a couple of linen napkins from the dining room chest of drawers. What else? he thought. Ah yes, ice packs. He went out to the garage and found his insulated cool bag. It smelt a bit musty inside so he took it into the kitchen and gave it a good wipe through and then dried it off with kitchen paper. In the bottom drawer of the freezer he found three blue plastic ice packs, put them inside and zipped up the lid. On second thoughts, he went down to his cellar and selected a nice bottle of burgundy, a 2013 Pouilly Fuisse, and popped it in as well.

He thought about taking two folding chairs but decided against it and went and fetched his big tartan picnic rug from the garage, much more informal than chairs, he thought. He loaded everything into Rosemary, the red Rover, checking she was immaculate inside, and went back in for a breakfast of a boiled egg (quite large, so 5 minutes and 40 seconds in boiling water), toast and marmalade and coffee.

He still had ten minutes to spare before he needed to set off for Winchester so he sat down and had a quick look at his *Observer*, reading the report on the Saints game and Andrew Rawnsley's column, which he always enjoyed for its insider insights and analysis of the UK political scene. He decided not to take the paper with him, looking forward to a day just enjoying the weather, the scenery, and Alison's company.

He was on the platform at Winchester ten minutes before Alison's train arrived at 9.50. He was very much looking forward to seeing her but, in truth, was a bit nervous. He had a feeling that, after Thursday night and that kiss, they were reaching an important point in their relationship. How should he play it? He didn't want to appear too sure of himself, on the other hand, not too cool. He sighed, the course of true love never... he thought. Was this love? He didn't know. He certainly thought about her a lot. But, he realised, not really in a physical way. It definitely wasn't just lust, he decided. He thought of her body, slim certainly, but not exactly boyish. Not his type? He chuckled to himself, nonsense!

The train arrived exactly on time and he watched her as she got down from the carriage, she was wearing bright yellow mid-thigh-length shorts, a navy blue v-neck shirt and an open white cardigan. Her hair was piled up on her head in a bun and she had pale blue sunglasses on. She looked stunning with nicely tanned bare brown legs ending in white ankle socks and Vans trainers in yellow, matching her shorts.

She walked up to him, smiling, and gave him a hug and a peck on the cheek. 'What a lovely morning, Harry! I'm really looking forward to our picnic.'

'Me too! Was your journey OK, Alison? It's out this way.'

'Call me Ali,' she said as they walked out to the car park, 'everyone does.'

'OK, Ali. I'm afraid I'm just plain Harry.'

'Not Hal? Hazza?' she laughed. 'Anyhow, I like Harry.'

'Good!' he smiled. 'Here we are.'

'Goodness,' she exclaimed, 'is that yours? What a lovely old car. I haven't seen one of these for ages!'

As they set off through the streets of Winchester, Harry explained about his business with George and his passion for these old Rovers. 'Three!' she exclaimed.

'Crazy I know. This one's called Rosemary. The other two are Rhoda and Ramona.'

'You must have a big garage, Harry. Tell me about your house.'

He decided not to go down the motorway to the New Forest and as they set off down the country roads towards Romsey he told her about The Dower House, the pub, and his neighbours. They passed by the Mountbatten estate and stopped at a big Sainsbury's supermarket where they bought crusty rolls, ham, smoked salmon, pate, stilton, tomatoes, lettuce and peaches for their picnic. Harry explained he already had a bottle of chilled white so they settled on a bottle of Beaujolais as their red, a Morgon Harry had drunk and enjoyed before.

Alison insisted on paying half when they got to the checkout and, as they walked out to the car each carrying a bag, she slipped her hand into his. He looked at her and they smiled at each other. It was going to be a great day!

Chapter 14

As they headed towards Cadnam on the A31, Harry recounted his conversations with Jack Chau in Jakarta, breaking off to explain why he was unshaven. 'I thought you might be wondering.'

'No, I didn't really notice, Harry, but it seems like a good idea to be incognito,' she replied.

'He's a good friend, Jack?' Alison asked when he'd finished.

'Uh-huh, a very good friend. He was my partner for nearly 20 years. We originally had a restaurant in Kuta, in Bali. It did really well but Jack has family in Jakarta so we sold that one and transferred the operation there. He would have had plenty of chances to ease me out or shortchange me financially, but he didn't, he's an honest man and, as I say, a good friend. I got an email last night with the details of the sleuth in Hong Kong, evidently he speaks very good English – most of his clients are English, or at least English speakers.'

'So...' a pause, 'there's no reason not to go?'

'No.'

'Yippee! When do we start?'

Harry grinned at her enthusiasm. 'When did you say you can start your leave?'

'Wednesday. I'll need a day to arrange things, but I could go on Thursday.'

'Great. I'll book flights for Thursday, from Heathrow. We'll be going business class so I should be able to leave the return date open.'

'Business class? Not up the front!' she teased.

'No, sorry,' he laughed. 'But two business class tickets gives me quite a saving on first class, so we'll be able to splash out on a suite at the hotel. I'll make the bookings tomorrow. I'll book for a week but explain we might need to change the leaving date. If that's OK with you.'

He thought about saying that the suite he'd priced up had two separate bedrooms as well as a lounge but decided it wasn't quite appropriate. Alison likewise was wondering about the same point and, also, decided against mentioning or querying it.

'Sounds great! Sorry if I'm coming across like an excited schoolgirl, Harry, but... but I can't tell you how much I'm looking forward to it. Hong Kong! Business class! Hotel suite! Pinch me, I must be dreaming.'

It was coming up to mid-day when the gleaming red car pulled into the parking area in the forest. It was quite a large car park but there were only a few other cars already there. A short walk from the car park there was a large tree-studded area with plenty of picnic benches, the ones with built-in seats.

As they undid their seat belts, Harry explained that he'd brought a rug, thinking they could carry it and the picnic into the forest, but asked if perhaps they'd be better off having a walk and coming back to one of the benches.

'I think so, Harry,' she replied. 'It's lovely here, not too busy, and I guess there'd be a fair bit to carry – hamper, cool bag, shopping, rug.'

So they set off on foot, unencumbered. A noticeboard at the end of the car park gave details of the different signposted walks they could take and they decided to follow the green posts on a circular three-mile walk.

Again Alison slipped her hand into his. 'Shame about the rug, though, looks very comfortable.' She kept a very straight face as he glanced at her. 'Perhaps we'll be able to try it out another day!'

Harry squeezed her hand, not knowing quite what to say. They walked for half an hour or so, taking pleasure in the fresh air, not too hot yet, the beautiful woodland scenery and each other's company. The light had that morning brilliance which illuminated everything softly, without any glare. The signs were easy enough to follow but they decided to branch off to what looked like a stream – elegant willow trees bending low in all their summer glory.

'I think willows are my favourite trees,' Alison said, 'stately but so graceful with their fronds waving gently.'

Harry thought of the amazing huge red flowering trees he'd known in Asia and was just about to answer when a great clap of thunder interrupted. They'd both been too busy admiring the forest to look up much at the sky and had failed to notice some huge dark clouds gathering a little to the west of them.

'Golly,' Harry said. A strong breeze picked up suddenly as they looked at each other. 'We'd better head back.' They set off back in the direction they'd come, walking quickly, but within five minutes the clouds were overhead and a thick, pelting rain began falling. Lightning flashed across the sky and the sunshine was blotted out. They took shelter under a huge spreading oak tree which kept them dry as the rain splashed down through the leaves a few feet away.

'This wasn't in the weather forecast,' Harry said. A huge flash of lightning created momentary shadows around them. They counted the four or five seconds until the enormous crash of

144

thunder echoed around them.

'That's really close,' Alison said, 'I'm sure I've read you're better off in the open than under a big tree the lightning might strike. Perhaps we'd better run for it!'

'Definitely,' he said, 'I can't see this stopping very soon.' An equally bright flash of lightning, seemingly right overhead, made their minds up for them. They looked at each other, nodded, and dashed out into the teeming rain.

Alison in her trainers was the faster runner and led the way back to the car. By the time Harry, in his sandals, arrived, gasping and fumbling for the keys to open the car, she was standing waiting, water streaming down her face, mascara running down her cheeks, shirt clinging to her arms and chest as she looked at him without speaking. He opened the doors with the key and they clambered inside, breathing hard.

Harry was about to say something jocular about their wet experience when he felt a certain coolness coming his way from the other front seat. 'Really sorry about that,' he offered, expecting the reply that it wasn't his fault. But she only sniffed, and then sneezed.

'No towels, I suppose?'

'No. No, sorry,' he said, 'but I'll get the napkins and rug from the boot.' She sniffed again as he got out into the rain, now slackening off a bit, and came back a minute later with the napkins, fairly large, and the rug. He handed her both the napkins and was again a bit surprised when she didn't hand one back to him.

'The rain's easing off now, it looks as though the storm's passing over,' he said, 'shall we wait it out, or...'

'Harry,' she replied, towelling her hair with the napkins, 'I'm wet and I'm cold and I look like I've been dragged through a hedge backwards. I just want to get home.'

He could see she was really upset so, rather than raise any objections, he started up the engine. He turned the heater up to maximum and said 'It should soon warm up.'

'Can I have that rug first, to put over the seat? Otherwise I'm going to stick to the leather.' Her tone was still not in the least friendly and Harry decided not to say anything, a bit baffled as to why she was quite so upset. The rain had now stopped and they both got out of the car so Harry could spread the rug across the two seats, making sure he could still get to the handbrake.

They got back into the car and set off in silence.

Men! Alison thought. They expect you to look nice and feminine and attractive and, when you don't live up to what they expect, they couldn't give a damn about how you're feeling. They still expect you to be happy and put up with it. She thought back to her father, he'd always wanted a perfect pretty daughter and when she, a bit of a tomboy, had fallen short of his idea of feminine perfection, he'd been cold towards her and withdrawn his love. It still hurt, a lot. Her sister, Penny, had been his favourite. When, after their mother had succumbed to breast cancer, Alison had insisted on going off to university, Penny had taken a dead-end job in a shop to stay home and look after him.

She was deep in these thoughts when Harry asked 'Warming up a bit now, Ali? There's a service station not far ahead now, would you like to stop and use the Ladies?'

'Yes please.'

He pulled into the Rownhams services on the M27, now back in brilliant sunshine. They eased themselves off the rug and went together into the crowded food and shopping area,

146

Alison taking her shoulder bag and the two napkins with her. Avoiding the curious glances at her bedraggled state, she went straight into the Ladies without looking at him.

He went into the Gents, had a pee and dried himself off as much as he could with paper towels and the Dyson hand drier, wondering what he could do to improve the situation with Alison, without coming to any sensible conclusions. Women! He thought.

He waited a good twenty minutes until she emerged, looking considerably brighter, and drier. She walked up to him and smiled, 'A really nice lady from Nottingham took pity on me, went out to her car and brought back a towel and a hair dryer. I'm still a bit damp,' she said. 'How about you?'

'Rather more than a bit damp,' he grinned, 'I won't need a shower for a week!'

She laughed and they set off back towards the food area. 'Would you like a hot drink, warm us up?' he asked.

'No thanks, Harry. The sooner I can get out of these wet things the better.'

'I've been thinking, would you like to come back to the house, put everything in the tumble drier, have our picnic there? Or would you rather go to the station?'

Alison was feeling considerably happier, hair and make-up restored to something resembling normality, and although she was inclined to accept his suggestion, the spirit of mischief remained. 'Do you really expect me to get on a train in this state, Harry Benson? Couldn't you drive a girl home?'

To his relief, Harry could detect that the mischief contained a kernel of good humour, and he replied in kind 'Heavens, do you expect me to drive you all the way to London and then back home in these wet things?'

147

They both laughed, glad that the brief hiatus in their friendship was over. 'Let's go to your house,' she said, 'I'd love to see it.'

'Great, we'll soon get your things dried. And mine!'

By the time they reached Upper Rossett they were both a bit more comfortable, and ravenously hungry. Harry showed her to the largest of the guest bedrooms, the one with an attached bathroom. 'You'll find a big dressing gown and towels in there,' he said, 'if you want to pass me out your wet things, I'll put them in the tumble drier.'

Alison had of course foreseen this situation and decided that she really didn't want to hand over her knickers and bra to him. 'I can cope, Harry, thank you, if you can show me where the drier is?'

'OK,' he grinned, 'the laundry room is down the stairs, through the kitchen towards the back door, and on the right. I'll go and get myself changed and leave you to it.'

He changed quickly out of his wet clothes and went out to the car to unload the picnic. By the time Alison reappeared, half an hour later, he had everything set out on the patio, the white burgundy opened and in an ice bucket.

'How do I look now?' she smiled.

'Mmm... good as new!'

Chapter 15

'TOUR OF THE ESTATE first, or picnic first, Ali?' Harry asked.

'Food first, definitely, I'm starving. I see you've started without me!' she replied glancing pointedly at the glass of wine by his side.

'Sorry, just couldn't wait any longer!' He poured out a second glass and handed it to her.

'Fair enough, I'm sorry I was so long, but I found your ironing board, didn't want to look too creased and ragged on my first visit here. It's a lovely house, and the garden...!' She took a long sip at her glass and relaxed back in her chair as she smiled at him.

'You look wonderful. It's so nice having you here. Ali, I'm sorry about this morning, should have checked the weather forecast more carefully, I guess.'

'Not your fault, and, and – sorry I got upset. But this is just as nice as it would have been in the forest. And we did get a walk in – and a run!'

'I didn't know you could run so fast,' he grinned, 'left me well behind. But let's eat, can I pass you a roll?'

After they had demolished almost all the food and were halfway into the bottle of Morgon, they took their glasses inside to sit in comfort in the lounge, glad to be out of the sun for a while. How nice she looks, Harry thought, her tanned legs highlighted by the cream-coloured sofa they were sitting on. He got a tray and went back outside to gather up the remains of their meal, leaving her looking at the colour supplement of his *Observer*.

When he'd finished clearing up, putting the uneaten pate and ham in the fridge, he returned to the lounge to find her with eyes closed and breathing gently through her nose, the magazine splayed out on her lap. He sat down quietly, so as not to wake her, and started to read the review section of his newspaper. After a few minutes, succumbing to the food, the wine, the sunshine, and the exertions of the day, he too fell into a gentle slumber.

When he awoke, half an hour or so later, it was to find her smiling at him. 'What a heavenly afternoon,' she said, 'I must have drifted off – lucky I wasn't holding the wine glass!'

'Me too, can I refill it?'

'No thanks, I've still got quite a bit left.'

While she was waiting for him to wake, Alison had been thinking about how he would look naked. She could see his smooth muscular calves and thighs as he sat next to her in his maroon-coloured shorts and sandals. His white Polo sports shirt showed only a slight paunch to his belly. The stubble around his chin and top lip made him look a bit younger, she thought. How would it feel against her skin? She shivered slightly in anticipation.

She'd done her best, not really deliberately, to test him, to put him off that morning, but his calm reaction had made her mind up. Drawing closer to him on the sofa, she murmured, 'Harry, I suppose that's the first time we've slept together.'

Finding no words to reply, Harry moved even closer to her, put a hand behind her head and, feeling no resistance as he gently pulled her head towards him, moved his own head forward and kissed her full on the lips. Her mouth opened for a full lingering kiss, after a short while he caressed her breast as she rubbed her palm against the front of his shorts. She

150

pulled her mouth away and whispering, 'Last one naked is a sissy!' jumped up from the sofa and started unbuttoning her shirt.

Harry watched in fascination as her cleavage and pure white bra was revealed as she reached round behind to unclip it. 'Come on Harry, get on with it!'

Within ten seconds he had pulled down his shorts and underpants and yanked his shirt up over his head, standing fully naked five seconds before her shorts and knickers joined her shirt and bra on the floor. They gazed at each other's bodies for a long moment and then she said 'Mmm, glad to see you know how to rise to the occasion, Harry! Now take me to bed.'

An hour later, as Harry came back with their glasses of wine and got back into the big double bed, she snuggled up to him. 'Did you mind me being so forward, playing the hussy, Harry? I do feel rather wicked.'

'Mind?' he laughed, 'do I look like I minded? No, sweetheart, I'm very grateful that you took the initiative. I guess I'm one of those who can't recognise "token resistance" and–'

'Good,' she interrupted, 'now belt up and come here. I haven't quite finished with you yet.'

Four days later, they met up again at Terminal 3, Heathrow to get the plane to Hong Kong. Harry had been busy booking flights and the hotel. On the way back to Winchester station on Sunday, he'd suggested sharing a bedroom on their trip. Ali had immediately agreed – 'Yes, please', so he'd switched from the suite he'd planned to book to a single luxury room at a better hotel. He'd also arranged for Pat to have Rosie, organised for George to go with Alan, his gamekeeper friend, taking his season ticket for the Saints opening home game of the season, apologised to Mick Taylor, the cricket team captain, for missing the big game on Sunday against local rivals Netherdene and met with the colonel, Tony, and Rose for their quarterly review of the pub business; all seemed to be going along very nicely.

He'd had dinner on Tuesday at the Forshaw's, taking Geraldine the bottles of Chateau Palmer he'd bought in Bordeaux. Apart from the pleasure of their company, it had been a useful evening for him as Frank and Geraldine were quite frequent visitors to Hong Kong and had been able to suggest some restaurants, evidently the restaurant scene had changed quite a bit since his day.

He'd known that a man as well-informed as the colonel would be aware of the Simon Oliver case and his involvement, and had decided that there was no need to be secretive about it all. When Geraldine had retired, leaving them to their coffee and cognac, he told Frank the full story. 'Goodness, Harry,' the colonel said, 'quite the adventure! You'll need to be careful, but I don't see why you shouldn't be able to put your finger on what's goin' on. It's a small world there, they all know each other. So a lot of people must be in the know, at least to some extent.'

'That's what Jack thought too.'

'I don't know if it'll be any help,' the colonel went on, 'but I have a good friend out there who used to be in their police force. He's retired now, but I'm sure he still has good contacts. Let me see,' he paused for a moment, 'he's a conservative sort of chap, I think the best thing would be if I write a letter of introduction for you. If you should need help, give me a call and I'll give you his address.'

'That might be very useful, Frank. Many thanks, I think getting the right evidence might be the hardest part.'

He'd also called Andy Pelham and asked him about the kind of evidence that would be needed if it came to a trial.

'Well, Harry,' the policeman replied, 'ideally, a police report, but your French friends don't want it made public, do they? If it were possible, then an official report into what happened. Let me see... it would need to include details of how that case came to make its way to Henry Yiu. If we had that, then I think we could make it stick. Otherwise... a signed, witnessed confession by whoever was behind it might do the trick. Photos, juries always like seeing photographic evidence, photos of fake labels, bottles, that kind of thing would help. Make sure the camera has a time and location stamp... can't really think of anything else right now but I'll have a chat with the boss and I'll email you if there's anything else.'

He'd wished Harry luck and told him not to hesitate to call if he needed to. Harry was impressed that he gave him his personal mobile number in case, with the time difference, he needed to call outside working hours.

Alison had not discussed the purpose of the trip with her boss on the two days she was in the office before leaving. He hadn't asked or mentioned it at all and she knew him well enough to take that as a signal. He was professionally involved and she was not. However, he'd left his office door open during his conversation with Harry, so she knew she had his support, even if he couldn't show it.

She'd decided not to tell Penny about Harry yet, and just said she was having a break in Hong Kong with a friend. The two of them got along well enough but they weren't exactly intimate. She'd called her best friend Julie, to cry off from their regular Saturday morning brunch in Shepherd's Market with a group of their friends. Naturally Julie couldn't be fobbed off with going to Hong Kong with 'a friend' so she'd opened up a bit about Harry, without going into too much detail about the trip.

Julie, who knew her well enough to guess she was well smitten, was encouragement itself. 'Fantastic, Ali! It's time you had a nice man, all to yourself!' Of course she'd known all about Martin. 'He sounds like a keeper to me. I want to meet him as soon as you get back, mind!'

She'd called Harry to check what kind of clothes and jewellery she should pack. Neither of them felt the need to refer to what had happened on Sunday, but they talked with a freedom and intimacy that was different, interrupting and laughing at each other's little jokes. She called him 'honey' which pleased him, she was 'sweetheart'.

'Our cover is that we're wealthy people that run a wine business.' He explained about using his company credit card. 'If anyone asks, and I don't really see why they should, we're on holiday, no, a combined holiday and business trip, ah, looking into the combination of fine wines and Chinese cooking… we're hoping to sell more wines to Chinese restaurants.

'So I suppose we do need to dress fairly smartly –'

'Rolex for you, Cartier for me?' she interrupted him.

'Haha yes! Have you got one?'

'Yes, honey, a Tank, no diamonds on the face though, sorry. Have you?'

'Actually I have got a Rolex, I bought it a long time ago when I was young and impressionable. I never wear it, big flashy chunky thing. But I'll dig it out. By the way,' he said, 'do you know the difference between a goldfish and a mountain goat, sweetheart?'

'No, do tell.'

'One mucks about in fountains...'

Peals of laughter came down the phone. 'What happens when two clowns divorce?'

'Don't know,' he answered.

'Custardy battle!'

'Very good,' he chuckled, 'I must remember that one – nice and clean. I only seem to remember the rude ones.'

'You must tell me all of them, Harry, one day, I'm not easily shocked. Anyway, I've got a little black Chanel dress that I can still just about get into –'

'And out of, sweetheart, I hope,' he said making exaggerated lustful hohihohihor noises in his throat.

She laughed again. 'Let me see, Lancel bag, Dior bracelets... I'm getting my hair and nails done tomorrow... earrings! I haven't really got any very smart earrings.'

'Well, let me buy you some diamond ones, as a present for coming with me, our first trip together.'

No time for false modesty and protestations, Alison thought. 'OK, thank you, honey, if you're sure.'

'I'd love to.'

'Are we going to be married?'

'Sorry?'

'You know what I mean! Do we need to have wedding rings?'

'Ah-hah! Good question. We'll need to show our passports at the hotel, when we check in, but lots of married women keep their maiden names these days, so that won't matter – not like the old days, you practically needed a marriage certificate to share a room! But, yes, I guess it might arouse a bit less curiosity if we're Mr and Mrs. We can get a couple of gold bands when we get there, there aren't many better places to buy gold.'

Eventually, when they'd made all the necessary arrangements, they wished each other sweet dreams and rang off. Harry put on a CD of Mahler's Sixth Symphony, Simon Rattle conducting the Berlin Philharmonic, and putting all thoughts and cares aside, lost himself in the beautiful, moving music. Alison curled up in bed with her book, a life of Frans Schubert, perhaps her favourite composer. She soon found herself getting drowsy and, switching off her bedside lamp, was soon asleep.

Now, meeting in front of the British Airways check-in in on the ground floor of Terminal 3, they kissed briefly and had a quick hug, Harry resisting the temptation to put his arms round her waist and lift off her feet in his excitement at seeing her. Control yourself, Harry, he thought.
'Goodness, honey, you are getting hairy,' she laughed, 'never mind, I like a man with a beard!'
'Hmm,' he replied, feeling his chin with his hand, 'I'm not sure it looks very smart.'
'I'll trim it for you when we get there, it'll be fine. What I forgot to ask you is, do we need adaptor plugs for Hong Kong? For the phone chargers?'
'I can't really remember, I don't think so. But there's an electrical shop through when we get airside and we can

check there.'

'Is there? I don't think I've flown out of this terminal before.'

'Yes, there's more shops now than you can shake a stick at. You can get anything here now, including diamond earrings, I'm sure! But I remember when there was just one shop at the end of the departure lounge, selling booze, tobacco, perfume and high-end gifts. I read somewhere that it had the highest turnover per square foot of any shop in the world. It used to be full of Japanese buying Baccarat Decanters of Remy Martin at two hundred quid a throw – believe it or not they bought them in three-packs. All the Americans buying Havana cigars and hiding them in their hand luggage! The place must have been a goldmine.'

He does go on a bit! Alison thought, what do they call it these days? Mansplaining? But she smiled at him affectionately. She'd been thinking back over their time together, did he perhaps lack a bit of oomph, of drive? Yes, he'd asked her out in the first place, but had he really ever taken the initiative since? She wasn't the sort that went for the super confident, dominating, Alpha male, but even so... Perhaps I'll try being a bit more passive, she thought, let's see what he comes up with.

There was hardly any queue at the Club Class check-in for their flight and they were soon through passport control and security. The helpful lady in the shop assured them that their UK plugs would work in Hong Kong and, after Harry had checked out the fine wine selection in the duty-free shop, (overpriced and exposed constantly to bright light, he grumbled), they found their way to Tiffany's. She selected a beautiful pair of diamond stud earrings, not ostentatious, but not invisible either, and they went to the business class

157

lounge to wait for their flight to be called.

'You know, Harry,' she said, as they sipped their complimentary coffees, 'one reason I'm so looking forward to this trip is the chance to taste these fabulous wines. I don't think I've ever drunk any of the grands crus, even from the not-so-good years. I've always wanted to try a Chateau d'Yquem, I do love Sauternes, but I've never been able to bring myself to splash out. The prices!'

'Yes, crazy. But a glass of d'Yquem with foie gras! One of life's greatest... what's the word... pleasures? No that's not adequate –'

'Culinary experiences?' she grinned.

'That's it, sweetheart! We'll definitely have to try it while we're there, compliments of those *grands crus*!'

Chapter 16

'THIS IS BEAUTIFUL, HONEY,' Alison said as she surveyed their big, luxurious room in the Hilton. She went out on to the balcony in her big fluffy white dressing-gown and gazed out over the crowded harbour. 'So much room,' she went on as he came out and joined her, 'and I just love that circular bath!'

Their twelve-hour direct flight had arrived at eleven in the morning, local time, six hours ahead. They'd been lucky that their room was ready for them when they got to the hotel two hours later, expecting to have to leave their suitcases until the four o'clock check-in time. They'd both managed to get some sleep during the flight and now, after a soak in the bath, easily big enough for both of them, they were refreshed and ready to go out.

'I think we should just have a relaxed afternoon and evening, sweetheart,' Harry said, 'let's leave the posh meals and detective work until tomorrow, shall we? By then we should be really over the jet-lag.'

'Good idea, honey. A nice stroll, a little quiet bar somewhere and a light meal would be just right. Those flat beds on the plane were lovely, so much better than being all cramped up in Economy! But even so I think I'm going to be ready for bed quite early. '

'Me too.' Harry thought about making a joke about not getting much sleep when in bed together, but decided against it. It had seemed quite natural when they were naked in the bath together. They would make love when they were ready to, Ali seemed perfectly relaxed about it, why on earth make it a subject for humour?

159

He turned the subject over in his mind while he was getting dressed and Alison dried her hair and did her make-up in the large ornate mirror above the dressing table. He knew he'd always used facetiousness in his relationships, as a kind of protection, he supposed, against being hurt. Much easier to laugh off a rejection that way. But this was different, no, he didn't want to get hurt, but he did want Ali to get to know him as he really was, warts and all. He believed that she'd been open and honest with him. She'd certainly made most of the running and had been the one who risked being rejected.

Alison's intuition kicked in as she looked over and saw his serious face in the mirror. She could see, or perhaps feel, he was thinking about her, about their relationship. 'No regrets, honey?' she asked.

'Well, yes.' He walked round behind her and, placing a light kiss on the back of her neck, and looking directly into her face in the mirror, went on, 'I feel maybe I've been taking you for granted. You've been so open and trusting with me, so wonderful, and I'm not sure I've really been the same.'

'Oh, Harry.' She got up from the dressing table and put her arms round him. 'Is that all it is? I thought maybe you'd felt you'd made a dreadful mistake.' She kissed him gently. 'No need to worry, honey. I know you're the kind who needs to go slowly. I've been worrying that it's been me, going too fast. I couldn't believe I said it when I complained you hadn't taken me to Bordeaux with you!'

'Thank you, sweetheart, you're very kind, but I want to be honest with you,' he drew a deep breath, 'I've never really been in a proper relationship. Infatuations when I was younger, plenty of girlfriends along the way but now I'm 46, single, no children. Maybe I just haven't met the right person, but maybe I've been scared of exposing myself, of making a commitment.' He sighed.

'Come and sit on the bed,' she said, taking his hand, 'I really do appreciate that, honey. But, honestly, you needn't worry. We're doing just fine, aren't we? No need to rush things, I love being with you. But thank you for opening up like that.'

'You're right. And I love being with you, Ali, thank you. By the way, did I ever tell you about the time I was a penniless student?'

'No?'

'Well, I met this very posh girl at a student union disco. We got on very well until she invited me home to meet her parents. Well, I managed to get my clothes clean and pressed, got my long hair cut and cleaned out my fingernails in preparation for the meeting. The trouble was that I was absolutely skint, had no money to buy any food and all there was in the larder was two tins of baked beans, which was all I'd had to eat all day before going round to her house for dinner in the evening.'

'Ah-hah, I can see an explosive ending coming! Go on.'

'It was a big, posh house and her parents were dressed up for the occasion. The small talk went OK and then we went into the dining room to eat. We were just eating the soup when, unfortunately, the beans decided to make their presence felt and I let out a loud smelly fart!'

'No!' she giggled.

'Yes! But, much to my surprise, her father just said "Down Rover!" I looked behind me and there was the family dog lying on the carpet, evidently he thought it was the dog, not me. Well, as you can imagine, after that I felt safe letting rip.

It happened twice more, during the roast beef, and each time he just said "Down Rover!", finally during the pudding the most tremendous fart erupted but this time...'
'Yes?'
Harry was almost unable to continue, shaking with suppressed laughter at the punchline to come, his face going purple. 'But this time' he stopped again, eyes screwed up and gasping for air as the giggles wouldn't stop coming, 'he said "Down Rover - before the bastard shits on you!"'

An hour later they were wandering hand in hand through a shopping mall down by the harbour. They'd been into a shop selling gold jewellery in every conceivable shape size and design and had ordered two plain 18 carat gold rings. To their surprise the sizes they needed weren't in stock but, after a quick call, the shopkeeper said he could get them from his cousin and they arranged to call back before the shop closed to collect them.

They were walking past the window of a shop selling beautiful, very expensive, furniture and objets d'art when Alison grabbed Harry's arm and said 'Look!'

He stopped and, following her pointing hand, saw, to his amazement, the most fantastic table lamp. It had a crimson conical shade, the ornate triangular base and lamp fitting appeared to be made out of solid silver, but the body, the upright, was a pristine bottle of wine, clear, Bordeaux style, with a Chateau d'Yquem 2007 label!

'Heavens, Harry! What a coincidence! Yquem!'

He looked in closely, trying to read the small price tag –
'Twelve thousand, nine hundred and ninety-nine dollars. That's about –'

'At todays exchange rate, one thousand two hundred and ninety-four pounds and... seventy pee.'

It was Harry's turn to say 'Heavens!' He looked at her in bemusement, 'Not sixty-nine pee, sweetheart, are you sure?'

'Sorry, honey, bad habit of mine. My mind loves playing with numbers. Tell me your date of birth and I'll tell you what day it was - my party trick.'

'OK, sweetheart. Twenty-first September 1971.'

A moment's pause. 'Tuesday. Tuesday's child is full of grace, suits you, honey.'

He looked at her fondly. 'Correct, a Tuesday, hidden depths, Ali, hidden depths! I've always been rubbish at maths, took me years to master the seven-times table!'

'It's always come naturally to me. Give me a test – two three-figure numbers to multiply.'

'OK. Three hundred and sixteen times four hundred and eighty?'

After two seconds, she replied 'One hundred and fifty-one thousand, six hundred and eighty!'

'Wow!' he laughed, 'I believe you, I won't check! But it's quite a price for a table lamp. I imagine it's all solid silver. I've never seen anything like it. Can we go in and have a look?'

'As long as you promise not to buy it! It's gross!'

They went in and were enveloped immediately in an atmosphere of luxury. Polished wood floors, delicate scents, silent air-conditioning. Money, it smelt of money. A very smartly dressed sales assistant moved smoothly towards them. 'Good afternoon, sir, ma'am,' she said, 'welcome to Liem's Emporium. My name is Gladys. Is there anything I can assist you with, or would you prefer to browse?'

Her English, like her manner, was impeccable. However she

made no real secret of the fact that she was assessing them – did they have money? Harry saw her focus on his Rolex, he'd put it on in order to get used to its weight. Evidently, they passed the test, would they like coffee, or a cold drink? Would they like a catalogue, with the new collection? A consultant could visit if they needed help to decide how to furnish their home.

Harry thanked her but said in fact they were interested in the wine bottle table lamp in the window. They moved over towards it and Gladys asked if they were wine lovers.

'Very much so,' Harry replied, 'may I pick it up?'

'Of course, sir. It's quite heavy.'

'Solid silver?'

'Yes, also available in platinum, sir.'

Harry picked it up and saw that the top of the bottle contained what appeared to be a genuine cork. A thin silver tube ran through it, presumably taking the wiring down through the bottle, although no wires were visible. 'Remarkable, very well done. Can I ask the price of the platinum one?'

'Around five hundred thousand. On order we can also have Petrus, Lafite, Latour, top vintages.'

'Not in gold?' Alison asked.

'It's possible, ma'am. Two months for order, around a million.'

Harry put the lamp down. 'I think I prefer the silver. Do you sell many, may I ask?'

'Yes, very popular. Platinum sells best.'

'Really? Well, thank you, we'll have a think about it. Thank you so much for your help.'

'A pleasure, sir, ma'am.' If the sales assistant was

164

disappointed, she hid it very well.

They moved out of the shop and headed for a bar they'd spotted down by the waterfront. The Friday evening crowds were building up now and they had to walk in single file along the crowded pavement, so it wasn't until they were in the dimly lit bar that they were able to talk.

'Goodness,' Alison said, 'half a million dollars, around fifty thousand pounds, is the best seller!'

'And they sell other grand cru bottles as well!' Harry replied. The waiter came, so they quickly perused the cocktail menu and ordered two Gin Fizzes.

'The big question,' Harry continued after he'd taken their order and returned to the bar, 'is, where do they get the bottles from?'

'Yes, and, is it connected to the switching? The plot thickens, Watson!'

'Hmm, most intriguing. I'm absolutely sure the chateaux wouldn't be supplying bottles to whoever's making those lamps. They must be getting them locally.'

Their cocktails came and, putting other thoughts aside, they concentrated on planning their weekend, looking through the Lonely Planet guide and the leaflets they'd picked up in the hotel reception.

When they returned to the hotel, after a meal of dim sum in the Lin Heung Tea House in Wan Chai, washed down with Tsingtao beer, they were both ready for bed.

'It's only four in the afternoon at home' Alison said, 'but, honey, I'm whacked.'

'Me too, sweetheart. A good night's sleep will set us up for tomorrow's adventures.'

The silent air-conditioning kept the room pleasantly cool. Alison put on a thin silk nightdress and Harry a t-shirt and a pair of boxers. They pulled the thin duvet over them and cuddled up, spoon fashion. Within a couple of minutes Harry heard Ali's breath changing to slow deep breaths and he knew she was asleep. After a couple of minutes musing on what had happened that day, he gently disengaged himself from her sleeping body, turned over on his side and he too was soon fast asleep.

Chapter 17

NEXT MORNING, THEY WERE on the balcony eating a light breakfast, courtesy of room service, of coffee, croissants and toast. The sun was rising behind their hotel and they watched as it gradually illuminated more and more of the harbour. The sky was cloudless and it promised to be another perfect day.

They'd had to move quickly when room service knocked on their door, not five minutes after they'd ordered, putting on the big white dressing gowns and scrambling to pick up the night attire strewn on the floor when they'd woken in the early hours and enjoyed each other's bodies again.

They said little as they absorbed the changing view unfolding, sipping their coffee, a very companionable silence had lasted for five minutes when Alison suddenly said 'We forgot the wedding rings!'

'So we did,' Harry replied, 'I hope he kept them for us. I'll have a quick shower and nip round there.'

'OK, honey. I'm going to enjoy that bath again. When you come back I'll trim your beard. Give me a kiss before you go.'

Fortunately, there was no problem picking up the rings and Harry was back at the hotel within forty minutes. He stopped at reception on the way back in, gave his name and room number, and asked the receptionist to order a taxi to take them to the restaurant they had decided on for their evening meal. It was one that Frank and Geraldine had recommended, its website had revealed a very extensive, and expensive, wine list.

'Certainly, Mr Benson,' the impeccably dressed young man in

reception replied, 'what time would you like it to arrive, and where will it be taking you?'

'At seven-thirty, please. The Chang Dining Room. Is it possible to get one of those big BMW saloons?' He'd noticed the BMW 7-series taxis driving around the previous afternoon and had decided that it would be as well to arrive in a style fitting the kind of bill he was going to run up.

'Yes, of course. Would you like me to make a reservation for you?'

'Oh, no, thank you, it's already made.' In fact it hadn't been, but he didn't want a reservation in his name. 'Thanks once again for your help,' he said as he turned away from the desk.

'My pleasure, sir, have a good day!'

Harry took the lift up to the fourteenth floor and let himself in to the room. Alison was sitting on the bed drying her hair. She looked up enquiringly. 'No problem,' he said and, walking up to the bed, he took the ring box from his pocket, holding it out, he dropped onto one knee, saying in a pompous voice, 'Madam, would you do me the honour...?'

She laughed and replied 'Heavens, sir, I trust you have my father's approval for this surprising request?' They both laughed and Harry sat down on the bed beside her. They put the rings on and looked at each other contentedly. Alison burst into song:

'Third finger, left hand
Is where he placed that wedding band'

'Martha Reeves and the Vandellas,' Harry said, 'great song!'

''One of my favourites – the b-side of Jimmy Mack, also a great song.'

'Weren't they wonderful, those early Tamla Motown days? The Four Tops, Supremes, Stevie Wonder...'

'Marvin Gaye, the Temptations, Martha, Junior Walker,' she added, 'amazing.'

'You've got a nice voice, sweetheart,' Harry said, 'unlike me. My voice broke when I was about eight and, although I do enjoy singing, I'm reliably informed that I sing flat. Growling, rather than singing, I believe.'

'It's good that you like singing, honey. It's really good for you. Sing me something and I'll let you know.'

'OK, but I did warn you!'

Harry sang 'Old Man River' in the style of Paul Robeson, dropping his voice down really deep on "free" in the line "what does he care if the land ain't free" and "jail" in "you shows a bit of grit and you lands in jail".

'Good style,' Alison smiled, 'but, yes, definitely flat!'

'I was once shushed by the lady next to me, singing a hymn at a wedding! Ever since in public I've just mimed and kept quiet. I love music but, really, I can't tell a crotchet from a quaver.'

'Never mind, you can sing to me as much as you like. I used to be in the church choir, but I haven't sung properly for years.'

'Can you sing me something?'

'Now?' He nodded.

'OK, let me think… I know. 'Amazing Grace'.'

Alison launched into the song, hitting the high notes beautifully.

At the end, Harry applauded. 'That was beautiful, Ali. Reminded me of Joan Baez.'

She laughed, 'That's high praise indeed! Now I'd better finish getting ready. Ready for you to show me the delights of Hong Kong.'

He grinned. 'OK! I'll just call the restaurant and make the booking for dinner. Mr and Mrs Winchester, in honour of our first day out together.'

That evening, the taxi arrived at the Hilton on time and, after a brief luxurious journey in the big car, they were soon being ushered to their table in the red- and gold-themed restaurant.

'Good evening, Mr Winchester, good evening, madam. I am James, the maitre d', your server will be Emily. Have you eaten here before, sir?'

'No,' Harry replied, 'our first time, but we've heard good things about it.'

'Indeed? I'm happy to hear that.' The maitre d' looked at them approvingly. As well he might, Harry thought, Alison looked like a million dollars in her Chanel dress and discreet, expensive jewellery. He'd brushed up pretty well too in his dark Savile Row suit, his white-collared, blue and white striped shirt and his Hermes tie, beard trimmed. All in all they looked like a prosperous couple.

'Our cuisine here is a fusion between the finest Asian food and European techniques. I hope you will enjoy it. Would you like an aperitif while Emily is bringing you the menu and the wine list?'

'Please, James. A glass or two of champagne would be lovely. Cristal, if you have it?'

'Certainly, sir. We have the 2012 vintage in half and full bottles, a lovely wine. Or the non-vintage of course.'

'I think a bottle of the 2012 would make a lovely start, don't you, darling?'

'It sounds wonderful,' Alison replied, 'I must say James, I love your décor here. It's sumptuous.'

'Thank you so much, madam. Now, if you'll excuse me, I'll go and arrange the champagne. Emily will be with you shortly.'

The champagne soon arrived and they sipped it as they saw the restaurant gradually filling up as people arrived for their eight o'clock reservations. Mostly Asians, Harry noted, although there was a large table of elderly Americans close to theirs.

They soon decided on the multiple dish tasting menu, starting with shark's fin soup and ending with tanghulu and Harry started to leaf through the wine list. The selection shown on the website had by no means done it justice, Harry decided as, with mounting amazement, he read through page after page of rare and ancient bottles of wine.

'Goodness,' he said, 'they've got some clarets pre-phylloxera! I've only ever tasted one.'

'Wow!' Ali replied, 'that was the 1870s, wasn't it?'

'Yes, that's right. Here's a Lafite 1858! Three hundred and eighty thousand dollars!'

He read on for a while. 'They've got dozens of vintages of all the grands crus! They must have a huge cellar to store them all in. The only wine list like it I've ever seen was the old Forge, in Miami Beach. Its wine list ran to nearly 300 pages. People used to buy them as souvenirs. I think I've still got one somewhere.'

He concentrated on the grands crus red Bordeaux wines, probably the most likely to be switched, looking at the price difference between adjacent vintages. 'Let's see, sweetheart, Lafite eighty-two is fifty-two thousand dollars, the eighty-three is twelve thousand five hundred. I've tasted both so...'

'Heavens,' Ali whispered, 'that's over five thousand pounds!'

'Let's hope Alain and Christian can afford it.'

Emily came to take their order and, when Harry said he was thinking of the 1982 Lafite, she said immediately, 'I'll send the sommelier over, sir.'

'OK, thank you,' Harry replied. While they waited, he said 'I wonder if they really have it, or if they just put it on the list. They must have a really big cellar... and it's not that big a building.'

'Perhaps it goes down a long way underground.'

'Maybe. Here he comes.'

The sommelier hurried over, his silver tastevin on a chain round his neck. 'Good evening, sir, good evening, ma'am.'

'Good evening,' they both replied.

'Emily tells me that you would like a bottle of the Chateau Lafite Rothschild 1982. A wonderful wine, now at peak maturity.'

'Yes,' Harry said, 'it's a wine we'd like to try. Not cheap, but we're on holiday! It's been kept in good condition of course?'

'Oh, yes, definitely, sir. We have a special location, perfect conditions, for our high-value wines. There's not room to store them all here so, if you decide you want it, it will take half an hour or so to bring it here.'

'I see,' Harry said a little doubtfully, 'it won't be shaken around and disturbed on the way?'

'Goodness me, no, sir! We move it, still lying flat, in a container double-insulated against vibration. It will be in perfect condition, I do assure you.'

'OK, we'll have it. We'll continue drinking the champagne until it arrives.'

* * *

They'd eaten the first two courses, both delicious, and were talking about their afternoon at the spectacular Ocean Park, and its amazing aquariums, when the sommelier returned with their wine. He showed them the bottle before opening it and Harry tried to decide if the capsule was the right colour, he thought it perhaps was.

The sommelier carefully cut round the capsule, firstly cutting out a perfect circle where the cork touched the side of the neck, removing the cut-out disc with the tip of his knife, then cut round the edge of the outer rim, stopping before completing the circle, leaving a couple of centimetres uncut. He bent back the foil ring thus created and very carefully drew out the cork. He placed the cork inside the ring, with its dark red bottom uppermost, and then pinched and slightly twisted the ring so that the cork was held firmly in place against the neck of the bottle, neatly displaying 'Pauillac-Medoc 1982' on one side and 'Lafite Rothschild' on the other. Harry had seen this done before but even so was impressed with the man's smooth dexterity. 'You've done this before,' he joked.

'Oh, yes, sir,' he replied smiling, 'many times. Our customers really like the great Bordeaux wines. Will you permit me to taste a little?'

Harry nodded his assent and the sommelier took from his pocket a small plastic box containing shining silvery three-inch discs. He took one out, rolled it into a tube and put it inside the neck of the bottle, ensuring absolutely drip-free pouring. He took his tastevin from his neck and poured a very little wine into it. After sniffing it, he tipped the wine into his mouth and rolled it around for a second or two.

He looked at Harry and smiled, 'In perfect condition, sir, I think you will find. Would you like to try it?'

'Yes please, both of us.'

The sommelier poured a little into each of their glasses and waited while they both swirled the wine around their glasses, sniffed and tasted. Harry glanced at Alison and they both nodded, the wine was superb.

He filled their glasses and left them to their meal. 'It's definitely kosher,' Harry said, 'Lafite eighty-two or I'm a dutchman.'

'It's wonderful,' Ali said, 'the depth of flavour, the balance, I've never drunk anything like it.'

The superb meal drew to its close as they savoured the wonderful wine.

'I think I must have died and gone to heaven,' Ali said, 'I can even, just about, see why people pay a fortune for it.'

'It really is wonderful wine. I wouldn't be surprised if it's still as good, or even better, in twenty years' time. Still, it doesn't really get us any further, does it?'

'What a shame! We'll just have to try again tomorrow!'

Chapter 18

THE NEXT EVENING, HOWEVER, they struck gold. After a day spent on a relaxing and spectacular boat trip around the islands, at another excellent restaurant they ordered Chateau Petrus 2000. It was even more expensive than the Lafite of the previous evening, and what was poured was, Harry was convinced, the 2007. A difference in price of around forty thousand dollars! There had been a bit of a delay before the wine came to the table. Nothing was said this time to explain the delay, but they noticed while sipping their aperitifs that diners at other tables who'd been seated after them received their food before they did.

Harry gave no outward sign about the taste of the wine and cheerfully paid the enormous bill at the end of the evening. The maitre d' fussed over them as they were leaving, asking where they were staying, how long for, and how they'd enjoyed their wine. Were they great lovers of Petrus? Of other wines from Pomerol? How did they think it compared with the grands crus of the Medoc? They avoided displaying any real knowledge in answer to these questions, and gave their prepared answer about being in the wine trade, before they were smilingly escorted out to their waiting limousine taxi.

Alison knew, from the sideways glance Harry had given her as they tasted the wine, that it wasn't the real thing but they didn't discuss it until they were safely back in their hotel room.

'Forty thousand!' she exclaimed when Harry told her, 'someone's making some serious money here, honey.'

'True,' he said thoughtfully, 'and although two restaurants is a very small sample, if anything like half the restaurants in Hong Kong, never mind in Shanghai and Guangzhou, are at it, it's very serious money indeed. But how do they do it? Another thing,' he went on, 'a lot of the wines on the wine list were the same as last night's, the prices were a bit different, mind you, but it does seem very coincidental. Even if they've both been in business for years and bought the wines a long time ago, at much lower prices, the investment involved in holding those stocks must still be pretty enormous, especially for restaurants that aren't that big.'

'Hmm,' she said, 'time to talk to Sam Spade! The good thing is that now we've got something concrete for him to work on, not just suppositions.'

'That's right,' he replied, 'I'll give him a call first thing in the morning.'

'I should tell him too about the lamps, honey.' Before boarding their cruise, they'd looked in some more high-end furniture stores and found the same lamp, one with a Chateau Margaux label and the other Chateau Haut-Brion, in two of them. 'That must be a sizable business too, and something tells me that they could be related.'

He called the private investigator's number at nine the next morning.

'Hello, you must be Harry,' the voice at the other end of the line said immediately.

'Y – yes,' Harry spluttered, 'how did you know?'

'Uncle Jack gave me your phone number and said you might be in touch around now, no mystery! My name's Francis, by the way, Francis Teo.'

'Great to speak to you, Francis. Did Jack say anything about why I might need your help?'

'Yes, but let's not discuss anything on the phone, Harry. You never know who might be listening! Let's meet and you can tell me all about it.'

Francis thought it would be better to meet in their hotel than at his office and they arranged a meeting for three o'clock that afternoon.

When he arrived they instantly took a liking to each other. Francis was a nondescript kind of man, small and wiry with a straggly moustache stained yellow in places, from smoking presumably, and a smile permanently hovering about his lips. He was charm itself to Alison and they all chatted amiably for a while about what they'd been doing in Hong Kong and the things he said they shouldn't miss, before getting down to business.

Francis outlined his fees, which Harry thought reasonable enough, especially in view of what he was spending on dining.

'So, tell me all about it, Harry, and please don't leave anything out. You never know what information might prove useful in an investigation,' Francis said.

Harry went right through the story from the Oliver murder, the involvement of Scotland Yard and the French, to their two meals in Hong Kong, with such similar wine lists, and their discovery of the lamps. At the end Francis whistled and said 'I knew people spend serious money on wine, but I had no idea it was that much! I'm a beer drinker.' He thought for a while. 'It shouldn't be too hard to find out from the waiters what's happening, but I'll need to be careful. It'll probably take me a couple of days.'

He accepted another cup of coffee and then asked 'Are you planning to visit any more restaurants?'

'Well, yes,' Alison replied, 'we've booked another one tonight. Don't you think we should?'

'I don't really see any harm and, if it does turn out the same as last night, it could be a useful lead. But be careful, it's not every English couple that are spending big bucks on wine, night after night. You're not using your real name, are you?'

'No,' Harry replied and explained about the company credit card.

'Very good,' Francis said. 'Are you using the same name every night for your bookings?'

'I'm afraid so.'

'No, no!' Francis exclaimed, 'that's good. If you'd changed it, I'd say don't go, these people talk to each other and, well, you never know, someone might smell a rat. But perhaps I wouldn't go again after tonight, at least not until we talk again.'

He left soon after, promising to keep in touch.

'That reminds me,' Harry said, 'I promised to keep Andy Pelham in the loop, and the French. I'll go and send a couple of emails to them on the laptop, then do you feel like a bit of a walk, Ali?'

They pottered around for an hour or so and then found themselves back in their quiet, cool bar. After two heavy evening meals, with lots of fine wine, they were both feeling a bit fragile so they stuck to coffee. What Francis had said about being careful had put them a bit on edge, so they chose a table well away from all the other customers, and talked quietly.

'Francis seems like a very nice man,' Alison said, 'and very competent and confident.'

'Yes,' agreed Harry, 'I think we're in good hands there. A good job I didn't think to change names for the reservations.'

'Mmm... it's Argentinian food tonight, isn't it? I could eat a straightforward steak tonight. I've really enjoyed the food but I don't think my stomach is really accustomed to such a variety of tastes and textures.'

'I know just what you mean! I could just eat a plate of baked beans on toast. But duty calls, someone's got to sample one of the finest bottles of wine ever made! It sounds like it might be the last one on this trip, so let's make it a night to remember!'

Less than six hours later, as they sunk into their seats on the plane bound for Jakarta, Ali said wearily, 'Well, that certainly was a night to remember, honey.'

The restaurant that night was close to their hotel so they had decided to walk. The Argentinian beef had been outstanding, so tender it could be cut with a fork. This time Harry, mindful of what Francis had said, decided to go for a less expensive wine, Chateau Cheval Blanc, from St Emilion, across the other side of the estuary from the Medoc. He'd seen from the wine lists from the other restaurants, as well as this one, that there were several more recent vintages of Cheval Blanc available, which made it a reasonable candidate for being switched.

He ordered the 2009, at around a thousand pounds, and was confident that the 2006, worth around half as much, was being poured. Again he showed no sign of awareness and their meal drew to a pleasant conclusion. While he was paying the bill, Alison went to the Ladies, which involved a walk round behind the bar area.

As they left the restaurant, she said quietly to Harry, 'I don't want to worry you, honey, but I saw the maitre d' from last night's restaurant in the office behind the bar, talking on the phone.'

'Maybe just a coincidence,' Harry said as they emerged into the cool night air. Alison slid her arm through his and they began to walk quickly back towards their hotel. The Monday night street was quiet, strangely quiet, Alison thought, with a shiver of apprehension, of what she couldn't say, but all her senses were on high alert. She heard the sound of a motorbike coming up the street behind them and, somehow sensing danger, looked over her shoulder towards it. To her horror, it accelerated and changed course to mount the pavement, driving directly at them. In panic she grabbed Harry's arm and sent them both tumbling into the side of the walkway. Fortunately they were level with the entrance to a souvenir shop and their fall took them nearly clear of the pavement. As she fell, she looked up and caught a glimpse of the rider, entirely covered in black, with a black helmet and a black scarf covering all his face except his eyes. He seemed to swerve at the last moment and roared off down the street.

'Jesus!' Harry said as he scrambled up and helped her to her feet, 'what the hell was that?'

'He drove deliberately at us. Heaven knows how he didn't hit you. Let's get back quickly.'

'OK. I'll call Francis now and tell him what happened.'

Francis listened for twenty seconds and said 'Go straight to your hotel. Pack enough clothes for a couple of days. I'll call you in ten.'

They'd just flung their things into Alison's onboard case when the phone rang. Francis. 'Get a taxi and go straight to the airport. You're booked on the Emirates midnight flight to Jakarta. Uncle Jack will meet you there. Hurry! Don't worry about your things at the hotel, I'll sort it out. Have you got your passports?' He rang off.

Harry dived into his sock drawer and pulled out his passport. He called reception to get a taxi, saying he wasn't sure where to, but wanted to find some nightlife. 'Don't want them to think we're doing a runner! I'll stroll down casually, when the taxi comes, I'll text you and you can come straight from the lift down the steps.'

'OK, honey, wilco!'

What a woman, he thought as he waited for the taxi, not a word of complaint or reproach. How did I get her into this?

The taxi purred up beside him. 'Mr Benson? Where to, sir?'

'Yes, that's right,' he opened the rear door, 'the airport, please but could you just wait two minutes? My wife is just coming.' He sat in the car, leaving the door open and texted 'OK' to Ali. 'Won't be a moment,' he said, 'please do set the meter running.'

'It already is,' the driver chuckled. Within ninety seconds Alison was walking down the steps, looking cool and unhurried. 'Sorry to keep you waiting, darling. Call of nature.' She put the flight bag on the middle of the bench seat and closed the door.

The driver chuckled again as he pulled out into the traffic, but to Harry's relief didn't try to start up a conversation or ask them where they were going in the middle of the night. Harry supposed that working in Hong Kong, a real 24-hour city, he'd seen it all before.

181

''Which terminal?' the driver asked as they approached the airport.

'Er, Emirates to Jakarta?'

'Terminal One.'

They'd checked in with ten minutes to spare and now, able to relax at last, they held each other's hand and kissed before she said 'Well, that certainly was a night to remember, honey,' and they relapsed into an exhausted silence.

Chapter 19

'IT WAS DEFINITELY JUST a warning,' Jack Chau said as they met for a very late breakfast in his sprawling comfortable house in the swish Jakarta district of Menteng. They'd arrived around six and had been grateful when Jack had said 'Let's not talk now, get cleaned up, get some sleep and we'll talk later, after I've spoken to Francis. You know the way to the guest quarters, Harry my old friend?'

'Yes, thanks so much, Jack.' After a couple of hours sleep and a shower, he felt infinitely better. Ali had perked up too, looking in wonder at the marvellous array of fruit on the breakfast table. Hairy rambutans, star fruit, guavas, huge mangoes, jackfruit, dragon fruit, purple mangosteens and small bananas. Jack caught her gaze and said 'They call them here *pisang raja* - the king of bananas, in English. Do try one, Ali.'

She did and was surprised at the soft firm flesh and sweet, delicate flavour, unlike any banana she'd ever eaten before. 'Absolutely delicious,' she said and they both smiled at her.

'Wonderful, aren't they?' Harry said, 'but where are the durians, Jack? I know you love them.'

'Ah, you're teasing me again, Harry, you Brits, always joking. Are you sure you want to get involved with this facetious hairy man, Ali?' he chuckled. 'I'll have one put in your room if you wish, Harry. You know of durians, Ali?'

'I've heard the name, I think.'

'Well, they taste of heaven, but smell of hell – rotting flesh is perhaps the best description. Not to everyone's taste, certainly not mine. Harry used to want to have them in the restaurant, but I refused!'

'They're divine,' Harry protested.

'With a peg over your nose, yes!'

'Guys, guys!' Alison said, and they both laughed. 'What a wonderful garden, Jack.' She gazed out at the exotic bushes and flowering trees among the towering date palms. 'Are those peacocks?' Just as she asked, one of the birds spread out his amazing multi-coloured tail, as if in answer. 'It all feels like a bit of a dream – the motorbike, the rush to the airport, the flight – now this, this... paradise.'

'I know just what you mean,' Harry said, it's all been a bit unreal, that bike could have seriously hurt us.'

'It was definitely just a warning,' Jack said, 'I spoke to Francis first thing and he agrees. If they'd wanted to kill you, they could have, no problem. And you said you think he swerved away, Ali?'

'Yes, I think so. As we fell it seemed inevitable that the motorbike would hit Harry.'

'Francis thinks they must have recognised you, Harry. He Googled you and found an old Facebook page with your photo. They must have guessed who you are and did the same, your facial hair wasn't enough!'

'Goodness. I'd forgotten that! I set that up ages ago, haven't looked at it for years.' He paused for a moment. 'Well, that's a comfort, I suppose, that they weren't trying to kill us, I mean. But it's clear that we're well out of Hong Kong. Thanks to you and Francis.'

'You'd better stay here for a couple of days,' Jack said, 'while Francis gets to work unravelling your mystery. Your hotel is booked until the weekend, is it?'

'Yes, until Saturday morning. Francis said he'd be able to sort out our things, but I'd like to get back if possible. There'll be the hotel bill to settle, and Francis's fees, as well as our luggage. Who do I owe for the flights here?'

Jack waved away the question. 'I don't see why that shouldn't be possible. They'll know for sure you've left and will assume they've scared you away. Even so, if you do go back, you'll need to be careful.' Jack thought for a minute. 'Anyway,' he continued, 'let's leave that for later when we have a better idea of what needs to be done. Francis definitely thinks there's a link with the lamps, so he's got multiple avenues to explore. I'd be surprised if he didn't have something for you before the end of the day. But what would you like to do in the meantime? I have to go to work soon, but I'll be back here around five for a couple of hours.'

Harry and Alison looked at each other and grinned. 'Absolutely nothing! Just laze about and enjoy your garden,' Ali said, as Harry nodded.

'Fine. Just ask the houseboy if you need anything to eat or drink. You haven't forgotten your Bahasa Indonesia, Harry?'

'*Belum*, Jack, *belum*! Not yet,' he translated for Alison.

'OK, see you later then.'

They spent a lazy late morning and afternoon dozing and reading books in hammocks spread between shady trees in the garden as the brilliantly coloured birds and dragonflies flitted around them. Wayan the houseboy brought them excellent Bintang beers when they became thirsty, but neither of them was hungry. They didn't talk about the investigation, both happy to forget about it for a while and relax. After all, Harry reflected, there's really not much we can do.

* * *

185

Jack returned as promised a little before five and, after checking they were OK, and not thirsty, went to call Francis in Hong Kong. 'It'll be quicker and easier in Cantonese, if that's OK?' he said.

'Sure,' Harry replied. He would have quite liked to speak to Francis, but had absolute confidence in his friend.

Jack returned a few minutes later, carrying a glass and bottle of Bintang, dripping with condensation in the humid late afternoon air. 'Francis sends his best,' he began, 'and he's definitely made some good progress. The company that makes the lamps, HK Fine Lighting, pays a few dollars, fifty or so, to waiters who supply them with the empty bottles, if the labels are clean and the cork is intact. It's widespread, so Francis had no trouble in getting confirmation from waiters in different restaurants. Some restaurants forbid it, some don't know about it, but most turn a blind eye, he thinks, seeing it as a harmless way for waiters to supplement their wages, and keep them happy.'

'Makes sense,' Harry said.

'Absolutely,' Jack continued, 'this kind of thing goes on all the time. Where was I? Oh yes, HK Fine Lighting is a reputable business, it does plenty of business in China as well as Hong Kong and Macau and, evidently, those wine bottle lamps do sell well.' He broke off, poured out his beer and took a long pull at it.

'That's better, such a hot day and the Jakarta traffic is awful. So, Francis has also been looking into the matter you raised, Harry, about the similarities in the wine lists. It seems that the biggest restaurants and hotels buy their wines direct from the official agents, mostly Kowloon Fine Wines for French wines. They have the turnover and the finances to be

186

able to buy by the case of six, or twelve as it may be, which is the only way Kowloon supplies. All above board.' He took another swig of his beer. 'The smaller restaurants also buy some wine from these official agents but, when it comes to the really expensive wines, the cost of buying a case is prohibitive, so they buy from a wholesaler, who can supply single bottles.'

'Ah-hah!' said Harry excitedly, 'light begins to dawn! The wholesaler buys from the agents in cases, of course.'

'Yes,' Jack went on, 'and in the case of the really fine wines, they don't even hold them in stock at all. If the customer orders a bottle, like you did at Chang's, the wholesaler quickly delivers it to them, obviously that's why your Lafite took half an hour to come. These smaller restaurants like to compete with the best in terms of an extensive wine list, so essentially they just list the fine wines the wholesaler has.'

'That's why the lists are so similar,' Ali cried.

'Just so.'

'What's the wholesaler's name?' Harry asked.

'I don't know, Francis didn't say. But he's looking into it. The obvious implication is that some bottles are finding their way from the lamp company to the wholesaler, and that's where the switch is being made.'

'Yes, yes, I see,' Harry burst out, 'they buy the lesser wine from the agent, get the empty bottles from the lamp company, pour the cheap wine into the expensive bottles, and hey presto!'

'What do they do with the empty bottles of the cheap wine, though?' Ali asked.

'Send them back to the lamp company, I guess,' Jack replied. 'A very neat little business. But, I wonder, how do they get it

187

past their auditors? If there are, say, six bottles of your 2005 and sixty bottles of your 2006, Harry, invoiced in to them, how can they invoice out sixty bottles of 2005? They must have to keep stock records.'

'Maybe the auditors are in on the game,' Harry said, 'but it's wonderful what a bit of human ingenuity, muddled stock records and lost or misleading invoices can do.'

'That's true. And if the maitre d's or sommeliers in the restaurants are involved, money could come back from the restaurant in cash, no invoice, and the bottle of the cheaper wine written off as broken, or damaged,' Alison put in.

'Quite so, Ali,' Jack said admiringly, 'no, how do you say it? No flies on you!'

'Scotland Yard training, Jack.'

'It all makes good sense,' Harry said, 'but, how come the case of wine, the one that began all this, evidently came from the Mandarin? They surely don't buy by the case from this wholesaler?'

'Excellent point, Harry. That doesn't make sense at all. I'll call Francis later and raise it with him. Now, it's thirsty work, this sleuthing, isn't it? Are you sure you wouldn't like another Bintang?'

'Why not?' Ali smiled, 'I think we're really getting somewhere, that's cause for celebration!'

'Quite right, sweetheart. Yes please, Jack, that would be very welcome.'

'OK, good. Wayan,' he called, '*dua Bintang lagi, terimah kasih*. Yes, I do think we're getting somewhere. Now, for this evening, Jonah, my chauffeur, can take you to a nice quiet little restaurant, after dropping me, or, if you'd like a quiet evening here, Susi, my housekeeper, makes the best *nasi goreng* in Jakarta, she'd be very happy to make it for you, I'm sure.'

They opted to stay in and have an early night. Ali had had *nasi goreng*, fried rice, before, in a Vietnamese restaurant, she thought, but nothing like this. It came as a pyramid of warm rice, dry to the touch but still somehow moist in the mouth, containing delicious pieces of prawn, chicken, ham, mild green chillies, peppers and cool cucumber, alongside really crispy fried onions. The finishing touch to the pyramid was moist fried slivers of beaten seasoned egg, cascading down its sides.

'Golly,' Alison said as she wiped her plate clean with a piece of bread, 'that is, definitely, the best rice dish I have ever eaten!' How do you say "thank you very much" in Indonesian, honey?'

'*Terima kasih banyak*,' he replied, 'yes, that was wonderful. Susi is an artist, Jack's lucky to have her.'

When Susi came in to clear away their plates, Ali put her hand on hers as she moved to pick up her plate, and said '*Terima kasih banyak*, Susi, that was wonderful.'

Susi's face burst into a huge bashful smile and she launched into a stream of rapid Indonesian that Harry could only catch half of.

'She says, I think, that she's very happy that such a beautiful lady enjoyed her cooking!'

Susi bowed, Alison blushed, then bowed back as well as she could from her seated position. Harry added his thanks and praise and Susi gathered up the dishes and went back towards the kitchen, still beaming.

'Sweetheart,' Harry said quietly, 'Susi's right. You are

beautiful. I'm not sure why I haven't told you so before.'

'Most remiss of you, Harry Benson. Never mind, take me up to our room and you can make it up to me!'

Chapter 20

HARRY WOKE EARLY THE next morning and slipped out of bed, leaving Alison still sleeping. He went down to the kitchen to make himself a cup of coffee and found Jack, already dressed, sitting at the big table, tapping away at a laptop.

Jack looked up as he entered and sat back from the computer. 'Coffee?' he asked, 'there's a fresh pot over there on the side. Can you refill this one for me?' When they were both seated with their coffees he said 'Alison is a lovely woman, Harry.' He waited for a reply but, when none came, went on, 'I must say I had you down as a confirmed bachelor, like me now. Those days – what fun we had, playing the field; love them and leave them!'

'Hang on, Jack, that's not really how I saw it! Most of them left me, not the other way around.'

'Huh! That's your story! But tell me, old friend, how come such a lovely girl, from Scotland Yard too, comes to be in Hong Kong with an old reprobate like you?'

Harry would really have preferred not to talk about it but Jack was a really old and close friend so he briefly related how they'd met and what they'd done together.

'So, you've only known each other for about a month! Quick work!' But Jack could sense his friend didn't really want to talk about Alison too much so he changed the subject and updated him on his call the previous night to Francis. There wasn't really anything new, Francis was thinking along the same lines as them, and would look into the Mandarin case question. 'He expects to be able to give you a pretty full report by the end of today.'

'Really? Now that's what I call quick work!'

'Very quick, now what are you going to do today? We can't let Alison leave without seeing the sights of Jakarta. I've arranged not to go in until this evening, so I can be your guide.' Jack couldn't resist a last dig at his friend 'As long as you promise to invite me to the wedding!'

Jack had a friend who ran a company offering private city tours and at eleven, promptly, a big Mercedes limousine collected them and set off on a tour around the bustling city. Jack sat in the front and supplemented the driver's commentary with remarks about some of the restaurants they passed, their owners, chefs and menus, that interested Harry, but meant little to Alison. She stopped listening to their chat and gazed intently at the teeming colourful crowds and the contrast between huge impressive buildings and shabby little side streets, smartly dressed people and hawkers and beggars, Ferraris and Lamborghinis and dusty little motorbikes and scooters overloaded with two, or even three, people mostly clutching bags and packages.

They saw the huge MONAS national Indonesian monument, with its enormous red and white flag alongside, piercing the sky, and the stunning curves of the great Istiqlal mosque, before having a late lunch by the waterside in Jakarta Old Town, alongside some lovely old colonial buildings erected by the Dutch, when the city was known as Batavia, Jack said. They finished off with a visit to the Grand Indonesia Mall where they were able to supplement the few belongings they'd brought with them with some new toiletries and clothes.

They arrived back in Menteng around four thirty, tired, not

so much from physical activity, as from the kaleidoscope of sights and sounds they'd experienced.

'Whew!' Harry said when they were back inside, sipping gratefully at cold beers, 'that was a great tour, thanks, Jack. Really nice to see the old town again. Goodness how it's grown.'

'Absolutely unforgettable, thank you so much, Jack,' Alison chimed in, 'a real eye-opener.'

'My pleasure. It's not Hong Kong. It's of course a bit chaotic, but, I must say, I've grown to love it. Now, if you want to go and freshen up, or whatever, I'll just attend to a couple of things and then I'll get Francis on the phone. Shall we say back here in twenty minutes? I'll put him on speaker-phone and we can all hear what he has to report.'

When they came back down, Jack was already talking to Francis, in Cantonese. 'Here they are,' Jack switched to English, 'I'll put you on speaker, Francis, so we can all talk.' He placed his phone into a cradle on the table and they all clearly heard Francis say, 'Right, good evening, Harry, good evening, Alison.'

'Hiya, Francis,' Alison said, 'thanks so much for your help on Monday night.'

'Yes, thanks so much, Francis,' Harry echoed.

'No problem. Maybe you would have been OK remaining here, but better to be on the safe side, I think.'

'Definitely,' Jack said.

'Now I have plenty of news for you. It took me quite some digging, I must say. People have heard about you and are clamming up, but I believe I've got to the bottom of it. The warehouse manager at HK Fine Lighting, the people who make the lamps, turns out to be a relative of the owner of Kwun Tong Import and Export, the wine wholesaler. I won't say the owner's name over the phone. I'm using an unregistered burner phone for this call, but, even so, you don't need to know it. The owner's name doesn't appear on any official documents connected to the company, the ultimate ownership is well hidden, in Macao, I think, but it's definitely controlled by him and his family.

'So that's where the connection lies. The warehouse manager supplies the expensive bottles and replaces them with the cheaper ones; as far as I can see, HK Fine Lighting is unaware of this. Are you with me so far?'

'I think so, Francis,' Harry replied. 'If I've got it straight, the lighting company collects the empty bottles from the restaurants. They use them to make the lamps. But some, the ones which have contained high-value wines, are diverted, by the warehouse manager, to his relative, who owns the wine wholesaler. They pour the wine from less expensive bottles into the empty high-value ones supplied by the warehouse manager. So they can sell them at the high price. Then they send the empty, less expensive bottles back to the lighting company, and no one's the wiser.'

'Exactly. Kwun Tong has plenty of staff, but all the management roles are filled by the family, logistics, finance, everything. So it's probably safe to assume all the family members are involved. It would cost me, or rather you, Harry, plenty but I believe I could get proof of what's been going on from someone who works there, a disgruntled employee.'

'No problem, whatever it costs.'

'OK. Now, the question of the case from the Mandarin Grill.

It's very simple. We know that Kwun Tong Import and Export delivers fine wine to the smaller restaurants. It really does have excellent storage and transport facilities for high value wines and has a very good name for it in the trade. They offer a transport service for wine that is widely used by other restaurants and hotels who need to move wine around, I guess they all have overstocks and understocks from time to time. And, tah-dah! The Mandarin is one of their customers!'

'So simple,' Jack broke in, 'they must have collected two genuine cases of the 2005 from the Mandarin for delivery to Sotheby's, switched one of them on the way for one of their phoney ones containing the 2006, and that was the one that found its way to England!'

'Absolutely,' Harry said, 'Francis I'm so grateful.'

'Good, Harry, I'm glad. But, when I said I **could** get proof, I spoke advisedly. If we have proof, and just turn it all over to the police, without doubt Kwun Tong will get closed down, this is quite a major fraud, you know. If Kwun Tong is closed down it will reverberate through the whole restaurant and hotel trade here, and will be impossible to keep quiet. Even if the family plead guilty, which is not very likely, and there's no trial, everyone will know what's happened and it'll be all over the press. Not what your French patrons want, I think.'

'No, indeed, you're right. This is a very, very important market for them,' Harry thought quickly and then said, 'I did discuss this question with the police at home. Basically it comes down to either a police report or a signed, witnessed confession. I guess that's not very likely.'

'No, no chance whatsoever.' Francis replied. 'So it has to be a police report. But without the police taking action, or, let me see, at least any action that exposes the wine switching.'

'And doesn't result in the wholesaler being closed down,' Jack added.

'This needs thinking about. The police here are not particularly well disposed towards private investigators, so I really don't have any strings to pull. I know some of them, of course, but nobody high up. But I'll see.' Francis paused and then went on, 'However, if it has to be a police report then I guess it makes sense to go ahead and get the proof. There won't be any police action, or report, without it. As I said, Harry, it's going to cost plenty to get it, are you OK with that?'

'Oh, yes definitely. As you say, without that we won't have anything. Please go ahead, whatever the cost. If your man can get photos, photos of empty bottles, of the fake capsules they put on the bottles, corking machines, anything like that it would be very helpful. If it comes to a trial. But, Francis, talking of strings to pull, it's possible I might be able to help. A friend of a good friend, who is retired now, was something senior in the Hong Kong police, perhaps he might be able to help.'

'Great! Who is he?'

'There's the thing. I don't know. My friend said he's a conservative, old-fashioned sort of man. So I just have a letter of introduction to him. I don't even know how to contact him, my friend said to ask him for the address if I really needed help.'

'Well,' Francis said, 'I guess that's better than nothing. But it sounds as though you might need to come back here, which might not be without risk. Let me think,' he paused, 'yes, we should be able to manage that if we're careful. But it's up to you, Harry.'

Harry looked at Alison, who smiled and nodded. 'I've come

this far,' he said, 'I'm not going to stop now!'

'Good,' Francis said, 'I'll go ahead with getting the proof, you get the address and we'll talk again tomorrow. I think we've covered everything, but is there anything else? Uncle Jack?'

'No, I don't think so,' Jack replied, 'Harry, Alison?' They shook their heads. 'OK, Francis,' he switched back into Cantonese and taking the phone from the cradle, walked into the kitchen to continue their conversation. Harry and Alison relaxed as the tension that had been building during the call subsided.

'Phew!' Alison said quietly to Harry, 'things are moving fast, honey. But, I've been thinking, do you really want to go back there? As Francis said, it might be dangerous and, forgive me, honey, but, as the Yanks say, have you really got any skin in this game? Getting a conviction for Courtenay, or not, won't change your life, will it?'

'No, it won't, of course you're right, sweetheart. And, thinking about it, we've now got enough information to enable Alain and Christian to put a stop to the whole thing – they can just exert pressure, via the agents, on the restaurants to stop supplying the bottles to the lamp company, or threaten to sue the lamp company for breach of copyright, or something, so they'll be happy, just pass it off as a minor affair, no damage to them. We'll get paid and can go home, job done.' He broke off and, as he pondered, she came and put an arm over his shoulders and squeezed softly, saying nothing.

'On the other hand, I don't want to let Andy down. I was there, in that room, with James Courtenay, he watched me, tasting the wines. How must he have felt? How is he feeling now? Laughing down his sleeve? I do feel personally involved in bringing him to justice. Sorry,' he laughed, 'that must sound really pompous, but I know how disappointed Andy was that he couldn't nail him, there and then.' He sighed. 'Maybe we should call Francis back and call the whole thing off. But a large part of me feels, as I said to him, that, having come this far, we shouldn't stop now.' He paused again for thought.

He turned to the side and looked up at her, into her eyes. 'If you say you don't think I should go, I won't, sweetheart, you mean more to me than any of this.'

'Oh, honey, that's sweet of you, but I can't decide for you, I really can't. But my intuition, which I value highly, I may tell you, tells me that you really want to finish what you've started.' She felt his shoulders relax as she said this and, knowing she'd hit the right note, added, 'Anyway, I haven't forgiven that bastard for aiming his motorbike at us, frightened the life out of me!'

'Bless you, Ali, you've helped me make my mind up, thank you, sweetheart. I'll give Frank a call right now and get that address.'

Chapter 21

JACK CHAU HAD LEFT for his restaurant while Harry was still trying to get hold of Frank Forshaw. Alison had refused his invitation for them to eat there that evening, pleading tiredness. 'Very well,' Jack chuckled, 'but you must come tomorrow, or I'll really be offended!'

He eventually got hold of Geraldine, with his fourth call to their home number. There had been no answer from Frank's mobile, which apparently was turned off. She'd been out in the garden, deadheading the roses. Frank was on the golf course and, no, he hadn't taken his phone with him, as normal. He ought to be back around six, she said, doubtless he'd have a drink or two after finishing his round. He might even stay there for dinner but, if he was going to, he'd be sure to call her, from the club's landline, so she could let him know Harry would like to talk to him. Harry had to be satisfied with that and pleasantly, though rather unwillingly, fielded her questions about Hong Kong and his trip. She could sense his impatience, though, and, promising to get Frank to call him as soon as possible, ended the call.

Six UK time was midnight in Jakarta so Harry prepared for a long evening, sitting downstairs to avoid disturbing Alison who had gone up for another early night. In fact it was about 11.45 when Harry's mobile rang, and Frank's name came up on the screen.

'Hello, Frank, thank you so much for calling, sorry to chase you.'

'Not at all, Harry, sorry to keep you waiting. I gather from Geraldine that it's somethin' a bit urgent?'

Harry filled Frank in with the outline of what had happened, ending, 'So you see, Frank, if your friend in Hong Kong could help it might make all the difference.'

'I see. Quite a delicate situation, really. I can't promise, of course, but he's a very clever man. If he wants to help, I wouldn't put it past him to arrange something. He's a bit of a wine buff as well, as it happens, so I think it might well interest him.'

'That's encouraging, Frank. But, to add to the complication, I'm actually in Jakarta at the moment and it might be tricky to get back to Hong Kong. I don't suppose it would be possible to contact him by phone, or email?'

Frank resisted the temptation to ask why it might be difficult for him to return to Hong Kong. His military training had long accustomed him to focus on the important when planning an operation and to leave the unimportant until later, and he sensed his friend's urgency. 'I'm afraid not, Harry. I don't know if he even has a phone, I certainly don't have his number if he has. I don't suppose he even knows what email is. We always contact each other by letter, or snail mail as they call it these days. As I said, he's a very conservative, private kind of man.' He paused, 'His name is Somerset McLennan. Evidently his mother was a big fan of the author, Somerset Maugham, but no one ever called him anything but Jock. I got to know him pretty well when I was stationed out there in the eighties. I think he later rose to be Assistant Commissioner, something like that. He's a golfer too, a lot of the police force played in those days.' Another pause, 'Sorry, Harry, I'm waffling on and you're probably ready to be in bed, but I've been thinkin' about the best method for you to contact him. You'll have to go there, of course. It might not be a good idea for you to go straight to his house, it might feel like an intrusion on his privacy. I think you should send him round, by taxi, my letter with a handwritten covering note saying, very politely of course, that you are sending him a letter of introduction from a mutual friend and that you would be delighted to have the opportunity to meet him. Send the taxi around nine in the morning, he won't have left for the golf course.' Another pause. 'Suggest a time for a meeting, early evening would probably suit him best, but leave it up to him to suggest something different. Say you'd be happy to visit him there, or to meet anywhere else he'd prefer. Tell the taxi driver to wait there for his reply. He does speak Cantonese, of course, but it would be best to send a taxi driver who speaks good English and can explain politely, when he delivers the letter, that he has a letter of introduction from an English gentleman and will wait outside in case there is a reply. I know it all sounds a bit ridiculous, in this day and age, but that's how introductions were made, in those days.'

'OK, I see. That's enormously helpful, Frank. I'm sure I can get back there. I'll do exactly as you suggest. If he doesn't want to meet me, I'll just leave it at that, no pressure.'

'Thank you, Harry, quite right. But I think he will, I've told him in my letter that you're a wine lover and a golfer! Well, I think that's it, you'd better get to bed, must be past midnight there now. I'll text you his address. Good luck and let me know how it all works out.'

'Of course I will, Frank, again many thanks, and goodnight.'

'Sweet dreams, Harry.'

Harry again woke early next morning, but Alison had been up

before him. 'Jack's sent you up a coffee,' she said, 'it's there on the bedside table, should still be fairly hot.'

'Mmm, just the job,' he replied, taking a sip. They sat up in bed together, supporting their backs with pillows against the huge tubular pieces of bamboo which made up the frame of the large double bed. Harry checked his emails and texts, finding Somerset McLennan's address from Frank Forshaw as he'd hoped.

He told her all about the phone call, ending by saying 'So I'm definitely going to have to go, in order to meet him.'

'You are,' she said, 'but, honey, I've been thinking... your friends Alain and Christian, who don't want any fuss, just keep things quiet, how are they going to react when it all comes out at the trial? If that is, touch wood, all goes to plan.'

'Great minds think alike, sweetheart! I've been thinking about exactly the same thing. But I think it will be all right, touch wood, as you say. Firstly, Andy said that, confronted with the evidence, Courtenay might plead guilty in the hope of a lighter sentence and it wouldn't even go to trial. And, secondly, even if it does, all the prosecution will need to do is to prove that the case that ended up with Henry Yiu was, in fact, due to fraud in Hong Kong, Lafite 2006. All the details we've discovered about how it all worked won't really be relevant. I don't think it'll cause the French any concern. Anyhow,' he went on 'they know why I'm investigating this, so it's not going to come as a shock to them.'

'Makes sense,' Ali replied, 'did you talk about the possibility with them, specifically?'

'No, not really,' Harry admitted, 'they didn't ask and I didn't raise it. They made it clear that they want to avoid publicity, of course.' He thought for a minute. 'As I say, they know why

I'm looking into all this, so I don't think there's really going to be any problem. And I think whatever publicity comes out of the trial, if there is one, won't be a problem for them. Some unknown company in Hong Kong has been up to a bit of hanky-panky, they've acted decisively, discovered it and put a stop to it. They might even see it as a positive, a warning to others.'

'Good stuff, honey, I'm convinced,' she said, 'you've really thought it all through.'

Well,' he began but was interrupted by a call from Jack at the bottom of the stairs.

'Harry, Alison, Francis is on the phone, can you come down?'

'Coming!' Alison replied, retying the belt on her dressing gown as they hurried downstairs.

'Morning, Francis,' she said, 'how's things?'

'Morning, Alison, morning, Harry. Things are moving on and we may need to move quickly. Did you get the address, Harry, are you coming?'

'Morning, Francis, yes and yes.'

'Good. Uncle Jack and I have been discussing how to keep you safe. We think it's more than likely the family will have a contact at the airport here who has access to passenger lists, in and out. If so, they will know that you left for Jakarta, not London, so they may well think it's possible that they haven't scared you off entirely, and might return. They'll be looking out in case you do, so we don't think you should fly back into Hong Kong.'

'Right,' Harry said, 'goodness, this is getting to be like a movie!'

'It's possible that they don't have such a contact and that we're exaggerating the risk, but it's likely they do and we think it's better to be safe than sorry.'

'Absolutely,' Alison broke in.

Francis chuckled. 'I think we're all agreed. So, what we want is for you to fly to Shanghai and come on here by train. We'll have someone meet you in Shanghai and look after you. Is that OK?'

'Yes… yes, I'm in your hands entirely, I'll do whatever you and Jack think best.'

'Good, thank you, Harry. I wish all my clients were as trusting as you! Anyway, the reason for the early morning call is that you'll need a visa for getting into China, I don't suppose you've already got one in your passport?'

'No.'

'OK, you need to get to the People's Republic of China Embassy in Jakarta this morning to get one. Take your passport with you. Have you got anything about your wine business in the UK with you?''

'Yes, I've got business cards.'

'Good, that should do it, tell them that you need to visit some customers in Shanghai. Look up a couple of big restaurants on the net and give them those names if they ask you. If they ask you why you didn't get a visa in England, say they heard you were in Hong Kong, show them your stamp, and asked you to visit, but you'd already booked Jakarta. That'll be more than enough and they'll give you an appointment to get the visa stamp. I don't know how long you'll have to wait for the appointment, I guess it depends on how many people were there yesterday, but with luck it'll be tomorrow at the latest and you'll be able to fly tomorrow night. First come, first served, so get there as soon as you can. All is arranged for getting the proof, I won't say any more. Now I must dash, let's talk this evening. Bye, everyone.' He rang off.

Jack clapped his hands. 'Chop chop! Breakfast can wait till you get back, Harry. Jonah will be waiting for you in fifteen minutes.'

'OK, thank you, but hang on a minute, Jack. Everyone's assuming that it's just me going. Do you want to come with me, sweetheart?'

Jack started to say, 'I really don't think that's –' but Alison interrupted him.

'It's OK, Jack. Thank you for asking, honey, I really appreciate it, I do, I'd love to but I'd only complicate things. You'll need to concentrate on getting things done, not be worrying about me. And,' she drew breath, 'and as a couple we'd be more visible and recognisable, it'd be more dangerous. I'll be fine here, if Jack can put up with me a bit longer.'

'Hmm, I'm not sure –' Harry began.

'Don't argue, honey, it's sweet of you, but you know I'm right!'

'Yes, Harry,' Jack put in, 'Ali is spot on!'

'OK, OK,' Harry said uncertainly, 'OK, I know when I'm beaten. If you're really sure, sweetheart?' She nodded. 'We've come all this way together, I don't really want to split up now. But, yes, it does make sense, I suppose.'

'Absolutely,' Jack said decisively, 'now hurry up and get dressed!'

Chapter 22

NOT MUCH MORE THAN twenty-four hours later, Harry was back in Hong Kong, checked in to a small hotel in the suburbs. The owner had used Francis to discreetly help him with his divorce and was happy to ask no questions about registering his guest in the name of Richard, Harry's second name.

There had only been four people ahead of him in the queue when he arrived outside the PRC embassy in Jakarta. To his relief, the questions about his trip had only been perfunctory and after five minutes he was given an appointment at four that afternoon, when he had quickly got a stamp in his passport. The flight to Shanghai had passed uneventfully and he had been whisked off to the train station by a hulking young man who spoke almost no English and hardly communicated with him during the eight-hour journey on to Hong Kong. Harry had noticed, though, that the young man was constantly on the *qui vive*, scanning the crowd at the airport and the other train passengers for anything untoward. He wasn't sure whether this was reassuring or worrying. Eventually tiredness overcame the tension and he slept for two or three hours in his seat despite the noise and constant coming and going of the other passengers.

Francis had met him at the station and driven him to the hotel, taking the young man with them. On arriving, he took a seat in the hotel lobby with a good view of people coming and going; Harry knew a few words of Cantonese and thanked him, but he only grunted. Francis hadn't said very much on the journey from the station to the hotel and they didn't talk until they were alone in Harry's room.

Francis wasted no time in small talk, saying 'The taxi will be here in twenty minutes, have you got the letter to McLennan and the covering note ready?'

'Yes. As you suggested, I've proposed meeting under the clock in front of the Kowloon Tourist Office if he doesn't want me to go there. Five o'clock.'

'How will he know you?'

'Black- and red-striped tie.'

'Good.' Francis visibly relaxed. 'You look much better without all the fuzz, Harry!'

'Thanks. Alison suggested I'd be less likely to be recognised now without it. I'm glad to be rid of it, to be truthful, it was getting a bit itchy. I haven't had a beard since I was a student.'

Francis chuckled. 'Long hair too, I'll bet.' Harry nodded and smiled. 'Anyhow, Harry, all seems to be working out nicely. Our man stayed at work late last night and got into the room in the cellar where the wines are switched. It's kept locked, of course, but one of the skeleton keys we gave him worked, fortunately. He found everything you could wish for, Harry, empty bottles, corks, all different colours of capsules, and, a hand-corking machine! I've got his photos here on the laptop. There weren't any empty bottles of Lafite 2005, unfortunately, but there was quite a selection, they must have had a delivery from the lighting company recently. He couldn't find any stock records or anything like that lying around, he didn't like to delve into desks and cupboards, for fear of leaving signs he'd been there.'

'Golly,' Harry exclaimed, 'well done, Francis!'

'Not me, he's the one who did well. He's pretty sure there wasn't a security camera in there, but of course you can never be certain, they can be hidden. He's called in sick this morning and is probably already in Singapore, probably working out how to spend your money. I had to give him fifty per cent of his fee in advance. No,' he said, holding up his hand, 'don't ask. It'll all be in my bill, probably as "consultancy services" or something like that. Anyhow, let me show you the pictures.'

He pulled his chair to the side of Harry's and took a laptop out of his big briefcase. Opening it up he pulled up a folder. 'Folder name is New Year Photos 2014,' he chuckled, 'you can never be too careful!'

The photos were, as he said, clear and everything Harry, or the police, could want. Empty bottles with their corks sellotaped against their necks, metal capsules in the colours of all the great wines, full, opened, and half-empty cases of wines from lesser vintages (among them, Harry saw, Petrus 2007) and the corking machine, with its long metal lever which forced down a piston through a short narrowing cylinder, driving the cork into the bottle.

'Wow!' Harry said, 'the whole shooting match.'

'Quite. If you show these to your ex-policeman, I don't think he'll be in too much doubt about it, and that the police will be able to act.'

'Amazing,' Harry said. 'Let's hope he'll see me. I've promised my friend, who gave me the letter of introduction, that, if he doesn't want to, I won't put any pressure on him.'

'OK. I don't see how we could anyway. I've been thinking through my contacts and there really isn't anyone I could take a delicate matter like this to, so McLennan is our only hope.' Francis looked out of the window and saw the taxi pulling up. Looking at his watch, he said 'Very punctual. If you

208

give me the letter and your note, I'll take them down and make absolutely sure he's clear about his instructions. I won't wait around for his return, Harry. Things to do. He'll come up here when he comes back. Give me a call on this number,' he wrote it down, 'and let me know. If it's a yes, I'll put the photos on a memory stick and send it to you here – you've got your laptop?' Harry nodded. 'OK, you can probably do with a shower after that train! See you later.'

After calling Alison in Jakarta to let her know how he was getting on, Harry undressed and had a long cool shower, which he found really refreshing. Although the previous day had been action-packed he didn't feel at all tired. He was delighted at the progress they'd made and very hopeful that things could be brought to a successful conclusion. He had a great respect for Frank Forshaw and hoped that any good friend of his would be of a similar stamp.

He thought carefully about whether he should make a report, at this stage, to France and decided not to. He'd already reported on the three restaurants they'd visited, but hadn't mentioned the lamps, or Francis's investigations. He didn't want them to decide they'd got enough and call him off. Once he'd met Somerset McLennan, if he did, and, he hoped, put the wheels in motion to get the police report, there wouldn't really be anything more he could do. We can go home, he thought, as long as no one bumps me off first!

He also thought carefully about what to report to Andy Pelham. He decided not to say anything about McLennan, unwilling to risk the possibility that someone above Andy might intervene and demand pressure was put on him. Also he decided to only say that things were in hand to get the proof, he was worried that, once they knew the proof existed, some big chief might go in heavy-handed to the Hong Kong police, asking for action and precipitating the big scandal he needed to avoid. He sent off his careful email and whistled quietly to himself – goodness, things are getting complicated, he thought. I wish Ali was here to talk it all through with.

He was musing about how much he'd come to respect her opinion and, indeed, to rely upon her, when there was a knock at the door. He opened it and found a young man standing there, holding an envelope.

'Mr Benson?' the man asked.

'Yes, that's right. I was expecting you. Please come in.'

'Thank you, sir, you're very kind, but I just need to deliver this envelope.' He handed it to Harry and turned to go.

'A moment,' Harry said, pulling out his wallet, 'let me–'

'No need, sir, all arranged with Mr Francis.' He smiled and left.

Harry closed the door and sat down to look at the envelope. It was heavyweight paper, light blue. Basildon Bond! He thought. Haven't seen that for a while. His heart was racing as he saw *Harry Benson Esq.* handwritten on it. He opened it carefully and found a sheet of the same paper inside, folded exactly into three. He took a deep breath, unfolded it and read, in precise handwriting, written with a fountain pen in navy blue ink:

Mr McLennan presents his compliments to Mr Benson and would be pleased to make his acquaintance. Mr McLennan will be at home at five o'clock this evening and will look forward to receiving Mr Benson at that time.

There was no date and no signature. Harry breathed a sigh

of relief and, re-reading the note, wondered again what kind of man he would be meeting later that day. Would they get on? It was going to be quite a lot to ask of a total stranger, he would need to tread very carefully. He thought again about whether it wouldn't be better to call it all off now, pack up and go home. No, too late!

He sighed and picked up the phone to call Francis.

'Francis, it's Harry. I'm meeting him at his house at five.'

'Very good! OK, I'll send a taxi round for you at four-thirty, that'll give you plenty of time to get there. The driver will bring the memory stick. What are you going to do until then?'

'I don't really know. I suppose I'll need to get some lunch somewhere. Can you suggest anywhere not far from here?'

'Well, Harry, I think it might be best if you stay put for the day, keep out of sight. I don't want to scare you unnecessarily but I think they may still be looking out for you. My enquiries have been very discreet but, even so, they could be aware that someone's been asking questions. The hotel does reasonable food, have room service for lunch.'

'OK, will do. Francis, I've been thinking, and what you say has confirmed it, that the sooner I leave the better. Once I've met McLennan and, with luck, got things set in train with the police, there's not really going to be anything more I can do here, is there? I suppose he might ask for time to think about it and want to meet me again. If so, I'll have to think again but, if I may, I'll give him your contact details and, should he want any more information or anything, you'll be better placed to help him than me.'

'Hmm, yes, that makes sense,' Francis replied. 'OK, I think you should leave as soon as possible. Let's see, today's Friday, your room at the Hilton is booked until tonight, isn't it?'

'Yes, I'm due to check out tomorrow morning. So my plan is to change my flights, go back to Jakarta tomorrow, pick up Alison, and fly home from there.'

'I see, let me think.' A pause. 'I had thought of routing you back by Shanghai...' he paused again, 'but I think it should be OK. Even if they do find out you're here, they'll know you're leaving. Still...' he paused yet again, 'make the reservation in another name. Make it for Mr Harry, when you get to check-in say your secretary made a mistake, as long as you have the booking confirmation you'll be OK.'

'Thanks, Francis. You're an immense help, as always.'

'No problem. I'm just checking when the Emirates flight to Jakarta goes, let me see... twelve thirty, so you'd better get to the airport by eleven. The less time you're out and about the better, half an hour to check out, half an hour to the airport, so you'd better be at the Hilton at ten. I'll send someone to you there at nine-thirty, he'll help you with your cases and take you to the airport. I think that's it. Good luck this afternoon, Harry, let me know how it goes!'

Chapter 23

ONCE FRANCIS HAD RUNG off, Harry called Alison back.

'Hello, honey, how's it all going? Are you meeting him?'

'Yes, sweetheart, five o'clock at his house. He sent back a handwritten note, I'll read it out to you.'

When he'd finished reading, Alison giggled, 'Goodness, very formal. I wonder what he'll be like?'

'Me too. I can't say I'm really looking forward to it. It's a lot to ask of a stranger really, but Frank didn't seem to think it was a waste of time, so we'll see.'

'Better dress up smartly, Mr Benson. Good job we shaved that beard off!'

'Jack's best jacket and tie. But listen, sweetheart, there's not much point in me staying on here after I've seen him, so I'm flying back from here to Jakarta tomorrow and, if it's OK with you, I'll change our flights and we can fly home from there on Sunday.'

'Oh, Harry, that's good news. You don't know how much I'm missing you and worrying about you. Jack has been wonderful but, yes, going home on Sunday would be ideal.'

'I miss you too, Ali,' he said, 'I really do. Right, I'll book the flights for Sunday. Can you update Jack on what's going on? There's no need for him to meet me at the airport tomorrow, the flight gets in around five or six, I'll get a taxi there.'

'He might not be there, honey, but I certainly will! I can't wait to see you and give you a big hug. Besides you'll need a hand with our two big suitcases... that's a thought. How are you going to get them to the airport? You're going to go and check out tomorrow morning? Or will you stay there tonight?'

'Francis is arranging for someone to help with the cases and take me to the airport. No, I'm staying here tonight, Francis thinks it's best I'm out and about as little as possible. Straight from here to the Hilton, check out and straight to the airport. And, yes, it would be wonderful to see you at the airport.'

'That's settled then. I wonder if the hotel will ask you where you've been? We haven't been there since, when was it? Monday? I did put the "Do Not Disturb" sign on the door, though, when I left. But I'm worrying even more if Francis thinks you shouldn't go out. Do be careful, honey. But it's a great relief that you've got Francis there, where would we be without him?'

'Absolutely, he's great, such a nice guy too.'

'So how are you going to spend the time before going to meet the mysterious McLennan? Not going sightseeing, obviously.'

'I'll just stay here, listen to some music. Try to relax. I definitely won't spend hours agonising about what to say to him!'

'No, don't, honey. Just be yourself, he's bound to like you.' Harry snorted. 'Yes, he is. Just put the facts before him, he'll either help or he won't. Either way you've done your best. The guys in France, and Andy, couldn't ask for any more. *Courage mon brave!* You can do it. And we'll see each other tomorrow.'

'Yes, you're right, Ali. Thanks for cheering me up.'

They were coming to the end of the conversation and the time was coming to hang up. Both of them thought about saying 'Love you' but neither of them did.

'Take care, honey, please, and call me as soon as you get

back,' she said.

'I will, sweetheart, bye now.' He knew it was a bit brusque, but he couldn't bring himself to say something banal like 'have a nice day'.

As soon as she closed the call he regretted it. Why hadn't he said something more? He sighed again, he'd never really had the gift of the gab. But, he thought, there was more to it than that. He was still protecting himself, wasn't he?

To distract himself, he perused the room service menu. Was it too early, to order lunch? He realised he didn't really know what time it was and looked at his phone. Ten forty. Yes, too early. But, he realised, he was hungry. Apart from some practically inedible chicken and rice on the plane to Shanghai, he hadn't really eaten since lunchtime the previous day. He saw there was a breakfast menu, available until eleven, and had some coffee and rolls sent up. Oh! For some bacon and eggs, and proper bread toasted, with marmalade, he thought. He let his mind stray to how they'd enjoy getting back home. It's nice to get away, he thought, but...

He daydreamed for a bit until room service arrived with his breakfast. The bread wasn't up to much, the jelly-like jam thin and over-sweet, but at least the coffee was hot and strong. And it was all taking his mind off that afternoon's meeting. Despite himself, he went over, for the tenth time, what he was going to say to Somerset McLennan. He wondered what his place was like. Did he live in style? Francis had told him that his district, Repulse Bay, was one of the better residential areas of Hong Kong. He supposed senior policemen there would have had plenty of opportunity to make money, if they wished to, but he somehow thought that McLennan would have spurned such opportunities and operated strictly by the book. But perhaps he had family money.

He sighed again and rejected all this speculation as totally useless. It was going to be a long six hours until the taxi came. He decided on the fried rice with king prawns for lunch and settled down with his book, a John Grisham legal story he'd picked up at Jakarta airport. He read it quickly but soon got fed up with the shoddy editing and story lines left dangling, and put it aside. I suppose he has someone to write them for him these days, he thought. Those early ones were so good! He found a cryptic crossword on his laptop and thankfully lost himself in its mind-bending complexities. 'Desperate guy rejected by girl essentially in worst moment' he read out to himself. The story of my life. Don't be daft - five letters, a D in the middle. The cogs in his brain whirred gratefully, concentrating on the problem.

Desperate guy, he thought. An anagram? No. Can't be. Yug? Ugy? No. Ah! Desperate Dan, rejected, so Nad something. Nadir? Yes it fits – worst moment. Where does the 'ir' come from? Yes, of course 'girl essentially' the middle two letters of girl.

An hour passed in this way and his lunch came, just a bottle of Evian to drink with it, no alcohol he decided. Don't want to breathe alcohol fumes over him if he's a teetotaller. No, no, Frank said he likes wine. Still, even so. He enjoyed his simple lunch and, feeling a bit drowsy, set an alarm before falling asleep in the comfortable armchair.

He was woken by a knocking on his hotel room door. He started up, looking accusingly at his phone – four thirty! Why

216

hadn't it gone off? He touched the clock icon and saw he'd set it for four in the morning! He cursed himself and hurried to the door, finding behind it the same young man who'd come that morning.

'Hiya,' he said, 'sorry, sorry, I fell asleep. I'll just need two minutes to–'

'No rush, sir,' the young man said, 'plenty of time. It will only take us fifteen minutes to get there.'

Coming down in the lift, five minutes later, hastily brushed and dressed, Harry cursed himself anew. All day to get ready, trying to kill time and then having to hustle around, risking being late. He was reassured by the driver's calmness, but who knew with Hong Kong traffic? And it was rush hour. As he crossed the lobby he noticed that the large young man was still there, apparently reading a magazine. He didn't look up as Harry passed.

In the taxi, he relaxed a little but then started to worry again. How would, what was the man's name? Mac something. How would he react if he was late? He took the handwritten note from his jacket's inside breast pocket. McLennan, of course. Dear, oh dear, cool calm and collected I'm not, he thought. How could I forget his name? Somerset McLennan. Oh dear.

He opened up his laptop case and took the sleek silver-coloured computer out. He fired it up and slid the memory stick the driver had handed him in the slot at its side. The laptop murmured a little tune to welcome the new drive and opened up File Explorer, showing D drive. There was the folder named New Years Photos 2014, he opened it and there saw the ten pdf files, all neatly labelled. He clicked on one called Capsules 1 and was happy to see the photo appear, bright and clear. He closed the file and File Explorer, slid the stick out, replaced it in his other breast pocket and, checking the battery icon was still nearly full, closed the laptop down.

He tried to relax and enjoy the scenery passing by, but found he was perspiring at the temples, despite the air-conditioning in the taxi. He pulled a handkerchief from his trouser pocket and wiped away the beads of sweat. He checked his Rolex, twelve minutes to five. Relax, Harry, he told himself, relax.

He decided to Google property for sale in Repulse Bay on his phone and was amazed at the prices, even small apartments were over a million pounds. He wondered again what kind of place Somerset McLennan lived in, probably comfortable leather furniture, shelves full of books, and watercolours of the Cotswolds, he thought.

Eventually, the taxi pulled up at a gate at the entrance to a development containing several large tower blocks. The guard didn't come out from his room beside the gate and, after a cursory look at the car's occupants, raised the bar and they were able to move inside, passing through beautifully manicured lawns and flower beds. As far as Harry could make out there were around a dozen tower blocks, all identical in appearance, all, he thought, about twenty storeys high. There must be an awful lot of people around here who can afford multi-million-pound homes he thought, no wonder it's such a big fine wine market.

The taxi pulled up outside the entrance to a block identified by a small sign as number five.

'This is it, sir,' the driver said, 'you go up to the seventeenth floor and it's the apartment on the right. The commissionaire will call up for you.'

'Thank you,' Harry replied.

'I'll be waiting for you in that parking area over there.' He pointed to a shady area at the side of the building.

'Good. I hope I won't be too long.'

'No worries.'

Harry got out of the car, closed the door and walked towards the building. A glass door slid silently open and he entered into a cool, smartly appointed entrance hall. A uniformed commissionaire sat behind a desk, looking him over.

'How may I help you, sir?' he asked quietly. His hushed tone was in keeping with the quietly luxurious feel of the place, and Harry replied equally softly.

'I have an appointment with Mr McLennan, seventeenth floor.'

'One moment please, sir. Your name?' Harry told him and he picked up the phone on his desk. After a brief conversation he said 'You can go up, sir. Mr McLennan is expecting you. It's the apartment on your right as you exit the elevator.'

Harry thanked him and walked across the hall to where the two lift doors stood. He pressed the call button and the left-hand door opened immediately. He stepped in and was surprised to find the commissionaire following him into the lift. He saw why when he noticed that each floor number had no button to press, just a slot for a key. The commissionaire placed a key in the slot next to the number 17, turned it clockwise and then stepped back out of the lift. The door closed behind him and the lift whooshed upwards at high speed. No getting out at the wrong floor, Harry thought, very impressive security, they all have keys to access their floor.

Within a few seconds the lift came to a halt and the door opened. Harry stepped out and saw that the floor contained only two apartments, one either side of the spacious lobby in front of the lifts. Just two per floor, he thought, goodness they must be big.

Well here goes, he decided, and rang the bell at the side of the large polished wooden door.

Prepared as he was to be ready to smile at the man opening the door, he was completely taken aback when the door opened to reveal a small pretty Chinese lady.

'Mr Benson. Do please come in. My husband will be with you in just a moment.'

Chapter 24

Harry was so surprised he was barely able to mumble out 'Thank you, Mrs McLennan.' He was married! Why hadn't Frank said? No need to, I suppose, he answered himself. Or perhaps he doesn't know.

He was shown into a large airy lounge quite different in style and decoration from what he'd imagined, no watercolours of the Cotswolds or Lake District, no shelves of books, but instead abstract paintings, hangings with Chinese calligraphy and delicate pieces of pottery, all in the oriental style. Indeed, he thought, there's really nothing to show an English person lives here.

Another preconception was shattered when McLennan entered the room and greeted him in a cultured Scots accent. 'Welcome, Mr Benson. Please sit down, would you like a cup of tea?' Edinburgh, Harry guessed straight away – none of the broad vowels of Glasgow or soaring cadences of the Highlands.

'Yes, I'd love one, Mr McLennan, thank you very much.'

McLennan smiled, 'I'll be back in a wee minute, make yourself comfortable, do.'

Harry sat on a low sofa smothered in cushions, putting his laptop case down beside him.

If the presence of a wife, and his being a Scot had surprised him, his appearance had amazed him even more; none of the tweed jacket, cream-coloured shirt and tie above trousers with razor-sharp creases and turnups that Harry had envisaged. He wore a cross between a tunic and a jacket, white, with buttons up the middle and a round-neck collar.

His trousers were loose fitting and wide-legged, he wore sandals. In stature, he was quite tall, over six foot, with thinning, greying, sandy hair worn long and swept back from his forehead to a top-knot. Only his precise manner of speaking fitted in with the formal, military being Harry had imagined. Harry guessed he was around seventy-five, at least twenty years older than his wife.

The room had wonderful views over the bay and Harry watched as ferries criss-crossed between the islands and a huge cruise ship came slowly in towards the harbour. After a couple of minutes, his host returned and set a tray with a small teapot, a strainer, and two small cups on the table next to Harry.

'I'll just let it brew a minute longer.'

Harry had wondered if it would be Indian tea, with milk, but no, the aroma was lapsang souchong, no milk.

'Well, Mr Benson,' McLennan started, 'I can only imagine you're here because of my previous position in the Hong Kong police, er, force.' He paused, poured out the tea and handed a cup to Harry. 'Forgive me if I sometimes search for words, but it is some little time since I last spoke English,' he paused again. 'Before you tell me why you've come to see me, let me tell you something about myself. I came out here at the end of the sixties, a rookie detective. In those days Hong Kong was completely governed by the Brits, people came out here and made large sums of money, regulation was lax and there was plenty of corruption. I always played things by the book and came into conflict with people gaming the system and exploiting the local people. They didn't like me and I came to despise them, greedy ignorant xenophobes who had no time for the Chinese, thought they

222

were above them. I didn't fit in socially, and was glad not to. Frank Forshaw, though, was different. He treated the local people with dignity and respect. When the nineteen-year-old niece of his housekeeper was raped and made pregnant by a lieutenant in his regiment, Frank fought for justice for her, paid for lawyers with his own money. The man was dismissed from the army. Frank made a lot of enemies through that and that is why, I'm sure, he never received the knighthood he deserved. He's the only person from back home from those days that I'm still in contact with and, if the letter of introduction had been from anyone else but him, you wouldn't be here.'

Harry couldn't think of anything to say in reply, so kept quiet.

'Tell me, Mr Benson, what strikes you about this apartment, where I'm living?'

Harry intuitively knew that his host didn't want a paean of praise, but was driving at something. 'Well, Mr McLennan,' he said, 'to be honest, I looked up property prices in Repulse Bay, very, well, extremely, expensive.'

'Yes, exactly. You're right. And how does a man like me, from the back streets of the wrong side of Edinburgh, come to be living in an apartment worth more than three million? I'll tell you. It's not mine, it belongs to my wife, her family. I did well here but never had anything but my service pay and pension. I lived in a small rented apartment until I met her, at a tea dance. Her family has treated me like one of their own and I now feel much more Chinese than British.' He paused and looked straight at Harry. 'I'm telling you all this because you need to know that I will be... totally unwilling to do anything that will cause upset and distress here in my society in order to benefit whichever person or company from outside you may be here on behalf of.'

'Fair enough,' said Harry, 'I appreciate your frankness.'

'I'm sorry to be so, er, unwelcoming, but that's the way it is. I'm willing to listen to you, and, if I see fit, to help you if I can. Frank says in his letter that not only are you a neighbour, a friend, a wine lover, and a golfer, but that you and he are partners in a business, in a successful business. You must be a shrewd man if Frank trusts you like that. I have a great respect for him. So, tell me why you're here. But, first, the sun's over the yardarm, I think, would you like a wee dram?'

Harry could only admire the way the man made his point so forcefully and then smoothly broke the tension. He accepted the offer and, while his host was away collecting a bottle of scotch, Chivas Regal, and two glasses, no ice, no water, he wondered how to begin. What had Alison said? Just tell him the facts.

'Cheers,' McLennan said.

'Cheers, good health.'

Well,' Harry began, 'if I can take up more than a few minutes of your time, I'll relate the whole complicated business that brings me here to your door and why I need to ask for your help. I want to bring a murderer to justice and I think... I hope that, well, it will benefit, rather than hurt... well, I'll begin at the beginning.'

He began telling McLennan the strange series of events that had led him there. He was starting to explain why Scotland Yard had called him in when McLennan interrupted him.

'No need for false modesty, Mr Benson, you won the Wine Challenge and can recognise any wine. My wife looked you up on the Googlynet, or whatever it's called.'

'Right, well, after that...'

224

Harry spoke for a good quarter of an hour, leaving [   ]
out, pausing only to wet his whistle occasionally f[ ]
large glass of scotch. He spoke fluently and well. His
listened in silence, sipping at his own glass. After he rela[ ]
the motorbike incident, McLennan broke in, 'Tell me, M[ ]
Benson, what exactly is your reason for getting involved
here? In a dangerous situation? You're not a policeman.'
'Well, as I said, I want to bring a murderer to justice and, it
seems clear, I'm the only person who can bring it about.
Scotland Yard, can't, or won't take it any further. It's too far
away, too complicated, too abstruse.'
'I see.'
'But, I must be honest, it's also partly professional pride. It
hurt when, as far as everyone was concerned, including the
murderer, I couldn't correctly identify that wine.'
'OK, please carry on.'
Finally, after he'd come to the end of the sequence of events
and had shown McLennan the photos on his laptop, he said
'So you see, it would be possible to take the evidence to the
police and put a stop to it. But, if the police throw the book
at them, and there's a trial, what harm would that cause? To
the restaurant trade, to the reputation of Hong Kong, and,
for my friends in France, to the willingness of people here to
pay large sums for fine wines, that might not be what they
seem and be, to put it crudely, taken for mugs?'
'Yes, I see what you mean. No' good. My wife's family has
many interests in tourism and hotels. It's a very important
part of our economy.' He thought. 'But, if I understand
correctly, you want me to intercede with the police to, how
shall I say, proceed with discretion?' Harry nodded. 'And, if I
don't, or can't, what will you do?'

will just walk away.'

at's what I thought. You're very honest, Mr Benson. I appreciate that. Your French sponsors would, I presume, be able to put a stop to it straight away by pressurising the restaurants, or the lamp company, to stop the empty bottle business?'

'Yes, they would.'

'And they'll be happy. You'll get paid.'

'Yes.'

'They haven't called you off, though?'

'No. They haven't.'

McLennan raised an enquiring eyebrow.

'I haven't told them yet about the photos.'

'I see. And Scotland Yard, they're not about to jump in and demand action from us? I mean from the Hong Kong police?'

'No, again, they're not completely up to date. I wanted to talk to you before reporting back. If you're not able to help, Scotland Yard will never know about those photos. As you say, the French will be happy and I will get paid. Not the end of the world.'

'No. But. But, corruption and crime will have paid here in Hong Kong, again. They'll try and find another way to make the money they're making now. They'll probably succeed. And... and, your murderer will walk free.'

'Yes.'

'Hmm, a pretty conundrum.'

'I realise I'm asking a lot from—'

'Never mind that,' McLennan interrupted. 'Look, I can't give you an answer now. I must think, and consult. I suppose what you need, for Scotland Yard, is something that identifies the case sold at Sotheby's as the Lafite 2006?'

'Yes, exactly.'

'No need for all the details of how it came about to be made public in the trial? No big deal for your chateaux?'

'Your analysis is unerring, Mr McLennan. I can quite see why you made it to the top of the force here.'

McLennan seemed taken aback by this rather personal remark. He looked sideways at Harry for a moment, seemingly puzzled. Harry worried that he'd overstepped the boundaries of their relationship, but, inside, relief that he'd succeeded in explaining everything properly and been understood was bubbling up and he couldn't have stopped himself.

'Why, thank you, Mr Benson. Or may I call you Harry? I think, you know, we're on the same side! My wife said that any good friend of Frank's would be someone worth meeting. Another glass of whisky?'

It was a good hour later that Harry left the apartment and took the lift down to the ground floor – just a button, no key needed this time.

Jock, as Harry had been invited to call him, had asked his wife, Zheng, to join them and they talked amiably together for a good while as the whisky flowed. Jock explained the situation to her and she instantly suggested who they should talk to, people in the restaurant business, Harry gathered. Even though McLennan had no phone, Zheng had the latest iPhone and Harry left her his and Francis's numbers and emails, together with the memory stick.

'So, what are your plans now, Harry? I don't suppose you'll be staying in Hong Kong too long?'

'No, indeed, Jock. I'm flying to Jakarta tomorrow lunchtime, and back to Heathrow on Sunday.'

'Not going out tonight?'

'No, Francis thinks I'd better stay out of sight as much as possible.'

'That makes sense,' Zheng said, 'I know the family that runs Kwun Tong, they're bad people. Be careful, Harry.'

'I will, Zheng, thank you. And thank you for inviting me in to your beautiful home.'

'A pleasure. Come back any time you're in Hong Kong.'

'Yes, Harry, do. But, look, I can't make any promises. First, we need to decide what's the best course of action and, secondly, if we do decide to talk to the police, it's by no means certain that they'll play ball. But don't worry, we wouldn't give them your photos unless we were sure they would cooperate. Michael Leung, the deputy director, used to be my number two, he's a very smart guy. You understand.'

'Yes, of course.'

'I can't really say how long it's going to be before I can let you know. Just a few days, I would hope. You'll be able to hold off the French and Scotland Yard for a while?

'I think so.'

'Hmm, are you sure? Once they hear you've gone home, you might not find it too easy, Harry. They'll expect a final report. Perhaps you should stay in Jakarta for a few days until it all plays out. Still supervising enquiries.'

'I see what you mean. I'll give it some thought.'

'It's up to you, of course. But it would be a shame if your chateaux owners jumped in and stopped the empty wine bottles too soon. They'd smell a rat and destroy all the evidence straight away, I'm sure.'

228

'It certainly would. Thanks, Jock, you're way ahead of me, I must say. I'm glad I was never a criminal you were after!'

'Aye, well. We're on the same side.'

'We'll be in touch soon, Harry, take care,' Zheng said as he shook hands and went towards the door, 'and don't forget your laptop!'

Chapter 25

THE COMMISSIONAIRE SMILED POLITELY as Harry got out of the lift.
'Good night, sir. Have a pleasant evening.'
'Thank you.' The door slid open and Harry walked out into
the cooling evening air. The taxi was parked just inside the
parking area and the driver instantly started the engine as
Harry appeared and cruised up to the steps in front of the
building to pick him up. He'd obviously been watching out for
Harry's reappearance.

Harry opened the door and got in. 'Sorry to have kept you
waiting so long, my friend.'
'No problem at all, sir. It's what I'm paid for.' He set off back
towards the city and said no more until they pulled up in
front of Harry's hotel. 'Have a good evening, sir.'
'Thank you, you too, and thank you for all your help today.'
The young man smiled and drove away. Harry went into the
hotel lobby, interested to see if the man who met him in
Shanghai was still there. He was but, as Harry waited in the
empty lobby for the lift door to open, he picked up his
magazines and headed out down the steps. He's definitely
keeping an eye on me, Harry thought as he went up to his
room.

As soon as he'd got in and taken off his jacket and tie, Harry
called Alison.
'Hello, honey, how did it go? How are you?'
'Fine, sweetheart, fine. It went pretty well, I think.' He
described the apartment and his surprise at McLennan's
appearance and his having a wife. 'For some reason I
assumed he was a bachelor. I'm sure Frank didn't say he was

married.'

'Maybe he doesn't know.'

'That's what I thought. But his wife is lovely, really charming, and the good news is that her family has interests in hotels and tourism.'

'Why's that good news?'

'Well, because I think the bigwigs in that business will have influence with the police. Like the French, they won't want a big scandal to erupt. So, if Jock McLennan does decide to help, their influence will be in his favour.'

'OK. You said "if" he decides to help. He hasn't said he will, then?'

'That's right, sweetheart.' He went on to explain why McLennan, and everyone, might decide that it was best to let sleeping dogs lie. That he appreciated that the French chateaux could put a stop to the fraud. 'He said to me "They'll be happy, and you'll get paid" and of course I had to agree.'

'I see, honey, so why do you think he might help us?'

'Because, well, because he's a good guy. An old-fashioned copper, he hates to see crime pay, and also he's well aware that James Courtenay would walk free. Besides he thinks that these people would just find a new wine scam to keep making the money they're making now, unless they're stopped. He, and everyone he and Zheng discuss it with, might feel it's best to nip it in the bud now. I certainly hope so. If they think the police will play ball, I suspect all will be well.'

'Right, I think I see. And also, of course, he might help because he likes you! I told you so!'

Harry chuckled. 'He was pretty fierce at the start but, by the end, we were getting on very well. They asked me to come back whenever I'm in Hong Kong! I took it as quite a compliment because, apart from Frank, he has almost nothing to do with Brits any more. He's almost totally immersed in the Chinese way of life. He said he hadn't spoken English for ages. But he holds Frank in very high regard, which was the only reason they agreed to meet me. He said, as I remember, "If that letter of introduction had come from anyone else, you wouldn't be here".' He told her the story he'd heard about Frank and the nineteen-year-old rape victim.

'Wow! What a guy! I can't wait to meet him.'

'You will, sweetheart. He'll love you too. He comes across as a bit of an amiable, doddery old buffer, but, when you get to know him, you see he's really sharp. But I admit I didn't suspect that he was such a hero.'

'Honey, you're my hero. You've obviously done brilliantly. I guess you're eating in the hotel tonight?'

'Yes, the food's not great, but it's OK.'

'Never mind. We'll be home on Monday and I'll take you back to Wilton's for a slap-up fish supper!'

'Ah, yes, about that, sweetheart. I'm afraid I might need to stay in Jakarta a bit longer.' He quickly explained Jock's misgivings about the French moving too quickly if he had to make a full report.

'Did I hear you say "I might need to stay", Harry Benson? Not "we"? Are you trying to get rid of me?'

'I don't want to get rid of you, Ali. I just thought you might have had enough of Jakarta, that's all. I'd love you to stay, you know that.'

She heard the anxiety in his voice and felt a bit guilty. 'Honey, don't take me too seriously, I was only joking. But you needn't worry, I'll be very happy in Jakarta, as long as you're here too. I'm not sure how keen Jack will be, though – I get the feeling I may be cramping his style with his lady friends!' Harry laughed out loud. 'I wouldn't be surprised. I know, we can fly down to Bali for a couple of days! It's beautiful and I'd love to show you around. It's only an hour's flight so it wouldn't be difficult to get back to Jakarta if necessary. But I really don't think there's anything more we can do. It's out of our hands now. So we can have a proper holiday! And I think I can promise you the best Tom Yum soup in the world!'

'It sounds divine, honey, I can't wait!'

'Great, I'll get busy and book the flights and a hotel down there. The Grand Hyatt in Nusa Dua is the place. If you want to look it up, Nusa Dua is the little teardrop on the bottom of the island. It's much nicer than Kuta where all the tourists go. Anyhow, sweetheart, I'd better go, I promised to ring Francis and update him. Could you update Jack for me?'

Alison said she would and they rang off, Harry promising to call her in the morning from the airport with his arrival time in Jakarta.

Feeling thirsty, Harry opened a bottle of beer from his fridge before calling Francis. Not finding a suitable glass he took a swig from the bottle. 'Right,' he said, 'better call Francis.'

Francis quickly appreciated Jock McLennan's position. 'Sure, there wasn't any way he could give you an answer there and then, Harry, he'll want to be sure of support from the trade before he makes his approach, if he has a mind to get involved. But I must say it all sounds positive. It's good that he knows Michael Leung. It's very good that his wife is involved and that she's got good contacts in the trade. I know her now, she used to be called Zheng Li before she got married. Her father and uncle own a couple of hotels and have shares in, I think, a big tourist travel company, coach and boat trips, guided tours, that kind of thing. They'll know anyone who's anyone in the hospitality business. But I'm sure they'll ensure the family don't get wind of it.' He paused, 'So, yes, I'd say, it's looking good. Well done, Harry.'

'Thanks. It was a bit nerve-racking, but in the end we got on pretty well. I certainly got the feeling that he'd like to help, but he was firm in saying he couldn't promise anything.'

'OK, fair enough, we'll just have to wait and see. By the way, there obviously weren't any security cameras in the warehouse, there's been no comeback, my guy's returning from Singapore. Must have spent all your money.'

'That's good. Well, I don't think there's anything more we can do. I'll leave tomorrow as planned, but I won't be heading home just yet.' He explained again the reason. 'So we'll be spending a couple of days in Bali.'

'Very good, you'll enjoy it there. So the car will be there tomorrow as planned. We'll stay in touch. Night, Harry.'

'Goodnight, Francis, thanks for everything.'

'No worries. You'll be getting my bill,' he chuckled.

Harry had Singapore noodles for his supper and was sound asleep, completely exhausted, soon after. He slept well, straight through till the alarm on the phone woke him at seven thirty. He showered, dressed, and packed quickly, decided against breakfast and busied himself arranging flights and booking the hotel in Bali. He decided to book for three nights, what the hell, he thought, we deserve a holiday. He just had time to send an email to Alain de Bossenet, saying that enquiries were proceeding, and looking promising, before the knock came on his door at nine-thirty. He'd half-expected it to be the same driver as yesterday, but it was the large young man who'd accompanied him from Shanghai and had been in the lobby all the previous day.

'Good morning,' Harry said, but the man just muttered something incomprehensible, picked up his suitcase and headed towards the lift. They descended in silence. When the door slid open, Harry headed towards the reception desk, pulling his wallet from his back pocket, but the man put his hand on his shoulder and stopped him.

'No,' he said, 'Francis pay.' When they got to the entrance, he spoke again, 'Wait.' He strode off along the street, pulling Harry's suitcase behind him and disappeared off into a side turning. A minute later he reappeared, driving a fairly new mid-range Toyota, and pulled up alongside the hotel entrance, gesturing to Harry through the open window to get in. He did, and they drove off.

Harry decided that Alison would be awake by now in Jakarta and gave her a quick call, saying he was on his way, and that Francis thought things were looking positive. He'd call again from the airport.

The journey continued in silence until they turned into the entrance circle in front of the Hilton. Harry expected to be dropped at the door but, no, the man kept going and parked the car in the middle of a long double row of parking spaces at the side of the hotel, giving them a walk of around a hundred and fifty yards back to the entrance. Strange, Harry thought. They walked into the lobby and up to the lift, no sign of recognition or interest from the receptionist, the same man who'd arranged their taxi on the previous Saturday. Good, Harry thought, they haven't missed us.

The big man stared around the lobby suspiciously, but no one seemed to be taking any notice of them. However, as they disappeared into the lift and the door closed behind them, a young woman who had apparently been absorbed in working on her laptop stopped tapping at it and pulled her mobile out of her handbag. After a brief conversation, she replaced the phone, closed her laptop, zipped it into its case and left the lobby, walking quickly down the street.

When they reached the room, Harry was pleased to find that the 'Do Not Disturb' sign was still hanging on the door handle. He went in, the big man following him, and found that, indeed, the room had not been touched since their sudden departure on Monday. He opened up both of the suitcases and laid them on the bed. Then he went methodically through every cupboard and drawer, taking out the contents and packing them carefully into the two cases, taking especially good care not to crease Ali's Chanel dress. The young man sat in an armchair and watched him. When Harry was satisfied that everything was packed he zipped them both up and twiddled round the numbers on the combination locks. He'd forgotten to memorise the numbers on Alison's case before doing so and reproached himself the minute he'd done it. Never mind, he thought, Ali will know it. He decided to go for a pee before setting off for the airport and, walking into the bathroom, found a range of toiletries and some clothes that he'd totally forgotten about. He cursed himself again and, after washing his hands, carried everything out to the bed. Of course he had to reset the combination on his case and unzip it, all under the gaze of his companion. Eventually everything was packed away and he was ready to leave and settle his bill.

They descended in the lift, each pulling a large suitcase behind them. Harry was old enough to remember the days before some genius had invented wheeled suitcases, and was musing about all the ways travelling around the world had changed, when the lift came to a halt on the ground floor and they got out.

He walked across to the reception desk and waited for a couple of minutes while the receptionist checked out an elderly French couple ahead of him. When they had moved away, he went to the desk, put his credit card-type key on the counter and said 'I'd like to check out please, room 1407.'

'Certainly, sir,' the receptionist replied, consulting the screen in front of him, 'Mr. Benson?'

'Yes, that's right.'

'I'll just print off your bill, sir. Have you used the mini-bar since, let me see, since Monday afternoon?' If he's surprised housekeeping haven't been in since Monday, Harry thought, he's hiding it well. He considered saying he'd been called away on urgent business, but thought better of it.

'No.'

'OK. Do you have the other key?'

No, he thought, Ali must still have it in her handbag. 'No, sorry, I'm afraid we lost it.'

'No problem, sir.' The printer at his side whirred and produced two pieces of paper. 'Here's your bill, Mr Benson, how would you like to settle it?'

Harry quickly looked over the bill. Everything seemed to be in order. Expensive but within the budget. 'American Express?'

'Certainly, sir.'

The credit card transaction was quickly completed and Harry

went back to where his companion was standing with the two suitcases. Harry glanced up at the clock above the reception desk, twenty past ten, they were ten minutes ahead of Francis's schedule. He felt himself relax as they moved away towards the entrance. All was going as planned and he would soon be safely away from Hong Kong. Relax, Harry, relax.

Chapter 26

THEY WHEELED THE SUITCASES down the ramp at the side of the steps leading down from the entrance, turned right and walked along the side of the car park. The walkway was too narrow for them to walk abreast and the big man indicated that Harry should go first. They were about halfway along towards the car when Harry noticed a man walking towards them. Evidently he'd just got off a motorbike; he was in full leather gear and stout leather boots, still with a black scarf across the bottom half of his face, carrying a black helmet in front of him. If Alison had been there she would have warned him, but he thought nothing of the man's appearance, although he heard a sharp intake of breath from behind him. Harry stood to one side to let the man pass but, to his horror, saw the man produce a long, narrow-bladed knife from inside the helmet. The man was still a few yards away but Harry froze, unable to react or move, just seeing that dreadful knife coming towards him, thinking he was going to die. Then things happened very quickly; he was thrust violently to the side and crashed backwards across the bonnet of a car. The big man shoved past him as he fell and aimed a violent karate-style chop at the assailant's throat. He moved his head to avoid it, but it had only been a feint. The rigid arm and hand crashed down on the joint of his wrist and the hand holding the knife. The man in black yelped in pain, Harry thought he heard the crunch of breaking bone. The knife clattered to the ground. The assailant dropped down on one knee to try to retrieve it, spitting and cursing at Harry's saviour who ignored him and kicked him with enormous force in the side. He sprawled away, retching, then quickly pulled himself to his feet and ran away down the walkway, back the way he had come. The big man started to pursue him, he ran a few paces but then thought better of it and came back to where Harry stood, shaking and gasping for breath.

Harry opened his mouth to speak, to try to express his thanks, but the big man just picked up the knife and said 'Get in car.' He clicked a button on the car key and Harry saw the Toyota's lights flash, just twenty yards away. He staggered forward, still too shocked to think or speak coherently, and pulled the car door open. As he got in he heard a motorbike roaring past at high speed, he looked round and caught a glimpse of the man in black. He saw the bike exit the car park and turn left onto the busy road, causing an oncoming van to swerve to avoid him. Within twenty seconds the big man had the suitcases in the car's boot. He quickly got in the car, started up the engine, reversed out at high speed and drove rapidly towards the exit. At first Harry thought he was chasing the bike, but he turned right out of the exit, not left. He did not speak, but pulled out his phone and made a call. He spoke briefly, listened for a short time and then passed his phone back to Harry. 'Francis.'

'Are you OK, Harry? I heard what happened.'

'Yes, I think so, thanks. Thanks to your man. He saved my life. I'm a bit winded and dazed, but yes, I'm OK.'

'Thank goodness. I'd have never forgiven myself if I'd let you be killed on my watch. I still can't quite believe they'd do such a thing. Anyhow, listen, Harry. I suppose it's just possible that they'll try again at the airport, although it's highly unlikely. So I've told Yao to buy a ticket to somewhere and to go through security with you and stay with you at the boarding gate until you get on the plane.'

'OK, thank you, that's very k-k-k-kind.' Harry had never stuttered in his life before, he realised he was still shaking with shock. 'Sorry, Francis, it's all been a bit...' he stopped, lost for words.

'Yes, I understand. It'll take you a few minutes, but you'll be OK, don't worry. But, Harry, we ought to let McLennan and Zheng Li know what's happened. This could jolt them into action. A bit of fraud is one thing, an attempted murder quite another.' Francis kept talking, knowing it would distract Harry from the shock he'd undergone. 'I know you gave them my contacts, but have you got a number for them? I'll give them a call.'

'No, I don't think so. No, I haven't. Sorry.'

'Hmm, that's a pity. Let me think. Zheng Li, now who might know her number?' He broke off for a moment to think. 'Possibly my mother has a friend who knows her, they both play bridge, I think. I'll work on it, Harry, leave it to me, I'll get word to them if I can. It may well help.'

Harry had only half listened to this, his heart rate had slowed down but he was getting a headache and Francis's voice seemed to be coming from a long way away. 'Yes, thanks, Francis,' he said haltingly.

Francis could hear the hesitation in his voice and knew it was time to end the call. 'Don't worry, my friend, you're still in shock, it's natural. You'll soon be OK again. Just relax and let Yao look after you. OK?'

'Yes, thank you Francis. Sorry.'

'Don't be. Now can you pass me back to him?'

'Yes, but Francis, can you please thank him for me? We don't communicate too well but, well, as I say, he just saved my life.'

'I will, Harry. He's not much of a talker, but he's got a black belt in Karate.'

This left Harry speechless again and he just passed the phone back to the front of the car, settled back in the seat and closed his eyes.

That evening, sitting on the sofa in Jack's house, holding hands, he told Ali all about it. He hadn't wanted to say much when he called her from the airport, partly because he had a splitting headache and partly because he didn't want to alarm her. She'd immediately known from the tone of his voice that something was wrong but he reassured her that he was safe, was being looked after, and that there was no need to worry.

When he emerged into the arrivals area in Jakarta airport, pushing a large luggage trolley, she vaulted nimbly over the barrier and rushed into his arms, hugging him tight. A sudden tide of emotion, relief and happiness at seeing her, overwhelmed him and tears ran down his face, wetting her cheek as they kissed.

'My poor, poor man. Jack rang and told me what happened. Don't talk now, you can tell me all about it later. Let's get a taxi and go home.'

After a bath and another plate of Susi's *nasi goreng*, his headache gone, he felt much better and told Ali everything that happened, right up to when Yao, who'd stuck to him like glue throughout his time at the airport, said goodbye as he watched him go through the boarding gate. 'I know Francis had thanked him for me, but of course I wanted to try again to say it myself. He listened to me with a smile, the first time I'd seen him smile, and said, in perfectly good English, "No need to thank me, Mr Harry, just doing my job," you could have knocked me down with a feather! Talk about the strong, silent type.'

'Well, I'm extremely grateful to him, honey, and Francis too. They've got you back here safely, thank goodness. If I'd thought for one moment they'd try and, well,' she couldn't bring herself to say "kill you", 'do that, I'd never have let you go.'

'I wouldn't have gone either, sweetheart. Sitting here safe with you, talking about it later, describing what happened, makes it all seem like a bit of a story, doesn't it, all's well that ends well, but it wasn't like that. I really thought he was going to kill me. But, it's really good to be able to talk about it with you, Ali.' He paused. 'You know, looking back on it, what flashed through my brain for that second as I waited for the end was regret that I wouldn't see you again.'

She squeezed his hand, but said nothing.

'I'm not very good at expressing my emotions, as I'm sure you know, sweetheart, but... but, I think I might be falling in love with you.'

'Do you, my dear, dear man?' She paused. 'You've quite taken my breath away. I'm trembling too. You might need to try some mouth to mouth resuscitation, Harry Benson!'

They were holding hands again next morning as they came into land at Bali's Denpasar Airport, the plane apparently about to crash land in the sea before the runway appeared beneath them in the nick of time. Harry'd made this landing many times before but it was Ali's first time and she squeezed his hand tightly for reassurance in those last moments when the sea was just below the plane.

'Whew,' she said as the plane landed softly and braked, 'that was exciting!'

'It's quite a landing, isn't it? There used to be a little restaurant on the beach next to the runway, where you could eat wonderful fresh fish, grilled over burning coconut husks in halved oil barrels, drink beer, and watch the planes take off and land. Beautiful at night when all the planes have lights on and the runway is illuminated. I wonder if it's still there.'

'Let's go there if it is, honey. It sounds absolutely wonderful. I'm so looking forward to seeing Bali, seeing Bali with you, everyone says how beautiful it is.'

They collected their hire car at the slightly chaotic rental desk and were soon heading out on to the road to their hotel in Nusa Dua.

'What does it mean, Nusa Dua?' Ali asked.

'It translates, as "two islands" I think, but I've never really understood why.'

'Good roads,' Ali commented as they zipped along the bypass. 'Jalan By-pass Ngurah Rai, it's called, she said, reading from a sign.

'Ah-hah! Don't be fooled! This is the only dual carriageway on the island, or at least it used to be.'

'Look at that! That must be a whole family on that little motorbike!' Ali exclaimed.

'Yes, they've probably got the dog on there as well! You need to be careful driving here, people just pull out of side-roads without even looking. They're Hindus, you see, the Balinese, and they believe everything is written.'

'So there's no point in worrying! Not a bad way to be, honey, don't you think?'

'I think there's a lot to be said for it, sweetheart. They're certainly lovely friendly people. For them it's not perhaps the paradise that visitors see, there's a lot of poverty, but on the whole they're happy people, I'd say, and who can argue with that?'

They spent a happy afternoon relaxing by the enormous hotel swimming pool and headed out to a nearby restaurant that Harry knew for an evening meal. The restaurant was called Angsa Putih, which, Harry explained, means White Swan. It was more of a barn than anything else, Alison thought. A great arched ceiling, twenty feet above them, open on all sides for coolness, with a cool tiled floor.

'The food's very simple, and typically Balinese, baked fish and rice. But they make the best sambal on the island, or used to. I hope they haven't changed the recipe.'

'Sambal,' Ali said, 'that's the spicy chili paste, honey, isn't it? I liked it a lot when I tried it at home.'

'Yes, sweetheart. There's sambal and there's sambal. Here it's got a wonderful balance of spiciness and a fresh fruitiness. I can't really describe it but–' he broke off as his mobile rang. 'It's Francis,' he mouthed.

'Evening Francis. Good to hear from you.'

'Good evening, Harry, how are you?'

'Much recovered, thank you.'

'Good. Harry, I've got some news for you.'

Chapter 27

Hᴀʀʀʏ ʟᴏᴏᴋᴇᴅ ᴀᴛ Aʟɪ and slid up the volume control on his phone so that they could both hear Francis's news.

'Good news I hope, Francis,' Ali said.

'Oh, hi, Ali, how are you? Having fun in Bali?'

'It's absolutely lovely. Tomorrow we're going to the Bird Park, Harry's promised me a man-eating lizard and the best Tom Yum soup in the world. I told him that we'd better have the soup first!'

Francis laughed. 'For sure, you'd better! Tom Yum? Perhaps it's good there, but next time you're in Hong Kong I'll take you to a little restaurant I know where it'll be better.'

'Huh, don't be too sure,' Harry cried, 'anyhow, I'm not sure how soon we'll want to be back In Hong Kong, Francis.'

'Of course, I don't blame you. But my news may help.'

'Go on, Francis,' Ali said, 'I'm on tenterhooks here.'

Francis's English was well-nigh perfect, but this was a new one. 'Tent hooks? I don't get it, Ali, what are tent hooks?'

She laughed nervously, 'Sorry, just an expression. I mean I can't wait.'

'Right. Well, my news is that I finally managed to get hold of Zheng Li's phone number. She hadn't heard about the attack on you, Harry, in fact no one seems to know about it. She was horrified, absolutely horrified; you seem to have made a bit of a hit there. Anyway, McLennan wasn't in but he called back within half an hour. He wanted to know all about it, of course. Like me he was really surprised that the Kwun Tong family would do such a thing, he thinks their scam must really be making a great deal of money for them to go to such desperate lengths to stop a potential threat. I have to say Jock McLennan has a very sharp mind, his speed of thought and analysis was very impressive. And, in passing, I've never heard a European speak our language so well. It seems that he's really, together with Zheng of course, how shall I put it… a not insignificant cog in the wheels that turn this city. That's a big plus. He says that now the family know that not only were you willing to come back after the first warning, which suggests you're serious, but also they will suspect from Yao's intervention that you're not on your own, that you're maybe working with someone local. He says they'll be very worried about that, maybe worried enough to close everything down and destroy the evidence. But he doesn't think so.' He paused for breath. 'With me so far?'

'Yes,' they choroused.

'OK. More than likely, he thinks, they've no idea that you know about the empty bottles business. They think you've just verified the wine switching is happening and are trying to identify which restaurants are involved. And, of course, that you're smart enough to get protection. They'll know you've left again and probably won't be back in a hurry, so he doesn't think they'll panic just yet. There's too much money involved for them to stop it just like that. In fact he really thinks they've shot themselves in the foot with their attack on you. If there was ever any question that the big shots in the hospitality trade here would decide it would be best to just let the French wine suppliers close it down and turn a blind eye, there's not any more. He's sure that once Zheng has stirred them up about one of their best friends, did you hear that Harry? One of their best friends nearly being killed in broad daylight, they'll be of one mind and will act. Evidently everyone in the business really dislikes this Kwun Tong family anyway and will be glad to see them brought to book. This is giving Zheng and her friends the chance to do just that. And they will act quickly, before the family get wind of what's happening and pull the plug. It's going to have to be handled carefully. Someone, probably Zheng's uncle and a guy from the Chamber of Commerce, will go and see the top man to prepare the ground, then Jock will talk to Michael Leung, explain the position and try to get the action we want. I think this will happen tomorrow, Monday, and, all being well, there could be a police raid on Kwun Tong Import and Export in the early hours of Tuesday.'

'I'm stunned, Francis. You've worked wonders, you really have,' Harry said.

'Thanks, Harry, but, to be honest, your meeting with Jock and Zheng was the catalyst for all this. I've really only followed up. The credit belongs to you, I think.'

'No, Francis,' Alison butted in, 'you've been absolutely marvellous, we'd never have got anywhere without you.'

'Thank you, too, Ali. That reminds me, I must double Harry's bill.'

'Ha ha. But I mean it, I can never thank you enough for saving Harry's life, really I can't.'

'That reminds me, Francis, of something I've been meaning to ask you about.' It was Harry's turn to interrupt. 'How come your man, Yao, my saviour, never said more than three words to me before and then spoke perfectly good English to me when we parted at the airport? I was flabbergasted, I thought he spoke almost no English, just "wait" and "get in car".'

Francis chuckled. 'Was he that monosyllabic? He's a real

professional. He knows that if he develops a relationship with someone he's protecting he'll have to spend time talking to them, answering questions, and that will be a distraction. That'll be time he won't be able to devote to reading the room, looking out for threats. That would be the time, when his back is metaphorically turned, that a really cunning enemy will choose to strike. And there are some really cunning, and violent, people here, believe me.'

'I do,' Harry cried, 'and there I was thinking he didn't like me!'

'Not at all,' Francis chuckled again, 'and I'm glad he spoke nicely to you at the end.'

After the call from Francis, they settled down to enjoy their meal. Harry was delighted to find the sambal was still as good as he remembered and soon asked the waiter for another of the little dishes it was served in. Ali loved the flavour but soon found that her mouth was on fire from the chilis. Their waiter had obviously been keeping an eye on her because, unasked, he brought her a glass of Coke. She looked questioningly at Harry who said 'It's the sugar in it, best thing to take away the sting.'

Ali took a mouthful, rolling it around her mouth. 'Goodness, yes,' she said, 'it really does help, doesn't it?'

'Yes,' Harry replied, 'probably the only good reason for ever drinking it. Foul stuff.'

'Do you think so? I quite like it.'

'Do you? I guess I'm in a fairly small minority compared to the billions of people around the world who drink it. To me it's one of those things, like a Big Mac, that you only ever try once.'

'Bloody Americans, eh? Corrupting the world's taste buds,' Ali teased.

'Yes, sorry, pompous of me!'

Just then Harry's mobile rang again. It was Zheng. After checking that he really had recovered OK and saying how sorry she was, she passed the phone over to her husband. He wanted to know if Harry had anything that would help to identify the attacker, but Harry was unable to recall anything apart from his short black hair and dark brown eyes. 'He's probably nursing a broken wrist and must have severe bruising on his left side, but that's it. I couldn't see the number plate on the bike either.'

'No matter,' Jock said, 'I'd like to nail him, but we've got bigger fish to fry. He's probably just a hired thug, anyway, not part of the family. But I'll get them to look out for someone with a bad wrist when they go in.'

'You said when, not if, Jock?'

'Yes, Francis has updated you, I'm sure?'

'Yes, he rang twenty minutes ago. I hope you didn't mind him contacting you?'

'No, not at all, Harry. He's a very smart guy, you chose well there. Anyway, yes it's ninety-five percent certain. They've overstepped the mark with that attack on you. The trade are glad of a reason to be shot of that family. The police will be as well, I've no doubt, and will also be in no doubt that the trade wants it done discreetly. I'm meeting Michael Leung tomorrow afternoon for coffee. I'm hoping that they'll take them down for false accounting. It'll be enough to put away the top guy and finance director for a couple of years. Not enough to cause the company to close down. If it was me, I'd agree not to go after the other members of the gang in return for them agreeing that they'll sell the business on. Of course I can't tell Michael what to do but, well, he's a very clever man too. We go back a long way. You remember I told you about the nineteen-year-old girl Frank Forshaw stuck up for?'

'Yes, of course.'

'He's her brother.'

Having promised to keep Harry up to date as and when things happened, Jock rang off.

'So, honey,' Ali said, 'it looks like it's all going to work out just fine, doesn't it? You've won!'

'We've won, sweetheart. I couldn't have done it without you. And, it must be said, a terrific stroke of luck, Frank knowing Jock so well.'

'Not luck, honey. We're in Bali. It was all written!'

They had a wonderful relaxed day on Monday. The Komodo Dragon at the Bird Park seemed to be fast asleep in its pen and didn't look interested in moving a muscle, never mind eating anybody. Alison, sitting with a large macaw perched on one shoulder, pronounced the Tom Yum, replete with prawns and lemon grass, the best soup she'd ever eaten.

They wandered up a path from a little café where they'd had coffee and soon found themselves in a rice paddy, which rose in terraces up a gentle slope towards a dark green jungle, palm trees fringed the side of the field. Innumerable little channels ran intricately through the paddy, moving water around. Some were flowing, some dry, and Harry explained how the farmer could redirect the flow of water by just lifting a clod of earth here, and replacing it there.

'It's a method that's been perfected over centuries,' he said, 'really ingenious.'

'I can see,' Ali replied, 'but not just that, it's so natural, and so beautiful.' She gazed out again over the gently undulating rising slope, savouring the tinkling of water and the contrasting greens and whites of the swathes of rice plants and the browns of the earth that made up the channels. The sun poured down from the clear blue sky and a gentle breeze moved the fronds in the palm trees. Mount Agung, the volcano in the centre of the island, rose majestically in the distance.

'I really don't think I've ever been anywhere more beautiful, Harry,' she said, 'I can see why people call Bali a paradise.'

They went on to the artistic centre of the island, Ubud, where Alison enjoyed browsing through the little galleries and woodcraft and pottery exhibitions, deciding to buy a small carved wooden figure for her sister.

By silent mutual agreement they didn't discuss the investigation or what might be happening in Hong Kong. After days of tension they were content to lose themselves in the beauty of their surroundings and the pleasure of being together. Harry tried his best to avoid being the all-knowing guide after a hint or two from Alison about how peaceful she found everything.

They headed back to the hotel, driving slowly through the winding roads, coming to a halt in a little village as a religious procession came down the road towards them. Women with head-dresses constructed to carry baskets of fruit were flanked by men carrying very long brightly coloured parasols. Behind them walked a gamelan orchestra, making a music Alison had never heard before, a clinking, tapping and shrill banging that seemed entirely unmelodious at first. However, as the procession slowly wound past them, she began to find it somehow hypnotic, the sound, the colours, the stately movement and the beaming faces combined to make it a strangely moving experience, and she watched spellbound. Harry wisely refrained from giving a running commentary, letting the beauty and serenity of the moment speak for itself.

Their silence lasted until after the procession had passed and they were back on the road.

'Pretty special, eh, sweetheart?' Harry said.

'Wow, yes,' Ali replied, 'I'm not a religious person, as you know, honey, but that had a real, I don't know, a real spiritual feel to it, didn't you think?'

'I know exactly what you mean. They're very spiritual people, and these processions are an integral part of their culture. And spiritual life.'

'It's lovely. What a day we've had, the birds, a real live dragon, the soup, the rice paddy and now this. I really can see why people rave about Bali. Thanks, honey, for showing it me.'

Later after a light supper in the hotel restaurant, they sat out on the balcony, sipping strawberry daiquiris and reliving their stay.

'You know, sweetheart, we were talking yesterday about having won?' Harry said during a pause as they watched the huge moon rising over the palm trees.

'Mm-hmm?'

'Well, I hope we weren't tempting fate. I've got a feeling James Courtenay is not going to plead guilty and I'm going to have a date at the Old Bailey waiting for me.'

Chapter 28

THEY BOTH SLEPT SOUNDLY that night, oblivious to what might be happening two thousand miles away in Hong Kong. But when they woke they were both keenly aware that things should have been decided, one way or another, and that Harry's mobile would soon be enlightening them as to whether all their efforts had paid off. Had Jock been right, or would all the empty bottles and capsules have been removed before the police arrived?

The phone remained resolutely silent throughout breakfast, though, and they decided to have a lazy beach day. Harry suggested going to Kuta beach, with its scores of bars and restaurants nearby for lunch, but Ali said 'It's our last day here, honey, couldn't we just eat tonight at your little place by the runway? Is there a nice quiet beach nearby? I've never had a swim in the Indian Ocean, or would it be the South China Sea?'

'South China Sea, I think, sweetheart. Yes, you're right, Kuta will be packed out, and a real quiet lazy day would be just the thing. There used to be a very quiet little beach just down from where I rented my first house here, with just a little shack shaded with palm fronds that sold cold beers. Although it's probably a hipster bar by now, selling draft Fosters and overpriced cocktails to sunburnt perspiring Aussies from Perth. And the beach is probably plagued by those horrible jet ski things that ruin everyone's peace.'

Ali laughed. 'I know what you mean. I hired one once, it was for half an hour and I was bored stiff after five minutes. Once you've gone along the beach one way, balancing on just your right leg as it jumps over the waves, and then the other way, balancing on your left, there doesn't really seem very much else to do!'

In the event, Harry's fears were unfounded, the beach was still quiet and the shack, rather more solidly built now, and offering sun-loungers for rent, was still selling Bintang beers. They'd stopped at the Tragia supermarket on the dual carriageway and had bought some sandwiches, little plastic tubs of diced orange mango, and a packet of biscuits, and now settled down for the day.

The tide was low and they walked and swam in the warm, crystal-clear waters between the exposed little outcrops of rock and sand. Harry kept a sharp eye out for the sea urchins whose spines grew to a surprising length in those limpid waters. He'd once suffered the agony of getting the tips of some of those spines in his foot. He'd been there with a local, fortunately, who knew what to do and straight away started beating Harry's punctured sole hard with the heel of his shoe, breaking the spines up into small fragments and easing the pain immediately. 'I was just swimming past the bloody thing,' he told Alison, 'I saw it and was sure I'd avoided it, but I swear it swayed out its spines towards me to stab me! God, it was painful!'

They managed to avoid them and returned to their sun-loungers to dry off. No missed calls had registered on the phone. As they were sipping their cold beers, Alison wondered why they'd just drunk beer, and not wine, while on the island. 'Don't they have any decent wine here, honey? She asked. 'I know you like beer too, but wine's your first love, isn't it?'

'It certainly is. There is wine here,' Harry replied, 'but it's very hit and miss. The Balinese have no problem with alcohol but the Javanese, who really run the government here, are Muslims who do. They can't do anything about beer, which is locally produced, and anyway is drunk by a lot of the less strict Muslims, but they can interfere with imports of alcohol. I don't know the ins and outs of it but wine would appear in the supermarkets, be there for a few weeks and would suddenly disappear again, sometimes for months.' He chuckled, 'There used to be a restaurant where, if you wanted wine, you had to ask for "Number One Tea" and it came poured out of little white china teapots! You wouldn't even know if it would be red or white, it was just whatever they could get hold of.

'So, everyone just got used to drinking beer. There's no wine culture here, so even if anyone did bother to import decent wine, and didn't have it impounded by customs on some pretext or another, I'm sure it wouldn't have been stored properly in this hot climate. We had champagne in the restaurant, which you could normally get hold of one way or another, perhaps those government officials enjoyed drinking it, but that was it, no other wine. But I'm sorry, sweetheart, if you've been pining for a glass or two. I'm afraid I didn't think of it at all.'

'No, honey, I haven't been pining, I just wondered. I really like this Bintang beer.'

'Yes, it's OK, isn't it? Made under licence from Heineken, I think.'

They sunbathed for a while and had another swim before they ate their little picnic around one o'clock. After that they settled down to read their books, now decreasingly on alert for the phone. Alison dozed off first and Harry made sure that the little canopy above the lounger shaded her head and bare shoulders before he let himself drift off, first making sure, yet again, that his phone was on and had a signal.

He was well down in sleep, holing a twenty-foot putt on the eighteenth green at St Andrews to win The Open, when Ali shook his shoulder. 'Phone's ringing!'

He shook himself awake and peered at the little screen, a Hong Kong number, not Francis's. McLennan.

'Hello, Harry,' It was Zheng. 'Sorry to keep you waiting for news. I'll pass you over to my husband.'

Harry and Alison looked at each other nervously in the moment before Jock McLennan spoke. 'Sorry, I'm sure you've been waiting with bated breath but I didn't want to ring and give you just half the picture. The raid went off at three this morning and they found it all just as in your photos, they've got them as we used to say, bang to rights. Not only the physical evidence but, you'll be glad to hear, detailed stock records, too, together with notes about how they disguised the income stream. All good news but,' he paused for a moment and Harry wondered what had gone wrong, 'but it's taken the police all morning to get hold of, of Mr X, shall we call him. I've just this moment had a call from Michael. Evidently he cut up rough at first, denied all knowledge and challenged them to throw the book at him and be damned. Said he has friends in high places, he probably has. However the other guy, the finance man, obviously appreciated the hopelessness of their position and was being more co-operative. They gave them ten minutes alone together in an interview room, secretly filmed and recorded of course, and he convinced Mr X that the police were ready to do a deal. His daughter and her husband are in the frame evidently.

'So, there we are. They're negotiating the deal, which will probably take a couple of days to finalise, but in essence, Mr Benson, you're going to get everything you want. No big scandal and an official police report. You can go ahead and let the French and Scotland Yard know, and I hope they're grateful to you!'

'I'm sure they will be, Jock, but not as grateful as we are to you and Zheng. I'm, well, I'm lost for words, really, I... I don't know how to thank you both enough.'

'No need, Harry,' Jock said kindly, 'we're glad to be of help, really. And it's good for our city. Now I must go. Bridge club, social disgrace to be late. I take it you'll update Francis?'

'Yes, of course.'

'OK, good, bye for now.' He hung up.

Alison and Harry looked at each other, both grinning broadly.

'Yippee! I told you, honey, it was all written!'

Before returning to the hotel to call Francis, Jack, Alain de Bossenet and Andy Pelham, they decided to have a final swim. The tide had come in and all the outcrops had disappeared, leaving a shimmering, mirror-like surface, only rippled here and there, which reflected towering clouds building up in the distance.

'Looks like a storm coming, we'd better be quick,' Harry said.

'Let it rain,' Ali said. 'I'm not going to miss my last swim in the South China Sea!'

Harry laughed and watched as she ran down the beach, admiring the curves in all the right places under her emerald green bikini. Not exactly skimpy, he thought, but not covering more than it really needs to! He ran down after her, dived in and came up behind her. He put his hands on her waist, she turned, put her arms over his shoulders and kissed him, before suddenly pushing him backwards and falling on top of him, pushing him under the water. He came up spluttering and found her not a yard away, laughing. 'Catch me if you can!' she taunted and plunged under the water. He followed her movement under the water and when she surfaced was ready to sweep water into her face from close range. A vicious water fight developed until they collapsed, laughing and panting, into each other's arms.

The tension that had been building all day as they waited for news, peaking as they heard that "but" from Jock, was now well and truly broken. Anyone seeing them would have thought they were just two lovebirds having fun on their holidays. And that was exactly how they felt.

By the time they got back to the hotel, the rain was really hammering down and they got soaked to the skin as they ran, water sploshing out of their sandals, the fifty or so yards from the car park into the hotel reception, laughing as they skidded and splashed.

When they regained their room and opened the wood-framed glass doors onto the balcony the rain was, if possible, even heavier, the sky a uniform dark grey as thunder rolled around in a continuous roar.

They put on dressing gowns and rubbed themselves dry with the fluffy white towels the hotel provided, before sitting on the sofa and watching the downpour in companionable silence.

Eventually, Harry said 'You know, Ali, the first time I ever came to Bali, I arrived in weather just like this. Ah well, I thought, it'll be fine tomorrow. It wasn't! It rained continuously for five days, it was cold and miserable. I hadn't brought any warm clothes and I developed a nasty cold. I wished I'd never come, seriously! Rainy season here can be like that.'

'That must be why it's so green. Such a lovely island, but, honey, you'd better get on the phone. Francis will be on tent hooks!'

'Yes, true. I'm afraid we'll have to abandon the runway restaurant plan, though sweetheart, it'll never be open in this weather.'

They ordered an early meal from room service, having steaks instead of fish, for a change, with a passable bottle of Australian red wine. When it was all cleared away, Harry got cracking on the phone.

The calls to Francis (who said he would call Jack with the news), de Bossenet and Andy Pelham all took some time and Harry was getting hoarse by the time they were all finished. Francis was particularly happy to hear that the police had found stock records. 'I was worried about that, Harry,' he said, 'it might have been really difficult to prove that the Sotheby's case came from them otherwise. They could probably have obtained verbal testimony but I don't know if that would really have cut the mustard. Documents containing facts and figures are a different kettle of fish entirely.'

Ali, in the lightness of her heart, complimented Francis on his use of English idiom. 'Francis, your English is nearly perfect. It certainly cuts the mustard, although tenterhooks is a different kettle of fish!'

They all laughed and somehow they all knew that, aside from business, a lasting friendship had been created. Harry promised to keep in touch regarding the progress of the case in England and they finished the call promising to meet up again before too long.

Alain de Bossenet was delighted. 'Well done, Harry. That's fantastic news. Just to be on the safe side, our lawyers will contact the lighting company. Lamps in platinum and, even, solid gold! *Incroyable*. I suppose it's a compliment in a way, but even so. I don't think we'll say anything to the restaurants about not letting their staff take the bottles for a little while, though. You've got it all shut down and it might risk bringing attention to the whole business. I'll call Christian and the others today. They're going to be really happy. You've no idea how important that business out there is to all of us. Or perhaps you have, now that you've seen it for yourself.' He paused. 'Don't forget to send me your expenses, *mon ami*. I wouldn't be at all surprised if they decide that you've earned a bonus!'

Andy Pelham had been a bit more circumspect. 'It all sounds very promising, Harry. You've done wonders, my congratulations. I hope you've been looking after Alison properly, though.'

'Not at all, chief,' Alison broke in, 'I've had a horrible time, had to drink five-thousand-pound bottles of wine, spend time in Jakarta and Bali as well as Hong Kong, worrying about a man who did his best to get himself killed, I don't know.' She sighed theatrically and then burst out laughing. 'No, really, it's been wonderful, I've had a great time.'

The policeman laughed too. 'What's this about getting yourself killed, Harry?'

'Long story, Inspector. If I may I'll leave it till we get back.'
'Fair enough, Harry. But, much as I like to preserve my official persona, I really think it's time I invited you to, well, to call me Andy.'
'Well, well!' Alison exclaimed, 'you are honoured!'
'Thank you, Andy, I'm, well, I do appreciate that.'
'I think it must be the first time I've ever said that to, er, to someone who, er – what the hell, Harry. You've deserved it. But don't you get any ideas, Alison!'
'OK, chief, understood.'
'Good!' he chuckled, 'Harry, do you know when we'll be getting the police report? It sounds from what you've said as though it may be just what we need, but we'll have to wait until we see it to make a decision on whether or not to proceed with prosecution.'
Harry had to admit he didn't know. 'I'll get Francis, our guy in Hong Kong, to find out. I don't think it'll take long, but I'll check and let you know.'
'Great. We do have some contacts out there, so we could pursue it officially, I suppose. But it sounds from what you've said that it would be better for it to be treated as a minor, internal matter.'
'Definitely, Andy. There are some delicate negotiations going on and–'
'OK, understood,' Andy interrupted, 'we won't interfere.'
'On the other hand, it may be possible to get you a draft copy of the report, and for you to make suggestions to, er, clarify things, I don't know.'
'That would be great, but I'll leave it all in your hands. When are you coming home?'
'We're flying back to Jakarta tomorrow morning and getting

the overnight flight back, so we'll be in London, let me see, Thursday morning.'

'OK. I'm sure you'll need a bit of time once you get back but give me a call when you're free and we can meet up.'

'Will do. And I'll let you know when to expect the report. It should be sent to you, personally?'

'Yes, that's right. See you in the office on Monday, Alison, bright and early! Good night now, both of you.'

'Good night,' they chorused, and soon were in bed, totally exhausted. Lulled by the incessant rhythm of the falling rain, they were both sound asleep within minutes.

Chapter 29

Harry hadn't had a cigarette in twenty years, but would gladly have lit one up as he sat in the cafeteria of the Central Criminal Court of England and Wales, resisting the temptation to chew his fingernails, waiting for the return of the jury. They'd already been out for nearly three hours in the case of *R v Courtenay* and the prosecution barrister, Adrian Nicholls QC, had told Harry that he didn't think it would take them long to make their minds up. 'They really have no choice but to convict, but of course you never know with juries. My opposite number did everything he possibly could to put doubt in their minds. And, of course, they heard him last. You know, Harry, I've always thought it should be the other way round, the prosecution should have the last word.' He paused and chuckled, 'Except if I'm appearing for the defence, of course!'

Needing some fresh air, Harry strolled outside into the cold, grey February afternoon, feeling a bit lonely. Andy Pelham couldn't spare the time to be there for the verdict, Alison was at work, and Alain de Bossenet had returned to France after giving his evidence. He'd stayed with Harry while in England, travelling up to the Old Bailey together with him, and they'd struck up the beginnings of a real friendship, cemented when Harry had opened some lovely old wines from his cellar. Harry was flattered that such an important guy, one of the real movers and shakers in the wine world, now seemed to treat him as an equal.

He'd been most gratified when, on a long weekend visit with Alison to Bordeaux in October to make his full report to Alain and Christian, they'd been invited to dinner with the owners of four of the five *premiers grands crus classes* of the Medoc and three world-renowned properties in Burgundy. The wines had, of course, been fabulous and Harry had received the sincere thanks of all of them for his efforts in Hong Kong. His expenses, including Francis's sizable bill, had been waved through without question and they gave him a generous bonus as well.

During his visit, Alain had hinted that, after the trial was over, he might have another *chose interessante* that he might ask for Harry's help with. Harry was intrigued and more than glad to help. He'd found time had hung a little heavily between returning from the excitements of the trip to the Far East and waiting for the trial to come on. He found he'd gained a taste for adventure, excitement even, and would welcome more of the same. He still enjoyed his life in Hampshire, of course, but he knew there was more he could do.

Just then, a young man having a cigarette caught his eye and came over; it was Tony Taylor, crime correspondent for the *Daily Mirror,* they'd spoken two or three times before. 'Confident of the result, Mr Benson?'

'I can't really say, Tony, we'll soon know.'

'I see,' the reporter replied. 'Any more cases coming up for The Wine Detective? Our readers are really interested in you, you know. We're getting loads of comments and feedback on social media for this trial, it's really caught the public's imagination.'

'No, nothing at the moment, Tony, I'm afraid.'

'Shame. Well if there is anything, tip me the wink. Any time. You know where to find me. And good luck with the verdict.

It's a slam-dunk if you ask me, but you never know with juries.'

Harry thanked him and moved back inside and bought himself yet another coffee. The popular press had had a field day with the trial, a juicy murder among the rich elite of London, and Harry had been given his nickname, just as Andy Pelham had predicted. One tabloid had even put it in a front-page headline 'THE PERFECT MURDER – IF NOT FOR THE WINE DETECTIVE'. Peter Hill, of *The Times*, had been in touch, reminding Harry of his promise to let him have the inside story. Harry knew he could trust Hill to be discreet in what he wrote but, even so, put him off until after the trial was over.

He sat down at an empty table and looked around. The barrister for the defence, Rex Williamson QC, was sitting at a table nearby with a woman, who, Harry guessed from the family likeness, must be Courtenay's sister. Williamson smiled at him in friendly fashion before turning back to the woman to answer a question.

He's friendly enough now, Harry thought, but he wasn't so nice in court. His mind went back to the day he'd been called to give evidence. He'd been the main witness for the prosecution and, in introducing him, Nicholls had waxed eloquent about his victory in the Wine Society tasting competition and his gift for identifying wines. Harry had been nervous beforehand but found he was able to speak eloquently as he described his long career in the wine business, his wine-tasting experience and the way his gift worked. The QC expertly drew him out, asking whether he had faced any problems with the way wines could change over the years as they matured. Harry answered with the analogy with faces that he'd used when talking to Peter Hill, saying that although faces changed with age, the person was still the same. Likewise with wine. He was also asked about wines that had deteriorated, due to poor storage. He replied that, unless the wine had completely turned to vinegar, he could still identify them.

When asked if he'd ever got anything totally wrong, Harry drew a laugh from the public gallery when he said, yes, he'd lost a ten-pound bet when someone at a party had challenged him to identify a wine, which turned out to be a Bulgarian Cabernet Sauvignon purchased for £2.99 in Morrisons!

When Nicholls felt that the courtroom had warmed enough to Harry, the jury was shown the police video recording of Harry's tasting of the decanters. A big screen was erected at the rear corner of the courtroom so that it was visible from all sides, the judge twisting in his seat and putting on his thick-lensed spectacles to watch. Harry remembered later that you could have heard a pin drop in the courtroom as the film was shown. It was the first time he'd seen the video and it brought back vividly to mind the extraordinary tension that existed on that morning, with all the men, all the potential murder suspects, watching him in silence. He hadn't been there when the safes were opened and saw for the first time the bottles being identified and shown to the camera.

An excited buzz ran around the courtroom when the first wine was shown to be one that Harry had identified. When the Haut-Brion 1934 followed, the noise grew louder and the usher called for silence. The reporters from the press, seated near the exits, prepared to rush out to call their newsrooms. Harry's nickname had been born. However, when Henry Yiu's bottle was revealed to be Lafite 2005, a puzzled silence descended on the courtroom.

When the video finished and the screen had been removed, Nicholls asked Harry if he had any doubt whatsoever, about the identity of the wines he'd tasted and Harry confirmed he hadn't, he was entirely sure. Yes, he had tasted all of the wines before and each had been instantly identified in his mind the moment he had tasted it. Nicholls asked him why, in that case, he had twice tasted the wine he had identified as Lafite 2006, whereas he had only tasted the others once. He replied that he'd been surprised because he'd been told that the members of the tasting club had agreed a minimum value of £300 for their entries and that the Lafite 2006 could be purchased for considerably less. So he wanted to double check.

The QC thanked him and he returned to his seat. Shortly afterwards he was again summoned to the witness box to be cross-examined by Williamson, the defence barrister. He was prepared for a lengthy grilling and wasn't sure whether or not to feel relieved when it was all over in five minutes.

'Mr Benson,' the QC began, 'the jury has heard a lot about your so-called expertise. But I have a very simple question for you. We've heard about your Bulgarian wine failure, most amusing, if I may say so.' He grinned at the jury. 'But have you ever failed to identify a wine, a fine wine, an expensive wine, correctly?'

'Well,' Harry began, 'of course—'

'Yes, or no, Mr Benson?'

'Yes.'

'Thank you. My learned friend has expatiated at some length about the Wine Society challenge that you won. Perhaps you could recall for the members of the jury the precise nature of the contest in which you were successful. There were twenty wines tasted, and the maximum score for identifying all the wines was 100 points. Is that correct?'

'Yes, that's correct.' Harry had replied.

'And what was your score?'

'93 points.'

'93 points, not 100 points, so you did not identify all the wines correctly. Is that so?'

'Yes, but–'

Williamson interrupted him again. 'Yes or no, Mr Benson?

'Yes.'

'Thank you, Mr Benson. No more questions, m'lud.'

After a recess, during which Adrian Nicholls requested that he be allowed to re-examine Harry, Harry was recalled to the witness stand. The judge, Lord Justice Castle, a bit of an old fuss-pot according to Nicholls, had reminded him that he could only address matters that had arisen during the cross-examination, could not introduce anything new, and must strictly avoid asking the witness any leading questions.

Nicholls, rolled his eyes at this statement of what he knew perfectly well, and the judge knew he knew perfectly well, but just said 'Thank you, m'lud. I will endeavour to limit my questions in line with your advice.'

'Now, Mr Benson,' he said turning to Harry, 'my learned friend asked you if you had ever failed to identify a wine correctly. When you began your reply, he cut you off. Would you care to tell the court what your answer would have been?'

'Certainly. I was going to say that it happens frequently, when I taste wines for the first time. Which was the case with three of the wines at the Wine Society. To my knowledge, it has never happened with wines I have previously tasted. Which was the case with all the wines I tasted in Mr Oliver's cellar.'

'Thank you, Mr Benson. You've answered my second question as well. I think that's made things perfectly clear. No more questions, m'lud.'

Lord Justice Castle had been a topic of conversation the previous evening when Harry had met Andy Pelham and their QC to discuss the progress of the case. Harry was staying in Alison's flat that night so was able to stay after dinner, talking it all through as they sipped brandies after their meal.

Nicholls thought the judge's summing up that afternoon had been reasonably fair, but he had perhaps given a little too much weight to the defence's assertion that the fake case shipped from Hong Kong might have gone to Paris. He paused and signalled to the waiter for three more brandies.

'I can't really see the jury buying the theory that Simon Oliver himself could have been the source of the poison. So,' he continued, 'the only thing that concerns me slightly about his summing up, was that he took a very neutral position on your expertise, Harry, after that sustained attack by Rex. He didn't cast doubt on it, exactly, but by not really commenting at all on it, it could certainly be inferred that there is room for doubt about it.'

'I suppose,' Andy Pelham put in, 'he was worried about being criticised for taking sides in the event of an appeal.'

'Yes, I'm sure you're right. Judges do tend to play things safe, these days, there are some pretty fierce people on the

Appeal Court at the moment. But, going back to old kingof's, at best lukewarm, support for Harry's evidence–'

'Sorry, kingovs?' Harry interrupted.

'Apologies, Harry. Castle likes to have his own way all the time so his nickname is King of the Castle! If the jury do entertain some doubt that the wine you identified as Lafite 2006 is what we say it is, I mean if they think you could possibly be mistaken, if they think, as Rex Williamson suggested, that decanter may have contained Courtenay's wine, the Mouton Rothschild, then all the evidence we've presented about the identification of the wine may appear to be less important. Illogical, I know, because all that evidence really ought to make them believe us, that it was Lafite 2006, but that's the way some people's minds work. Some of the stories one hears back about juries' deliberations would make your teeth curl. The mental gymnastics some people can go to to dismiss evidence that doesn't align with the verdict they believe in are quite incredible. So, gentlemen, I think this is what it comes down to – do the jury believe in Harry's expertise, or not? That is the crux of the matter, I believe.'

'I see,' Harry said, 'I wonder if there are any wine lovers among the jury? People who understand wine? It might help if there are. I've spent some of the considerable time I've been in court studying our twelve good men and true, or good men and women and true, I should say, to see if any of them looked interested or not when wine has been the subject.' He stopped for a sip from his brandy glass.

'And?' Andy prompted.

'Not a clue.'

The other two laughed. 'Well,' Adrian Nicholls said, 'my

learned friend certainly did his utmost to discredit you in his final statement to the jury, Harry, didn't he? I'm not sure I could have done a better hatchet job myself! He knows, as we all do, that your credibility, or lack of it, is the issue on which this case stands or falls.'

Chapter 30

In Alison's flat, that evening, over slices of buttered toast, with Marmite, washed down with a mug each of cocoa, Harry recounted this conversation, and the QC's conclusion, to her. 'Goodness! That sounds serious,' she said, 'what did he actually say to attack you, honey?'

'He started off talking about how notoriously hard it is for even the most expert wine person to know what they're drinking. He went into great detail about the Rudy Kurniawan case in the States, where several eminent wine experts were duped into buying cheap wine in expensive bottles by this guy Kurniawan. Not only were they fooled but, when people began to suspect what was going on, they doubled down in support of him and insisted that, with their knowledge of wines, they couldn't possibly be wrong. Of course they looked extremely foolish when it all came to light.'

'Hmm, yes, I can see that might register with the jury, honey,' Ali said, 'what else did he say?'

'Let me see... yes, he started off calling me a self-styled wine expert. He more or less suggested that, as an unemployed man I might have much to gain by making a name for myself as a wine expert.'

Ali laughed, 'if he only knew, honey!'

'He probably does know that I'm not exactly short of a bob or two. However, he then went on to mention some cases where supposedly expert witnesses, whose evidence had condemned innocent people to years rotting in jail, had subsequently been exposed as frauds and charlatans. Of course he didn't explicitly accuse me of being a fraud, but he left the implication for the jury to pick up on.

'Then he got on to the nitty-gritty of the tasting. "Ladies and gentlemen of the jury" he said, "you are being asked by the prosecution to convict the defendant, a hard-working businessman, who, by his own efforts, has made a considerable success of his life, a man with ample funds at his disposal, a man who, his friends and colleagues called as witnesses have attested, has a good reputation, and boasts an unblemished record; you're being asked to convict him, on what? On the opinion, let me repeat, ladies and gentlemen of the jury, on the opinion, of this so-called expert about what? About a bottle of wine. A bottle of wine, ladies and gentlemen, a liquid, a drink made from grapes, which we all know can be bought for three pounds in Tesco, or Asda." I may have paraphrased it a bit, sweetheart, but it's pretty much seared on my memory, being in court and hearing myself being rubbished. The way he talked was very persuasive, I almost started to agree with him!'

'Go on, honey. I'm sorry I wasn't there to support you, it must have been a lonely feeling.'

'It was, sweetheart. Anyway, he then got more specific. "As to the tasting itself", he said, "the defence accepts that the decanters of wine filled from the bottles supplied by Messrs King, Ellison, Benezet and Mr Oliver himself, did not contain the poison that, sadly, killed Mr Oliver. We accept that they were correctly identified by Mr Benson. We do not contend that Mr Benson does not have the ability to identify some wines. Clearly he does. Plain straightforward facts have to be accepted and recognised as such, or else where would we be? But, reverting to Mr Benson and his abilities, it must be admitted that, as human beings, we are all susceptible to making mistakes, are we not?

"So, members of the jury, accepting that the poison was not present in the decanters filled from those four bottles, we know that it must have been present in the decanters filled from the bottles supplied by either the defendant, or Mr Henry Liu. The case made against the defendant, that you have just heard from my learned friend, counsel for the prosecution, is that, as they have identified to their own satisfaction, if not to anyone else's, that the fifth decanter tasted by Mr Benson, and incorrectly identified by him was supplied by Mr Liu, the poisoned wine must therefore have been supplied by the defendant. At this stage, let us remember that, by his own admission, the supposed expert, Mr Benson, is quite capable of failing to identify wines correctly".

'That's not fair,' Ali broke in, 'you only admitted that for wines you hadn't tasted!'

'True, sweetheart, but he went on to say that they only had my word for it that I had tasted them before.'

'By this stage, he had the bit between his teeth, I think he felt that the jury was warming to him. He went on, "The case for the defence is that the defendant, an honourable, upstanding man, did not poison the wine in his decanter. That the wine the self-styled expert Mr Benson misidentified as Chateau Lafite 2006 could entirely possibly have been the wine supplied by the defendant, Chateau Mouton Rothschild 2005." He even produced a map of Pauillac, pointing out to the jury how close the vineyards of Lafite and Mouton are. "And, therefore, that the poison could entirely possibly have been in the decanter filled from the bottle supplied by Mr

Henry Liu." He paused dramatically, gathering his cloak about him and, straightening his wig, looked for a long ten seconds at the jury to let this sink in. "Let me be quite clear," he went on, "the defence is not claiming that Mr Liu put poison in his wine. The defence does not wish to make wild, unsupported allegations against innocent people, we leave that to the prosecution. As I remarked just now, we must respect facts, but, of course we must also treat mere opinions with scepticism." He now really had everyone's attention, as you can imagine, sweetheart,' Harry said, 'I really couldn't see where his argument was leading, and it came as a real surprise.'

"So," he went on, "The prosecution would have you believe, members of the jury, that, by a process of elimination, it must have been the defendant who put the poison in the decanter. As the defence has just shown, it is entirely possible that the poison was in fact contained in the decanter containing the wine supplied by Mr Yiu. In fact, ladies and gentlemen of the jury, the defence, wishing to be entirely candid, does not deny that the poison could, in actual fact, have been in the wine supplied by the defendant!"

'After this bombshell, he really had everyone sitting up and taking notice.'

'I bet,' Ali said, 'that was surely the opposite of what he just said?'

'I thought so too, but he said that the prosecution's case entirely ignored the possibility that it might have been Mr Oliver, himself, who introduced the poison. Mr Oliver might have intended to poison the other members of the tasting club, he said, or he might have intended to dramatically

276

commit suicide, he pointed out that he was known to be in financial difficulties, or that he might simply have become confused and tasted the wrong decanter. "We simply don't know", he said.'

'Goodness, honey, I wonder what the jury made of all that?'

'Heaven knows what they were thinking. He laboured the point that there was no real proof that the wine in question was in fact the 2006, and that it was entirely possible I was wrong about it, as I had been about other wines in the past. He developed the theme that for the prosecution to succeed it had to prove its case beyond any possible doubt, and that they had manifestly failed to do so. There was no proof that Oliver had not supplied the poison, it was just an opinion. There was no proof that the wine in question was a Lafite 2006, that was merely my opinion and the opinion of some of the other witnesses. There was no proof that the case of fake wine from Hong Kong was the case that ended up with Henry Liu, there was no proof it hadn't gone to the restaurant in Paris. It was all just a matter of opinion. He rather ridiculed the amount of detail Andy had gone into in proving that the case had been falsified in Hong Kong and traced through to Yiu. "You may wonder," he said, "why Detective Inspector Pelham took up so much of your valuable time with his very lengthy exposition of how the bottle of wine mis-identified by Mr Benson had arrived from Hong Kong when, under cross-examination, he had to admit that there was no physical, tangible proof that the case in question was not, in fact, sold to the restaurant in Paris. Yes, the Hong Kong police report was very thorough, and the defence does not wish to suggest that a case of wine sold at auction in Hong Kong as Ch Lafite 2005 did not actually contain Ch Lafite 2006. The court must be grateful to the Hong Kong police for their thorough investigation. But there is absolutely no proof, members of the jury, no proof at all, that that case of fake wine did not end up in Paris".'

'And of course he went back to the Kurniawan case and how so many people, so-called experts he called them, had all been unanimously in agreement and had all been proved wrong. "You are to consider, members of the jury", he said, "that once one of these self-styled experts has arrived at an opinion, the next expert may be hesitant to disagree, for fear of appearing ignorant, or foolish. Mr Liu told you that he and his friends had doubted the bottle they had opened was really a 2005, but not enough, you will doubtless have observed, to complain to the supplier about it. What could be more natural than for him to decide, in hindsight, that he agreed with Mr Benson that it must be a 2006? And that Mr de Bossenet and his assistant in France should do likewise?"'

'Wow!' Ali said, 'I can see why the jury might have found him persuasive. I'm sorry to break the flow, honey, it was very mean of him but also fascinating to hear how he could paint a picture. However, I promised to phone Penny before she goes to bed. She's got a crisis with her neighbours, parking wars! She thinks Scotland Yard ought to intervene.'

While Alison went into the kitchen to make her call, Harry tried to relax and put thoughts of the trial to one side for a bit. He picked up a framed photo of Ali and her best friend Julie taken at a poolside when they'd been on holiday in Ibiza together. He'd been invited to one of the Saturday morning brunches, meeting Julie and half a dozen of Ali's close friends, and seemed to have passed muster. They'd subsequently gone out for a meal with Julie and her husband

278

Richard and had all got along together well. Ali had definitely made a hit with Frank and Geraldine when they had been invited to Rossett Hall for Sunday lunch. All in all their relationship was getting stronger, he thought. With Alison working Monday to Friday, they'd mostly been limited to weekends together. It had seemed odd at first, being apart for days on end, after the intimacy and shared experiences of their Far Eastern adventure, but it hadn't really caused any problems, let alone any feeling that they might be drifting apart. They didn't call each other every day, just for the sake of being in touch, but the weekends together had been free and easy, seeming to both of them, he thought, more natural and normal than when they were apart. The periods apart had been good for their sex life too, Harry reflected. Sex in the past for him had largely been about lust and performance; his mind went back to the night he had spent with Sandra, the night, in fact, he realised, when this whole business had started. He shook his head, as if to dismiss that night, and all the other nights strangers had shared his bed for money, from his memory. With Ali, it was totally different, sex just seemed like a natural expression of their feelings for each other.

By the time Ali had finished talking to her sister and had come back into the sitting room, she had undressed and put on a silk dressing gown, tied loosely at the waist. She came and sat next to him, ruffling his hair. They kissed and the front of her dressing gown fell open, exposing the valley between her breasts. He instantly forgot to ask about the parking wars and all about the finale of the defence barrister's speech and surrendered himself to exploring the contents of the dressing gown.

* * *

Next morning, Andy Pelham had called early to apologise for not being able to come to court that day, he had to go to the site of a double murder in Clapham. He'd had time for a chat though, asking for Harry's opinion of their dinner companion the previous evening. 'I like him well enough,' Harry replied, 'although it does sometime seem as though the trial is just a game for him.'

'I know what you mean,' Andy replied, 'but I suppose that for barristers, dealing every day as they are with the rawest human emotions, matters of life and death, they would need to disassociate themselves or they'd be nervous wrecks. Throw in hectoring judges and unreliable juries and it's not a job I'd like.'

'No, I suppose that's fair enough. And he'll get his fee whatever the verdict is today.'

'Uh-huh, today's the day,' the policeman replied, 'seems a long time ago now that we finally got that report from Hong Kong and decided to prosecute, doesn't it?'

When the report had come through it wasn't quite as clear as Andy would have liked and Francis had, reluctantly, put Harry's suggestion to Jock McLennan that Scotland Yard might put forward some minor amendments. It hadn't gone down well.

'We were speaking in Cantonese, of course,' Francis said, 'and the best translation, Harry, of what he said would be "who do those effing Brits think they are? Tell them to go and jump in a lake." I didn't tell him it was actually your idea, but I think he may well have guessed.'

Harry had written a long letter of apology to Jock, to his relief his apology was accepted. Jock sent back a friendly letter, telling Harry among other things that Kwun Tong Import and Export was in the process of being sold to a respectable Hong Kong investment company at a bit of a knock-down price, and that the hotel and restaurant wine business seemed to be continuing undisturbed. The trial wasn't due to take place until the following spring. Francis had also told him that the collection of bottles from restaurants had ceased. He was happy that all was well in Hong Kong but he frequently wondered about the man who had tried to kill him. He supposed he'd never know what became of him.

These reflections occupied Harry for a moment before he replied, 'Yes, it does, seems like ages. I'd hoped all along until the trial started that Courtenay would plead guilty, having seen the evidence, and we'd all have been spared all this.'

'Me too. I'm still surprised he didn't, but I suppose that, as he could afford to employ a top brief, he thought he might as well try. It's a shame the judge wouldn't let me say he did a degree in chemistry! I don't think he's got much of a chance, and although Rex Williamson did a good job yesterday, your testimony won the day, without a doubt. And that video!'

'Yes, that really was a special moment, Andy. Shame you couldn't be like Hercule Poirot.'

'Never mind, all's well that ends well, and Mr Courtenay will spend most of the rest of his life behind bars. Although I suppose I shouldn't tempt fate, you never can tell with juries.'

Andy was one of three people to say that to me about juries, Harry reflected, as he considered buying his fifth cup of coffee, maybe they know something I don't. Before he could start worrying again about the verdict a young constable, who'd been guarding the entrance to the court all though the trial, walked in through the cafeteria entrance and looked around. Seeing Harry, he came over and said 'Jury's coming back in now, Mr. Benson.'

Harry thanked him and went back into the court, resuming his seat in the first row behind the barristers. The jury was filing in and Harry, along with everyone else, looked inquiringly at their faces, hoping to be able to get a clue about their decision. Did they look sombre, perhaps because they were going to have to condemn a man to rot in jail? Did they perhaps look relieved, because they'd decided to pass up that responsibility? No, nothing to indicate either way, he decided.

When they were all seated, the judge came back into the court, and everyone stood.

The judge, old kingof, Harry chuckled inwardly, seemed vaguely irritated. Perhaps the jury's time spent deliberating had made him late for a round of golf, or lunch at his club.

He sat down and everyone else did too. He adjusted his wig, put on his glasses, glared around the court and started speaking, rather loudly, Harry thought.

'Members of the jury, as I told you yesterday, when you retired to consider your verdict, your verdict does not have to be unanimous. If ten of you have agreed on a verdict, and two disagreed, the court will accept your verdict. If three or more of you have disagreed with the majority, you cannot pronounce a verdict.'

The courtroom, packed now that all the press had come racing in, was totally silent. Harry looked at James Courtenay in the dock, how on earth was the man feeling? He certainly wasn't showing any visible emotion.

'Will the jury foreman please stand.'

A middle-aged woman wearing a smart navy-blue dress stood up. She looked straight ahead of her at the judge.

Should be forewoman or foreperson, Harry thought, not foreman.

'Have the members of the jury reached a verdict?'

'Yes.' The judge looked annoyed again, perhaps because she hadn't added 'my lord', Harry thought.

'Is your verdict unanimous?'

'Yes, it is.'

'Very well. Please tell the court, does the jury find the defendant guilty, or not guilty?'

She seemed to hesitate for a second, Harry felt his heart racing and closed his eyes, then heard her speak out clearly.

'Guilty.'

THE END

About The Author : Robert Stone

Robert Stone has lived and worked in many countries around the world, meeting many engaging and interesting people. Passionate about wine, wild asparagus, baseball, and not ever having tomato and egg on the same plate, he likes to relax with a cryptic crossword.

Other books in The Wine Detective series:

BURGUNDY AND BETRAYAL

Harry is asked to help identify a cellarful of fine wines, worth millions of pounds, that has been discovered in a derelict chateau near the Franco-Spanish border.
The area still bears the scars of the Spanish Civil War and the struggle between the Nazis and the French resistance during the Second World War.
Harry's researches awaken old memories and bitter hatreds there, threatening to put his life in danger as he enjoys some of the best wines ever made.

SHIRAZ AND SUCCESSION

Harry has been named as an executor in the will of an American friend, an eccentric millionaire who has left one of the largest collections of fine Californian wines ever assembled.
He'd cordially detested his sons and grandchildren and determined to make inheriting his estate as difficult as possible for them.
Harry has to find a way of satisfying the terms of his will while staying out of the vicious family feuding, which threatens to become very unpleasant indeed.

Printed in Great Britain
by Amazon